Whispers at Midnight

Edward Donohue

 **New Generation Publishing**

Other works by the Author

Novels
Billy's Crowded Hour
A Major Miracle
Demons of the Green Eyed Monster

Non-Fiction
Echoes in the Hills
Neither Pity nor Patronise
The House in the Hollow
Growing up in a Greedy Society

Children's
Bravo Bunny to the Rescue
The Girl Who Walks Through Time

I would like to thank Maureen for her invaluable assistance and hard work and Janet for everything.

Chapter One

It had not been a good night. Tom had awakened about four thirty with a hand around his throat and a second hand grasping the wrist and trying to force it away. He panicked and thought, she's trying to kill me again. 'Stop it Evelyn,' he gasped. 'You're choking me.' The second hand dug its fingernails into the first wrist and succeeded in pulling it away. As he lay there struggling for breath, he realised that both hands were his. He patted the bed on his left to see if he had disturbed his wife, Evelyn, and then remembered that she was no longer there. He lay, totally disorientated, still struggling to get his breath back. He then recalled the two previous occasions when he had awoken to find a pillow over his face suffocating him. Fortunately, he had been stronger than his wife and he managed to extricate himself without hurting her. Those last few months, when she had been alive but suffering from some form of dementia, had been very difficult. One minute she had been loving and clinging to him, begging him not to leave her and then in an instance, she would change and demand to know what he was doing in her house and telling him, she hated him. He became very nervous about going to sleep in case she did try to kill him. Today was different, he knew that it was not April the first and what had occurred was not an April fool's joke played on him. It seemed as if he had really been trying to kill himself. If not, it was a very strange hallucination. It was in fact the twentieth of April and his birthday. He had received some teasing when he was younger because it was the same date as Adolf Hitler's birthday but now half the population would not know who Hitler was. He did not expect to receive any birthday presents and very likely not even a birthday card. Evelyn's two daughters had not kept in touch after her funeral.

He had a splitting headache and he blamed the current crop of nightmares on the anti depressant pills that his GP had prescribed to help him relax, he had probably been taking them for too long. He decided to get up and while he shaved, he planned a programme of trivial activities which would help to get him through the day. Most of these were domestic chores, even though the house was always immaculate. It was a lovely spring morning so; he decided to go into the garden and try to keep it as tidy as she had for so many years. He thought back to the day when they moved into the neat three bed roomed semi after starting their married life in a flat; she had looked at the garden and clapped her hands saying she had always wanted a garden of her own. She would spend hours gardening while he was at work and then in the evenings give him a conducted tour, she was very knowledgeable and often remonstrated with him because he couldn't remember the names of the plants and flowers.

He went downstairs and it was much later in the day before he tried to understand why he had been trying to throttle himself. He had finished his breakfast and just after washing up he went into the nicely furnished dining room, which had been his wife's pride and joy. He heard the gate clang and looking through the window he cursed out loud. He could see that woman from social services coming up the path and he really did not want to be bothered. She had been coming every few weeks since his wife died, just over a year ago, and he really wasn't sure that her visits were much help. Little did he realise that on this occasion she was to set off a chain of events which would dramatically change his life. Tom was a good looking man, just over average height and pleased that he had not, like many of his contemporaries, developed a paunch or lost most of his hair, in fact he looked very fit and at least ten years younger that his age of seventy four. He was very conscious of his appearance; he shaved conscientiously every morning and never went out without a collar and tie. Some people might describe him as a dapper man, although this would not be his own description, just neat and tidy.

The doorbell rang and reluctantly he went to answer it. He knew there was no use pretending he wasn't in because his car was in the drive. The lady from social services was her usual bright and breezy self, showering him with 'good mornings' and 'how are you today' and 'may I come in'. Tom beckoned that she should go down to his living room and he politely asked her if she would like a cup of tea. There were two cups and saucers on the side, they were the ones he and his wife Evelyn always used and had she accepted his offer he would have got the social worker a cup from the cupboard. Everything in the house was just as it had been when his wife was alive and though he was a very neat and tidy man, he saw no reason to change anything. Indeed in the last two or three years of his wife's life, when she had developed the illness of dementia, he had been responsible for the shopping and the housekeeping long before she died.

The social worker said no, she wouldn't have a cup of tea, although it was very kind of him to ask but she was in a hurry as she had a dozen clients on her list and she had to get round them all that day. She said she knew he would be coping alright because he was one of her most able clients. Tom wondered how he had come to be a client, because he had never asked social services, or anyone else, for assistance. Even in the last few months of his wife's life they very rarely saw either a social worker or one of the community nurses.

The social worker, Mrs. Brooks, went on to say that the reason she was calling was to invite him to a new club just started by the local WI. She did hope that Tom would go along and see whether it was something for him. Tom grimaced. 'A sort of Derby and Joan club is it?' he said. 'Well, something like that, but I don't think it has a name yet. Anyway it will be in the Methodist Hall, just a couple of roads away, and will meet at two o'clock every Wednesday.'

Tom let her out and as he did so he looked at the leafy avenue where he lived, which ran up to a long road which was entirely council houses. In that road there was a small row of shops; a hairdresser, a fish and chip shop, a small ironmongers and a newsagent. The last one being Tom's main point of social contact, he often spent five minutes chatting to Mr. Patel, the owner, if the shop was quiet when he went to buy his daily newspaper. They were both cricket enthusiasts. He watched Mrs. Brooks cross the road and about five houses up disappear into a gate leading to a larger detached house where he knew a Mr. and Mrs. Harris lived. He knew them vaguely because when he went out for a walk they would both usually be working away in their very attractive garden. Mr. Harris was a tall man who had retired from the police force a few years ago and in contrast Mrs. Harris was a small, bird like, chatty lady who was at least a foot shorter than her husband. They were both very friendly and when Tom's wife had been alive, Mrs. Harris often gave him a bunch of flowers or a plant in a small pot to take home to her. Tom wondered what sort of response Mrs. Brooks would get from the Harris's.

Tom shut his door and decided that he would not be going to the club the following Wednesday. However, as often happens, fate decreed otherwise. That night he remembered his rough awakening the previous morning. His neck was still tender where he had been digging in with his fingers. Had he been trying to kill himself he wondered? If so it seemed a very unlikely method. After his wife died he certainly had wondered whether he should join her and had gone as far as stockpiling painkillers and sleeping pills. But then he wasn't at all sure about the concept of heaven and although the vicar had said one day he would be reunited with his wife, he was far from convinced. Also, it did seem a rather pathetic and cowardly way to end, what had been at the very least, an interesting life. He could understand and even empathise with elderly people, especially those with severe physical ailments, who wanted to end their lives. There were currently many discussions about euthanasia, voluntary or assisted, and he believed that everyone has a right to make their own decisions. There should be a proper counselling service to assist people to look very carefully at the alternatives and safeguard the risk of greedy people trying to take advantage of vulnerable relatives, he thought.

He personally was still grappling with the mixture of sorrow and guilt; naturally he missed his wife but had he done enough for her when she was alive? He had loved her of course, but there were days when her illness had made him very angry, although he had never once considered striking her back when she attacked him. In many ways the last three years of her life had been the loneliest of his. They were virtually housebound because there were problems if he took her out and he could not go out and leave her alone in the house. He had tried to take her out for a meal on a few occasions but on one attempt she did not like the food she had chosen and accused the waiter of trying to poison her. On another occasion, because they had a pleasant smiling waitress who was very attentive,

Evelyn had become certain that she was "making eyes at him" and created a terrible scene. He discovered that he could do most of their shopping on the internet and had the food delivered.

Very occasionally her sister or one of her daughters would visit and spend a few hours with her, enabling Tom to go out; unfortunately there was a down side to their visits as they did not understand Evelyn's illness and believed her when she said that Tom was ill-treating her. On other occasions, when Evelyn was having her afternoon nap, he would go for a short walk; she often begged him not to put her in a home but it was a lonely, artificial life and if he was honest, her death had come as something of a relief. The fact that he heard her voice sometimes and had even believed she was trying to strangle him, were probably symptoms of him feeling guilty, but he still was not sure what he felt guilt for. There was no doubt that the problems of living with someone who had dementia were severe, medical knowledge was constantly improving but what about the aftermath? When someone who has suffered from dementia or Alzheimer's disease dies they leave behind relatives who may feel a very confused mixture of relief, anger and guilt from which they may never be entirely free. He was still musing when he switched off the dreary television and made his lonely way upstairs.

On Wednesday morning his telephone rang, which in itself was a very rare occurrence. Practically the only calls Tom ever got were from foreign sounding people who wanted to sell him something. However, on this occasion it was Mrs. Brooks, sounding as cheery as ever. 'Ah Tom,' she said. 'Bloody hell,' thought Tom 'I don't remember giving her permission to address me as Tom. Yes, this is Mr. Burton,' he said in a cold voice. 'Oh good,' said Mrs. Brooks 'now listen Tom, I know you're going to the club this afternoon and I told Mrs. O'Brien, who lives just round the corner from you, that you will be giving her a lift. She can't walk very well, so it will be kind of you to pick her up as you go past; number thirty seven, Adstock Way, literally just around the corner from you.' 'But,' said Tom 'I wasn't intending to go this afternoon,' 'Nonsense,' said Mrs. Brooks 'you'll enjoy it, and anyway I've told Mrs. O'Brien that you will be picking her up, you can't disappoint her now.' With that, she said goodbye and put the phone down. To say that Tom was angry was an understatement. 'If ever there was an example of a busy body official taking liberties, that's it,' he said. 'Alright,' he thought, 'I'll go once, but I will make it quite clear that I will not be going again, nor will I be coerced into giving someone I don't know a lift.'

Chapter Two

Tom helped Mrs. O'Brien out of his car and held her arm while she walked into the hall. She was leaning heavily on two walking sticks and when they got through the door, a large, hearty lady took charge of her and said 'Come on dear we'll sit you down near the front.' Tom looked round the hall, there were about a dozen tables, each with six chairs, as he stood there he heard someone calling "Mr. Burton" and there were the Harris's sitting at one of the tables and Mrs. Harris vigorously waving him over. He went to join them and just as he was sitting down, he heard a voice softly say, 'Ah, Mr. Burton, may I sit here with you?' He looked around and there was Mr. Patel looking rather shy and anxious. 'Yes, of course,' Tom replied. 'You do know Mr. and Mrs. Harris.' 'Oh yes, they often come into my shop.' Mrs. Harris said 'Have you given yourself the afternoon off Mr. Patel?' 'Yes, my son and daughter-in-law are looking after the shop; he will be taking over soon, as I hope to retire.' He was a small, slim man and he certainly didn't look as old as many of the people in the hall. Tom thought, as he looked around, that they were a very elderly collection. Many people had sticks and Zimmer frames, some were in wheelchairs.

While he was daydreaming, a gruff voice said, 'Do you mind if I join you?' Before Tom could reply Mrs. Harris had said, 'No, the more the merrier.' The newcomer was a slightly overweight, balding man who looked even more uncomfortable than Mr. Patel. 'It's Jim, isn't it?' said Mrs. Harris. 'Didn't you use to work at the garage?' 'Yes, I did,' replied the man. 'But then when a new oil company took it over I was made redundant, so I'm working in the local cemetery, keeping the pathways tidy.' Their table was now almost full and just as a lady at the head of the hall was rapping on the table and calling for order the last chair was pulled back and a large but attractive lady, who was pulling off her coat to reveal a floral dress, said rather breathlessly, 'I forgot the time, and I've been rushing to get here.' Their table now had six occupants and as Tom looked round the hall he could see that most of the other tables had five or six people sitting around and he estimated there were somewhere between fifty and sixty people in total. In addition, there were about a dozen younger women, who could best be described as hovering and he assumed these were the helpers from the WI. The lady at the head of the hall was tall and rather elegant and one of the few people to be wearing a hat, although Tom could see at least two flat caps among the men. The lady introduced herself as the chairperson of the WI and bid them all welcome. She said that this was the first meeting of what they would call the Wednesday Tea Club and her and her colleagues from the WI hoped that it would become a regular event.

'Before we have tea,' she said 'we thought it would be nice if we played Bingo, but we should start off by every member on each table introducing themselves. My colleagues will come to every table to see if they can be of assistance.' 'A bit patronising,' thought Tom, 'I expect we can manage to remember our own names.' A woman appeared at the head of their table and announced that she was called Joyce and would they all like to introduce themselves. Bill Harris introduced himself and said 'This is my wife Beryl.' Tom was sitting next to Beryl, so he introduced himself and was followed by Mr. Patel and then Jim and finally the last arrival said she was Alice Johnson. 'Well,' thought Tom, 'not a bad collection. At least we all look as if we can move under our own steam.' Then chastened himself by thinking 'And we're damn lucky at that.' The helpers then distributed Bingo cards and coloured pencils and the chairperson introduced a large jolly man, whom she said was from the local Rotary Club and had volunteered to act as the Bingo caller. The game duly started and after a couple of false calls a woman sitting near the front on the same table as Mrs. O'Brien, successfully called "house". They all applauded and the lucky woman was given a Boots gift voucher. Off they went again and after several games no one on Tom's table had won anything, but he suspected that they weren't paying too much attention and showed more interest in chatting amongst themselves.

At half past three, they all stopped for tea and Tom admitted to himself that the selection of cakes was in themselves almost worth coming for. The chairperson had announced ominously that, after tea, with the assistance of Irene on the piano and Jenny on the guitar, they would have a singsong. Tom looked round his table and saw a varied collection of looks of dismay and horror. He himself thought, 'Now how can I decently leave?' There were two helpers standing by the door and escape looked almost impossible. 'This should be fun,' muttered Bill Harris, as they all took a song sheet being handed round by the helpers. Tom resigned himself to staying for a little while and the following three quarters of an hour was passed by fairly indifferent music from the duo at the front and a rather unmelodic collection of voices from the various tables. Just before five, the singing came to a halt, the chairperson told them what a lovely time they had all had, and how much, she was sure, they were looking forward to next Wednesday when they could do it all over again. 'Additionally,' she said 'we hope to get some very interesting speakers in to entertain us all.'

The duo then played God Save the Queen and they all stood more or less to attention. As they shuffled out the members of his table stood around his car, because he was waiting for Mrs. O'Brien. However, she called out 'Mrs. Jones is going to give me a lift in the future, thank you very much.' Tom said to his new friends, 'Well I definitely will not be upset over that because I'm not planning to come again.' 'No, nor me,' said Jim and Mr. Patel said 'I'm not sure that I will either.' Mrs. Harris then said, 'Well instead of coming here we could all meet at our house next Wednesday for a cup of tea and a look round the garden.' 'Good,' said Jim, 'but no singing please.' Thus the Windmill club was born.

Chapter Three

The following Wednesday Tom was preparing his lunch and wondering if he could possibly get out of the meeting they had planned for that afternoon. He decided that he had better go because it was only a few yards down the road and although he didn't know Mrs. Harris very well he suspected that she might come looking for him. They had arranged to meet at three o'clock and when he opened the Harris's gate, just after three, he could see that most people had arrived and were being escorted around the garden by Mrs. Harris. She saw him come through the gate and called out, 'Welcome Mr. Burton, I think we are now all here.' After a few more minutes of admiring the hyacinths and narcissi, which were magnificent, they went round to the back of the house to look at Mr. Harris's vegetable and flower garden. 'Blimey,' said Jim 'look at them tulips, a sight for sore eyes,' and the other members of the party made similar complimentary comments. Mrs. Harris had disappeared into the house and after a few minutes she called them and they all went into the spacious living room, where there was an array of cakes set out on a coffee table; it was obvious that she was not to be outdone by the ladies of the WI.

When they sat down, Tom realised that there were now seven of them; the new member was a West Indian lady with a very jolly laugh who introduced herself as Victoria. 'But everyone calls me Vicky,' she said. Alice said 'I do hope you didn't mind me bringing Vicky along but I'm a widow,' and Vicky promptly interceded, 'And I'm a sort of widow, as my husband has buggered off back to Barbados.' Tom almost choked over a mouthful of tea and Mrs. Harris patted him on the back. 'We are a bit of a motley collection,' he mused to himself, 'but none the worse for that as we should have lots of different ideas and opinions.' After they had finished their tea, they sat chatting amicably among themselves. Mr. Harris called the meeting to order. Tom had learned that Bill Harris had been a chief inspector in the police force and he had an air of authority. 'I think that we shall have to decide on the format of our group, are we to be a formal club meeting regularly or just a bunch of neighbours getting together now and then.' Tom, who had been an office manager, liked everything neat, and organised and said that he thought they ought to go for a formal club and have regular meetings. Alice said 'Well does it have to be formal, can we not just meet now and then when we're in the mood?' 'Ah,' said Jim 'how will we know who is in the mood and when?' They all laughed. Mr. Patel, who asked them to call him Lenny, thought that it would be nice to have a bit of regular structure. 'After all the world we now live in is pretty chaotic, I regularly read the newspapers I sell and I don't mind telling you they make me pretty depressed.' 'It seems to me,' said Vicky who was clearly no shrinking violet, 'we ought to have a vote and get it sorted out properly.'

After some further discussion, they agreed they would do this. Bill automatically took the chair and said, 'Well, we're going to vote on whether it will be a formal club or just the occasional meeting. Hands up those who think it should be formal.' Beryl Harris picked up the teapot and said 'I'm going to make a fresh brew; you can vote for me Bill.' 'Right,' said Bill again, 'hands up if you want it to be formal.' Everybody put their hand up except Alice and she said 'Whoops, I'm not going to be the odd one out,' and she put her hand up. 'There you are,' said Bill, 'our first decision is unanimous. That's a very good start.' Jim then asked if they were going to have a name for their group. Vicky said 'When Alice told me about your group and when I saw you all in the garden I thought, in the nicest possible way, we are a rather strange collection, my husband would have called us a bunch of screwballs.' 'Well,' said Bill 'we could do worse than call ourselves "The Screwball Club". They then decided to formalise it and to make Bill the chairman, Lenny Patel the treasurer and Alice, who had been a school secretary, would be the secretary.

'What will Lenny be the treasurer of then?' asked Tom. 'Are we going to have subscriptions?' 'Well yes,' said Bill, 'we might need money for postage, secretarial materials and travel, so we really do need a small fund to fall back on.' More discussion followed and they decided they would put into the kitty two pounds a week each. 'We can always supplement it if we have to,' said Bill. Beryl came in and refreshed the cups and they then discussed what kind of subjects they would discuss at their meetings. Tom said, 'Why don't we just let it float and discuss whatever happens to be currently relevant.' They decided to do this for the time being, 'But,' said Tom there will be times when we need to prepare material in advance.' The meeting closed about five o'clock and Tom went home feeling much happier than he had on the previous Wednesday. He and Lenny Patel walked along the road together and Lenny said as they parted at Tom's gate, 'Oh, this is your house; I often wondered where you lived when you have been in my shop. A few years ago we had a newspaper delivery service but kids nowadays are not interested in working for pocket money.' They shook hands rather formally and said goodbye. Tom went in his front door and for once it did not feel that the house was quite so empty.

The following morning, Tom was just clearing away his breakfast dishes when there was a long persistent ringing of his bell on the front door. He went to the door and there was a rather flushed and angry looking Mrs. Brooks. 'You didn't come to the meeting yesterday,' she said without any preliminary "good morning" and "how are you". 'No,' said Tom 'please come in and I can tell you about it.' She followed him into his sitting room and sat down without being asked. 'I already know about it,' she said 'I have just been to see Mr. and Mrs. Harris and he as good as told me that they would not be going again and it was none of my business. I have to say that I feel you are all being very ungrateful.'

Tom decided that it was his job to pour oil on troubled waters. 'I'm very sorry that you feel that way Mrs. Brooks but a small group of us felt that we would prefer quiet little meetings, such as the one we had yesterday. After all, surely from your point of view, it is simply a question of elderly people getting together socially. 'Yes,' she said 'that's all very well but I went to a lot of trouble to liaise with the chairperson of the WI and she and her fellow members went to a lot of trouble to arrange the meeting.' 'Yes, I'm sure that's true,' said Tom 'but there must have been fifty or sixty people at the WI meeting and surely half a dozen of us will not be missed.' 'It's the principle of the thing,' said Mrs. Brooks. 'We of the social services go to a lot of trouble to think up ways of caring for you old people and we do not appreciate being told that we are wasting our time.' Tom was not happy about the way she described himself and his new friends. 'You can't just label us as "you old people",' he said quietly. 'We are individuals and we still have the right to make our own choices. I'm afraid our little group will continue to meet and we will not be coming to the meeting organised by the WI, I am sorry if this upsets you or anybody else but we would like to be left alone to do things our own way.' 'Well, if that's the way you want it, I hope you won't come running to me or my colleagues when you want something.'

Tom really did not know whether to be angry or laugh out loud. 'Obviously I cannot speak for the others,' he said 'but I assure you that I will not come running for help or anything else.' He escorted her to the door and bade her a civil good bye.

Less than half an hour later his doorbell rang and he could see through the frosted glass one very tall figure and one small figure. When he opened the door they proved to be Bill and Beryl Harris. 'Have you had a visit from Mrs. Brooks?' Bill asked. 'Yes indeed,' said Tom 'Please come in and I'll put the kettle on.' He made some coffee and produced a plate of chocolate digestive biscuits. 'Not quite the hospitality you offered us Beryl,' he said apologetically. They sat quietly for a moment and Tom thought to himself that this was perhaps a sign of a meaningful friendship. People who don't have to fill all the empty spaces with chatter are obviously relatively more comfortable with each other.

After a few minutes, Bill said 'Well, what are we going to do about Mrs. Brooks?' Tom replied 'We appear to have two choices, we can ignore her and pretend the whole thing never happened or, we could write to her as a group thanking her for her help but explaining that we have established a group which is more suitable for us.' 'That's not a bad idea,' said Bill, 'I'll compose a letter and if the others agree next Wednesday we'll send it off.' They agreed that this was the better alternative. They chatted for a while, Beryl about her garden and Bill with a few anecdotes from his police service. They suddenly realised that it was almost lunchtime and Beryl said that they had better get home. Tom showed them to the door and after they had disappeared down the avenue he felt a distinct sense of loss

Chapter Four

When he arrived at the Harris's on Wednesday, Tom was pleased to see that everyone was present. He wondered if it was loneliness that was partly responsible for bringing them together. Both he and Alice had lost their partners, so too had Vicky in a slightly different way. Jim had told them that he had never been married, but had lived with his mother until she died three years earlier. She had reached ninety-eight years old; he had said proudly and was still cooking the day before she died. Their ages ranged from Alice and Jim, who were the youngest at sixty-eight, through to Tom who was the senior member at seventy-four, although they all looked very healthy. Vicky was a bit vague about her age. 'Never saw any birth certificate,' she laughed, 'but I think I am a bit younger than Alice.' Lenny Patel said he was seventy-two but he certainly didn't look it and Beryl said 'Bill and I were born in the same year and the same month. We will be seventy four next month; we've known each other since primary school,' she said proudly. 'Oh good,' said Alice, 'We can have a birthday party.' They were then called to order by their chairman. 'We really must discuss what to do about Mrs. Brooks,' he said. It transpired that everyone but Vicky had received a visit from Mrs. Brooks, although Jim said he saw her through the window and didn't answer his doorbell. 'She used to call when my mother was alive,' he said. 'Don't need her now.'

Bill read out the letter he had drafted and they all agreed that it was polite enough but firmly established their independence. 'How do I sign it though? Do I put chairman of the Screwballs Club?' Again a lengthy discussion followed and they decided that the

Screwballs title was their own private joke and a more formal title might be better for "official correspondence" as Tom put it. 'It might even be worth having some letterheads printed,' he suggested. As Tom and the Harris's lived in Welton Avenue and they met on a Wednesday they half decided on the Welton Wednesday Club. 'Not to be confused with Sheffield Wednesday,' said Jim, who was a keen football supporter. They all agreed that this name was prosaic if adequate. 'Hang on,' said Tom 'I've got an idea,' they all listened in silence to their senior citizen. 'Why not call it the Windmill Club?' Again there was a silence and one or two of them looked rather puzzled. 'Well,' he said 'we are going to be tilting at windmills, aren't we? Or to put it another way, taking on puffed up officials and protesting at our bureaucratic society.' 'Blimey,' said Vicky turning to Alice, 'you've brought me to a revolutionary group have you?' 'I do hope so,' Alice replied, 'I'm sick of old people being regarded as wrinkled old nobodies, pushed and jostled by kids, patronised by do gooders and ignored by practically everyone else.' 'Exactly,' said Tom 'It's time some of us protested a bit more loudly.'

'Hear, hear,' said Jim. 'You should hear some of the abuse I get; cheeky kids knocking down gravestones and adults blaming me.' 'You should be in my shop sometimes,' said Lenny 'kids shoplifting and their parents being abusive, if I dare to protest. I get all sorts of unpleasant racist comments.' They all nodded and murmured sympathetically. 'Right,' said Tom, 'we may not have a Don Quixote, but let us begin as we mean to go on. Bill can make his letter a lot firmer by pointing out that we were not consulted in the first place about the WI Club and we have no intention of being treated like sheep.' Vicky laughed and clapped her hands. 'That's better; tell it like it is, although I've never heard of this chap Don Quixote. French is he?' They all agreed on Tom's suggestion and Bill said he would get some letterheads printed and then post the letter. They then had to decide a topic for the following week and who would lead the discussion. Again there was a long silence, and then Bill said 'Well I don't mind starting and as Jim and Lenny have both mentioned forms of vandalism that will be my theme. After all as a long serving police officer I saw more than my share.'

At that point Beryl wheeled in the tea trolley. 'I only come for the cakes,' said Tom with a smile. After tea the group started to break up, it was now pouring with rain and Alice said 'Oh dear, Vicky and I walked here and we'll get soaked.' 'Me too,' said Lenny. Don't worry said Jim, I've got my little car, I can give you all a lift, well three of you anyway.' 'That's just right,' said Tom, 'I only live a few yards away so I can run home.' He and Bill stood in the porch and watched the others climb into Jim's pride and joy, a beautifully preserved Morris Minor. 'Hope the springs will cope,' murmured Bill as Vicky and Alice squeezed into the back. Then with a wave and a toot of the horn they were off and Tom said 'I'll just scoot up the road, thanks Bill, see you soon,' and he half walked and half trotted up the road. The downpour was so heavy that by the time he reached his house he was soaked. As he went in the door he clearly heard Evelyn say 'Get those wet clothes off, you'll catch your death of cold.'

By contrast the following Wednesday was bright and sunny and Beryl had put the chairs and some small tables on the terrace behind the house. 'Gosh,' said Vicky 'this is very nice, sitting here in the sunshine reminds me of home.' 'Why, you haven't got a garden,' said Alice. 'No, I mean home in Barbados, silly.' When everyone was present Bill said 'You will remember that we were going to talk about vandalism.' He then went on to talk about some of the incidents he had had to deal with during his time in the police. 'It is always difficult to know where to draw the line; you can have quite artistic graffiti at one end and very nasty muggings at the other. As you will be aware young children and old people are the most vulnerable when it comes to mugging and bullying, but anybody can have their property damaged.' During the discussion that followed it transpired that they all knew of someone who had been mugged and they could fill a book on the incidents of vandalism that they had encountered. Jim talked about the youths and girls who frequented the cemetery at night and were not content with smoking and drinking. 'And much worse,' he added darkly. 'Then, when they've had their pleasures they have to knock down gravestones and scatter the flowers. If they knew of the distress this causes, particularly among some of the older widows and widowers perhaps they wouldn't do it.'

'I don't want to sound too cynical,' said Bill 'but in my experience very few vandals feel remorse or show any willingness to apologise.' 'And what about the kids who come shoplifting in my shop,' said Lenny. 'Not only do you get a mouthful of abuse but sometimes they bring their parents along to accuse me of wrongly blaming their innocent little dears. Sometimes I think it's almost better to let them steal and just turn a blind eye.' 'I don't think that's the answer,' said Tom, 'they will just grow up thinking that stealing is OK, providing you do not get caught.' 'I'm afraid that is already quite a prevalent attitude in society,' Bill added. 'It's a bloody disgrace,' said Alice. 'Kids today have no respect for their elders; I'd like to give them a thick ear. But then I would finish up in court.' Bill was sympathetic, 'I know a lot of people blame the police for being lazy or too soft, but the real problem nowadays is this so called political correctness and all the bleeding hearts in Town Halls and Parliament. The old fashioned bobby has gone for good.' They started talking among themselves until Beryl said 'Time for tea I think,' and she wheeled out the trolley with the usual splendid array of cakes. Tom said 'Perhaps we ought to consider having the meetings at different venues because at the moment you do all the work.' 'No, please,' said Beryl, 'I really enjoy baking and entertaining, and once a week is no hardship.' 'Well, tell us when you get fed up,' said Tom. 'And in the meantime,' said Vicky, 'keep helping us to get fed up. I don't cook on Wednesdays now.' And they all laughed.

Tom thought again how amazing it was that such a disparate group had jelled so well. During tea Bill disappeared and after a few minutes he came back onto the terrace wearing a broad smile. 'I have just been talking to my old Sergeant on the telephone,' he said. 'Since he retired he has been helping to run the local youth club, which meets every Friday evening in the same hall where we first met and I have issued a challenge.' 'What kind of challenge,' asked Alice? 'Well, I said that the Windmill Club would go next Friday and take on their best players. Let's see if we can earn some respect.' 'Blimey,' Jim said 'that could be tricky.' 'It could be a scream,' laughed Vicky. Bill said 'A few of the club members are among the vandals and Lenny's shoplifters so we may be able to exert some influence or at least build some bridges.' 'All we have to do then is polish up our old skills and hope for the best,' added Tom with a smile. 'Exactly,' replied Bill. 'We show them that all older people are not just waiting to die.' 'No,' said Tom soberly, 'but all over the world there are millions of old people who are starving and lonely and waiting to die and nobody really cares. There are millions in this country for that matter, and somehow we have to make more people aware of their situation. That is probably a task for older people such as us because the vast majority of young and middle aged people are not very interested unless possibly a member of their own family is involved.' They made their farewells and as Bill and Beryl stood arm in arm and waved them off Tom couldn't help thinking how fortunate they were to have each other.

Chapter Five

On Friday evening they travelled to the youth club in two cars. Jim picked up Vicky and Alice and Bill and Beryl collected Tom and Lenny. On the way Lenny said that he had been talking to Ronnie Wong, the owner of the fish and chip shop, and he had expressed a lot of interest in the Windmill Club. 'Perhaps you would like to bring him to the next meeting,' said Tom. 'That's if it's alright with Bill and Beryl.' 'Of course,' they replied in unison. 'But,' Beryl added 'perhaps we had better limit our final number to ten or else we will not have enough room.' Bill pulled into the car park just as Jim arrived. All seven of them then went to the hall door, it sounded very noisy in the hall and Harry Baines, Bill's friend, met them at the door. 'Come in,' he said, 'I hope you're all feeling fit.' The members of the Windmill Club laughed nervously and followed him in. There must have been about forty teenagers ranging from thirteen to eighteen years, engaged in various activities. A young, attractive, red haired girl dressed in a tracksuit came to meet them and Harry introduced her as Frances Summers, the club leader, 'Please call me Fran,' she said.

Quite a hush had now fallen over the hall and most of the young people were staring at the members of the Windmill Club. Fran clapped her hands and said that she was pleased to introduce the Windmill Club who are our guests and opponents for the evening. At this some of the teenagers laughed out loud and most of the others smirked or grinned. One tall lad shouted 'Blimey Fran we thought you were serious about the opposition, isn't it their bedtime?' Some of the others laughed, but Harry Baines said 'I should wait and see if I were you lad.' Fran then asked a slim girl, who in Beryl's eyes was wearing too much makeup and had large hoop earrings, to draw up a list of competitive activities. 'Ask our visitors what they would like to play Rose, and then pair them off with some of our best players.' 'OK Fran will do,' Rose said smiling at Beryl and Alice. It was decided that it would be best if they played in pairs where possible. They started off with Bill and Jim playing darts. Quite a few of the youngsters stood around and watched, but there were two side rooms, one in which a small group were playing music and the other was given over to boxing training. Bill and Jim got off to a flying start with Bill throwing nearest the bull, he had been a member of the police social club darts team and Jim still played occasionally in his local. Their opponents were two of the older boys and although they were useful the 'old timers' as the kids called them, won three games to two. 'We'll play a mixed team for table tennis,' said Beryl who had obviously given it some thought. So she and Lenny lined up at one end of the table against a boy and girl who seemed to be about fifteen years old. In the meantime Tom had wandered into the boxing room, he had been a navy boxing champion and he still loved the sport although Evelyn used to say it was barbaric. The coach was putting four lads through their paces, 'We are hoping Pete and Jerry will be in the ABA's next year,' he said to Tom. He suggested that those two might like to spar with each other but Jerry said he had to go as he had a 'hot date'. Pete looked disappointed and Tom suddenly heard himself saying 'I'll give him a couple of rounds if you like.' The coach was a bit surprised but Pete said eagerly 'Yes please.' 'OK,' said the coach 'but be sensible, this gentleman probably hasn't boxed for years, just sparring mind you.'

Tom took off his jacket and tie and the coach helped him on with some boxing gloves. He climbed into the makeshift ring and the coach said, 'Right, two, two minute rounds and if I say stop you stop.' He rang the bell in the corner and they set off, Pete was wild but rather slow and Tom found no difficulty in blocking or avoiding most of Pete's swings. He responded with quick jabs to the face and body and dodging most of Pete's punches. Halfway through the second round, Pete did connect with a swing to Tom's ribs and it was rather painful. He realised that, as well as some of the youngsters, Harry and Fran had been watching, the latter with an anxious frown. 'Well,' said the coach as he took the gloves off 'I wish this lad was a few years younger, he moves like lightning, Pete hardly laid a glove on him.' Tom saw that Pete was looking a little downcast so he quickly said 'I had no choice, Pete has a punch like a mule, and he's going to be very useful.' Pete shook Tom's hand and said 'Cheers mate, I hope I won't meet someone as good as you in the ABA's.' They went back into the hall where the table tennis was just finishing. Beryl had been a County tennis player and Lenny had played a lot of badminton in his time. The match was at two games all and the adults were getting on top with the fourth game ending 21-7. Beryl tactfully said 'I think I've had enough for one night,' and the opponents shook hands.

The tall lad was still making derogatory remarks and Pete said 'You want to try boxing with this one, he's mustard.' Alice whispered something in Bill's ear and he said to the cocky youth, 'Are you any good at arm wrestling?' 'Oh yes, I could but not with you, you're much heavier than me.' 'Oh no,' said Bill with a smile, 'I was thinking of one of the ladies.' 'Very funny,' said the lad 'no woman could beat me.' 'Right,' said Alice 'try me'. They put two chairs on the corner of the table tennis table and sat opposite each other. 'This is Mickey,' said Harry Baines 'he thinks he's top dog around here.' 'Right,' said Alice 'best of three.' But it was no contest, the Windmill Club learned one of Alice's secrets that night, in her youth she had been a lady wrestler in a circus and had toured Europe and America. She flattened Mickey's arm three times until he pulled away and said sullenly 'Well I hurt my arm when I fell off my bike, that's why it's not as strong.' 'Oh, I am sorry,' said Alice 'I was just lucky then.'

Just then, there was the sound of the very melodic singing of a Negro spiritual song. 'It sounds as if Vicky has found her niche,' said Tom. Fran moved the group into the main hall for refreshments and an impromptu singsong followed. Then she called once more for hush, 'I'm sure you would like me to thank the Windmill Club for coming here tonight and being such good sports.' Everyone clapped and cheered. There was a buzz of excitement in the hall and a feeling of camaraderie. 'Why did they come Fran,' asked Rose? 'Well, let's ask them.' Bill stood up and as he towered above most of them, he could be clearly heard. 'We want to build bridges between the younger and older citizens in our area and see if we can develop mutual respect. But only you will know if we've succeeded.' Fran said 'Hands up if you agree with Bill.' And there was a loud cheer and a forest of arms. As the Windmill Club left Fran and Harry shook their hands and asked them to come again. As they made their way to the cars Beryl said 'I bet I'll be stiff in the morning,' and Tom added 'And I'll definitely have bruised ribs.' They agreed that it had been an enjoyable evening and well worthwhile and bade each other goodnight.

Chapter Six

When they met the following Wednesday the first topic of discussion was the evening at the youth club. They were unanimous in their agreement that the evening had been worthwhile, although they could not know how successful it had been from the youngsters' point of view. 'But,' said Bill, 'we have a clue, they have presented us with this,' this was a poster on which a number of small sketches of activities had been drawn and a note in the middle saying, "We are friends of the Windmill Club". They were all pleased to receive this and Tom suggested that they had copies made and pinned them up in places where there had been trouble, such as Lenny's shop and Mr. Wong's fish and chip shop. Mr. Wong had been going to attend their meeting but had to postpone because of a family illness. Then Bill said 'I'm afraid I have to apologise, in all the excitement of the trip to the youth club we did not agree on a topic for today's meeting.'

'Perhaps we could use the time to find out a little more about each other,' said Alice. 'Well you were a dark horse for one,' laughed Beryl. 'We had no idea that you had been a lady wrestler.' 'Well, it was funny how that happened,' said Alice, 'I was mad about horses and I wasn't very happy at home because my mum died and my dad married a dreadful woman who hated me. I was only fifteen but I decided to run away and join a circus.' 'As you do,' murmured Tom. 'And I thought I could do acrobatics on horses, anyway I became too big for that and one of the wrestlers suggested I join them as it would be a novelty to have a lady. We used to take on all comers, although obviously I only wrestled women. Though I do say it myself I became very good and then my coach, Jack,

33

and I decided to get married.' 'But then you became a widow,' said Beryl softly. 'Yes, he took on one opponent too many, he won his bout but as he acknowledged the cheers he collapsed with a heart attack and died before they got him to hospital.' There were a few moments of sympathetic silence and then she smiled and said, 'Luckily he was one of life's savers and he left me very comfortable. I own the little bungalow I live in and I've got no debts.'

'You're lucky,' said Vicky, 'my old man is one of life's gamblers and when his debts got too big he cleared off leaving them with me. I live in a council flat and always just manage to make ends meet with a couple of pounds left over for the collection plate on Sunday.' Beryl said 'Haven't either of you got any children?' Alice replied that she and her husband never had time until it was too late and Vicky said, 'I've got a good for nothing son who takes after his father.' Beryl then said 'What about you Jim?' 'Here,' said Bill I thought I was supposed to be the chairman, are you taking over?' 'Don't be silly dear, it's just me and my great sense of curiosity, that's all.' 'Well, there's not a lot to tell about me,' said Jim, 'I became a motor mechanic apprentice when I left school and there's not much about motor cars that I can't fix, I lived with my mum and dad. Dad and I used to go to the pub twice a week for a game of darts and a pint but he died about twenty years ago. Then I just stayed with my mum until she died. The council house was in her name but after a bit of 'argy bargy' the council said I could take it over. I've lived there all my life and I've got a smashing vegetable garden. Then a year before I was due to retire the new company made me redundant, so I've now got a part time job in the cemetery.' 'Do the ghosts bother you?' said Vicky. 'No, I don't believe in ghosts,' replied Jim with a forced smile. 'I have much more trouble with the vandals.'

At that point Beryl said 'I'll go and get the tea.' 'Hang on a minute,' said Vicky 'what about you and Bill?' 'Oh we're not very exciting,' Beryl replied 'we first met at school and we were childhood sweethearts. I've never been with another man, although a few years ago Bill did have an affair with one of his women constables and I was very upset at the time.' Bill looked a bit embarrassed and said 'Not really an affair, just a bit of a fling when we were away on a course, I soon came to my senses.' 'Just as well,' said Beryl 'I would have given him what for.' The others looked at six foot three Bill and five foot two Beryl and Jim muttered, 'The mind boggles.' 'Anyway,' she went on 'we had our golden wedding a couple of years ago and as you can see we are still happily married.' With that she went off to the kitchen.

They waited until she returned and in the meantime the men argued about the merits of the two local football teams. As it happens Jim was a fervent City supporter and Tom and Bill supported United. They said that in their opinion City wasn't a proper English club, it had an Arab owner an Italian manager and in almost all of their games they had about nine foreign players in their team. The ladies commented that they thought it was a silly game, grown men rushing about a field, kicking a ball and knocking each other over. Lenny said he was a cricket man, 'You can't beat the sound of leather being struck by willow,' he said. Beryl came back in with the usual loaded trolley and they munched and drank with enthusiasm. Beryl then said 'Well, it's just you and Lenny now Tom, the rest of us have spilled the beans.'

Lenny turned to Tom and said, 'I'll start, it won't take long. I was born and brought up in Bradford, but after I got married my wife and I moved across the

Pennines. My dad was a shopkeeper and that's the only trade I've ever known. My wife isn't very well, she doesn't get out much and I'm afraid she doesn't speak very much English.' 'Oh, wasn't she born in Bradford then?' said Alice. 'No,' said Lenny 'ours was an arranged marriage, I went over to Karachi and we had the wedding there. We have three sons, one helps me in the shop, one has a shop in Birmingham and the other one is an accountant.' 'You must be very proud of your sons,' said Vicky 'it makes me feel quite jealous.' 'It hasn't been all plain sailing,' said Lenny, 'I know England prides itself on being tolerant, but me and my family have had an awful lot of abuse in our time.' 'Aye,' said Bill, 'the number of times I've had to be involved in racial arguments, mind you it's not always one sided, but I agree with you that foreign people, especially those with dark skins, do have a lot to put up with.' 'The other thing we worry about,' said Lenny 'is the growth of terrorism. I know for a fact that two of my brother's sons have gone back to Pakistan and are almost certainly involved in some kind of military training.' Tom said 'There is no doubt that there are many Muslims who would like to see the growth of Islam.' 'Well I'm not one of them,' said Lenny 'I like England and I like the English people.' 'What about you Tom,' asked Beryl 'you haven't told us very much?'

'Well it's all a bit complicated,' said Tom. 'I look back on my life wondering at which crossroads I took the wrong turnings and probably like the rest of you, I wonder where it has all gone. After I left school I went as a cadet into the Royal Navy then I spent the next twelve years wandering about the world. I finished up with the rank of Chief Petty Officer and saw little bits of action in the Far East. After I left the Navy I met a New Zealand girl in Hong Kong and went to live in

New Zealand working on her father's sheep farm. This was in the South Island and it was where I started climbing in the New Zealand Alps. We never did get married and after a few years of coping with the dust and the smell I moved to South America because I wanted to climb in the Andes.' 'I didn't know you were a climber?' said Bill. 'Oh yes,' Tom replied 'I like big mountains and after I left the Navy I felt I had to have some alternative to the sea. When I came back to England I spent most of my summers in the Alps.' 'What were you doing in England then after such an adventurous life?' said Alice. 'Well believe it or not I finished up as a sales rep for a builder's merchants and then became the office manager and finally the managing director. I only retired a couple of years ago.'

'What about your wife?' said Beryl, 'didn't she die just over a year ago?' 'That's right,' said Tom 'I got married rather late in life, I was in my fifties and Evelyn, who was of a similar age had been married before. She had just been divorced when I first met her and after a few months we got married. She had two daughters by her first marriage, but they both live in London and I haven't seen them since her funeral. The last few years of her life were very difficult because, as some of you may know, she developed some form of dementia and had enormous mood swings. But, I miss her terribly and I often find myself talking to her and asking her advice. Jim said he doesn't believe in ghosts but I think that when you have loved somebody they never really leave you.'

Again there were a few minutes silence and then Beryl said 'Goodness me, it's after five, how the afternoon has fled by.' 'Ah that's because you were in charge,' said Bill 'but before we break up we must determine the topic for next week.' 'What do you suggest,' Alice asked 'politics, religion?' 'Oh I'm not sure we're ready for those yet,' said Bill. 'What about entertainment, after all most of our lives are spent either reading or watching the television or listening to the radio? I'm sure that we will find plenty to talk about.' 'Alright,' said Alice 'I was in the entertainment business really, although circus's and fairs are not as popular as they once were. I'll lead the meeting next week, if that's alright with everyone?' 'It's fine with me,' said Tom 'providing you don't challenge any of us to arm wrestling.' They laughed and made their preparations to depart. Tom and Lenny walked down the road and once again shook hands rather formally at Tom's gate. 'I'll try to bring Mr. Wong next week,' said Lenny. 'Yes do,' said Tom 'it will add another dimension to our group.'

Chapter Seven

On Friday evening Tom was just washing up his dinner dishes and thinking about the youth club when the doorbell rang. He was surprised because he rarely, if ever, got a visitor in the evening. He went to the door and there on the doorstep was Fran, the youth leader. 'Hello Tom,' she said, 'I heard that your ribs were a little sore and I just called round to see if you were alright.' Tom couldn't imagine where she'd got this information but he assured her that although they were a little bruised after his episode in the boxing ring they were now fine. 'I was a little worried,' she said 'and I wasn't at all sure that we should have let you take on a young, fit youth.' Although Tom invited her in, she explained that she couldn't stop as she was on her way to open up the club. 'Although I suppose Harry will have beaten me to it,' she said. 'He is very keen and a great help.' She gave Tom her card and said 'If ever you feel that you want to get involved give me a ring, we're always glad of volunteers.' After she had gone Tom sat down in his sitting room and fingered the card, it still felt warm and had a faint trace of perfume, or was it just his imagination he wondered. Evelyn said 'She was a nice young lady, Tom; perhaps you ought to help at the club.'

Tom decided to think very carefully about helping at the club, he often made quick impulsive decisions but on this occasion, something told him to think very carefully. Perhaps he felt too attracted by Fran and at his age that was madness. He sat back and closed his eyes, he wondered as he had done so often before just where his life had gone. He thought about the people he had known, the ones he had liked and the ones he had clashed with. On the whole, he had made very few enemies but then if he was completely honest he had acquired very few real friends. He had a few intensive friendships while on climbing expeditions because when people are sharing danger they often draw closer to each other. However, once the expedition was over they had usually moved on to new expeditions and new climbing companions. Oddly enough, the friends he remembered most clearly were those who had been killed in the mountains. They were always with you, while the others came and went. He quite often thought about the climbers he had known who had perished on some distant peak. The wife of one friend had told him that men who climbed in high mountains should not get married and for many years, he had stayed single. By the time he married Evelyn he had just about finished with expeditions and she was definitely concerned that he should give them up entirely. The trouble with growing older, he thought, was that you spend too much time fretting about the past and not being optimistic enough about the future. Still, he thought, I have some new friends now and with any luck, the next few months could be very interesting. He thought about the differences in the group; from laughing, outgoing Alice, what a life she must have led; through to quiet and rather withdrawn Lenny. How much misery had he known? He must have dozed off because the next time he opened his eyes the room was in darkness so he decided to make himself a warm drink and go to bed.

He was a few minutes late on Wednesday afternoon and he apologised. 'Nearest to come and last to arrive,' laughed Vicky. Lenny had brought Mr. Wong and though they all knew him, at least by sight, he introduced him formally and Mr. Wong put his hands together and gave them a small bow. Bill said he was pleased that everyone had been able to attend and he handed over to Alice to continue with the meeting.

40

Alice had taken her task very seriously, she had drawn up a list of possible 'entertainments', and had it photocopied at a local stationers. 'Please tell me if I have left anything off,' she said 'I won't be offended.' There were the obvious home entertainments, such as radio, television and listening to music and the activities for which they had to leave home. These included the cinema, the theatre, sporting activities and of course Bingo; also the occasional visits of fairs and circuses. 'Not that I can go to a circus any more,' said Alice 'I tried it once and it made me cry.' 'That's very understandable,' said Tom sympathetically. They started discussing the list, all but Lenny listened to morning radio, he said that he had to be up at five o'clock to do the papers and was busy right through until lunch. 'My customers entertain me,' he said with a wry smile. Tom and the Harris's preferred Radio 4 and Jim said he always listened to Five Live. Vicky and Alice said that they preferred Radio 2, although they really missed Terry Wogan, and Mr. Wong was a surprise because he said he always listened to Radio 3 because he loved classical music. He surprised them even more when he said he particularly liked Wagner.

Only Vicky said that she watched television in the morning sometimes and the others agreed that they mostly watched in the evenings. 'I couldn't miss my soaps,' said Beryl 'it gives me something to look forward to, although I never watch Eastenders. I used to spend a lot of evenings alone at home when Bill was an active police man.' As Tom expected, their tastes in music were very diverse, he himself was a traditional Jazz man and in this he was joined by Lenny. Mr. Wong had already enthused about classical music but he did surprise them by his wide-ranging knowledge. Alice and Vicky said that they preferred pop and Vicky said 'Something I can dance to for preference.' But Bill

41

and Beryl said they rarely listened to music but they would go to a concert in the city if the performers interested them. Once again Tom thought 'What a disparate group we are.' Bill surprised everyone by saying rather vehemently 'There's too much smut on the television nowadays, too many double entendres and too much suggestiveness. I think we ought to write to some of the people who control radio and television and demand that they clean up their act, particularly before nine o'clock.'

Beryl said rather sadly 'Yes, even the soaps have deteriorated in the last few years, they used to be very suitable for all the family but there are some things now which you wouldn't want children to watch.' 'It's the people they employ nowadays,' said Lenny 'some of them receive as much as a million pounds and they're rubbish. I'm thinking of people I used to like such as Michael Parkinson and of course Terry Wogan.' 'Perhaps we can amuse ourselves by nominating our least favourite personality,' said Tom. 'I won't use the term celebrity because I think it is a stupid term. There is nothing celebrated about most of the performers we see on the box.' After some discussion they agreed that the following week they would each nominate somebody they would be happy never to see or hear of again. They continued to talk about entertainment and the afternoon seemed to fly by. Apart from Alice and Vicky none of the others had ever been to a Bingo hall and only Tom had ever been to a casino. 'I would love to go sometime,' said Alice and they agreed they would make up a party in the near future. Tom thought, 'How much more interesting life is when you have friends to share it with. Everybody should have friends, perhaps we ought to start a series of Windmill clubs in different parts of the Country.'

'We haven't talked yet about the theatre and the

cinema,' said Alice. 'I want to go to the cinema this week because there is a film I particularly want to see but Vicky doesn't want to come with me and I don't like going on my own.' Jim murmured 'Is that the film on at the Odeon?' When Alice said yes it was he said 'Well I'll come with you if you like, because I don't like going on my own either and I wanted to see that film.' 'That's a good idea,' said Bill, 'I mean for us to pair up sometimes and do things together, it's alright for Beryl and me we have each other.' 'Not that we always agree on who should see what,' said Beryl. They decided to keep an eye on the local theatres and see if there was anything that they might wish to see together and Vicky said 'I'm always willing to take someone to Bingo; it's a lot of fun.' It was teatime again and Tom said 'I'm sure your cakes get better and better Beryl. If you keep feeding us like this we will all want to move in.' Shortly afterwards they said their goodbyes and Tom and Lenny walked down to Tom's gate accompanied this time by Mr. Wong. He told them how much he had enjoyed the afternoon and he was glad that they had asked him to join them.

Chapter Eight

Tom could not get Fran Summers out of his head, in the end he decided to grasp the nettle and telephone her. She answered her phone at the second ring and for a few moments Tom was dumbstruck. 'Hello,' said Fran for a second time and then Tom managed to say 'Hello Fran, this is Tom Burton.' 'Oh thank goodness, I thought for a moment that I'd got a heavy breather.' 'No, nothing like that, I just wondered if we could talk about the possibility of my helping in some way at your club?' 'Yes of course, we're always looking for volunteers.' Tom swallowed, 'Uum, perhaps we could have dinner together and talk about it.' He hurried on 'There's a nice little bistro near the bus terminus, I'm told it's very good. Have you been there?' 'No, I haven't,' she replied 'it's very kind of you to ask me. When would you like to meet?' 'Well I wondered about Thursday, but only if it's suitable for you.' 'Thursday would be fine,' she said. 'Shall we say seven thirty?' 'Great,' said Tom 'I'll look forward to it.' 'Me too,' she replied. 'Bye until then.' 'Bye,' Tom whispered. He couldn't believe what he'd just done he had to sit down.

He hadn't been out to dinner or anywhere else since Evelyn died. Apart that is from his old firm's annual bash to which he was still invited. He went but he hated those kinds of functions. Watching people drink themselves silly and then stumble into lust only to bitterly regret it the following morning. 'I suppose I'm just old,' he murmured to himself, 'a silly old 'fuddy duddy'. Anyway, this is only a meeting about the youth club he told himself and it will mean little or nothing to her. 'And what will it mean to you?' asked Evelyn. 'Nothing at all, my dear, I'm an old man and she's a young woman.' 'A very attractive young woman,'

Evelyn replied, 'whatever you do, don't go making a fool of yourself.' He recalled when he and Evelyn first met; they were both in their early fifties. Evelyn had been married before and divorced and he had almost married his New Zealand girl but decided that life in New Zealand wasn't for him, she told him she did not want to live anywhere else. So they parted with some mutual regret.

When he eventually returned to England he started work at the builders' merchants and Evelyn eventually became a secretary there. When he first saw her there were no bolts of lightning or feelings of love at first sight, but he thought that she was an attractive lady. Evelyn gradually learned of his travels and adventures and decided, as she told him later, that he was just the man to provide her with a second husband. They were married in a registry office and had almost twenty peaceful and pleasant years together. Then she developed her dementia. At first it was just forgetful lapses, he had decided not to retire at the usual age but to keep working until he was seventy-two. The reason for this was to try and build up his pension fund and because he was so efficient his fellow directors of the company were happy to accept it. He would arrive home from work and there would be no evening meal or even food to prepare. 'I was busy in the garden and I forgot to go to the shops dear,' she would say. And he would kiss her and say 'Never mind, we'll go out for a meal.'

Then the mood swings started, his gentle and loving Evelyn would suddenly lose her temper and some of the scenes were too painful and unpleasant for him to recall. These would be followed by her becoming very contrite and begging him to forgive her. 'Please say you will never leave me,' she would sob. If he was ashamed about anything it was the very small sense of relief he felt when she died. Not for his sake, he told himself, but for her because she was at last at peace. In his heart, he knew that their love was gradually dying with each traumatic episode. The last few months she could not possibly have loved him, because for most of the time, she no longer knew who he was and he didn't know how much longer he could cope. The end, when it came, was surprisingly peaceful, they had had a quiet day, Evelyn gardening and him sitting in a deck chair and reading. At bedtime, he asked her if she would like a cup of tea. 'Yes please,' she replied 'and a biscuit.' He went into the kitchen feeling quite relaxed.

They sat drinking their tea together and then she said, 'Will you take my cup darling?' He did so and she lay back in her chair and closed her eyes. After a few minutes, he quietly suggested that they should go up to bed. She didn't reply and when he touched her hand, he realised that she was dead. He gently kissed her forehead and telephoned the Doctor. He had always been brought up not to cry, both his mother and his grandmother had told him that boys didn't cry. He remained impassive while the paramedics took her away but later in bed, he berated himself into exhaustion and fell asleep. Now here he was thinking wistfully about a girl young enough to be his daughter. 'There's no fool like an old fool,' he thought to himself and went to get his bedtime drink.

When he arrived at the following Windmill Club meeting, he found his friends were in the middle of a very animated and even heated discussion. He soon learned that the debate was about homes for the elderly. It transpired that Alice had been to one of these homes to visit an elderly aunt. It was her first visit and she said 'My god Tom it was a right dump. All the residents were sitting on chairs placed around the room and most of them looked as if they were almost asleep. They honestly looked as if they were just waiting to die. My aunt was awake but she didn't seem any happier than the rest. People should not have to spend their last years in a place like that.'

'One of the staff told me that they had their evening meal, usually soup and sandwiches, about five o'clock and then around seven o'clock they were given a cup of tea and a biscuit. They all had to be in bed by nine o'clock when the night staff came on. She told me that some staff gave them their last drink between six and six thirty and then had them in bed by eight o'clock so that they, the staff, could take it in turns to leave early. The manager was prepared to turn a blind eye providing all the jobs got done.' 'Yes, but surely this was an unusual home,' said Tom mildly. 'We don't think so,' said Beryl, 'we've heard quite a few stories about different homes.' 'Ah but only gossip,' said Tom, 'none of it substantiated.' 'Well, I think we're very lucky,' said Vicky 'that we don't need one of these places. But that doesn't mean that we should just ignore it and do nothing. Poor Alice called on me after her visit and she was really very upset.' 'But what exactly can we do?' said Bill. 'We will just get told that it is none of our business.' 'Ah yes,' said Tom, 'but we have actually called ourselves the Windmill Club, and perhaps here is an opportunity to do a little tilting.'

At this point Beryl said thoughtfully, 'Well we could split into pairs and visit some of the homes in our neighbourhood. Apart from the one Alice saw there are apparently another six within a two mile radius.' Bill stood up and assumed his chairperson role, 'Supposing we split into pairs and each pair visits two homes and then we compare notes.' 'Yes, but we can't just march up to a home and say we just want to visit, just like that,' said Jim. 'No,' said Bill, 'Beryl and I will go as a couple saying that we are looking for somewhere for our future; Jim and Alice can go to two different homes and say that they're looking for somewhere for an elderly relative.' At this point Lenny said, 'I don't think I could do something like that,' and Mr. Wong agreed. 'Well then, Vicky and Tom could go along saying that Vicky is his carer and because she has to leave Tom is thinking of going into a home.' 'He doesn't look decrepit enough,' said Beryl. Alice said 'Oh we can soon fix that, give him a stick to lean on and a bit of makeup, I used to do makeup in the circus you know. I'm sure we can make Tom look about ninety.' 'Thanks very much,' said Tom 'I'll really look forward to growing old that quickly. It is a pity that we have to resort to subterfuge but I doubt we would get much information if we just knocked on the door and asked. In any case we have a duty to look after the welfare of our fellow citizens.'

After further discussion, they got out the local directory and decided which pair would visit which two homes. 'We'll grade them from A to E,' said Bill. 'Well I certainly wouldn't give the one where my aunt is more than D,' Alice retorted. 'We'll make these visits sometime at the beginning of next week,' said Bill 'and report back at the next meeting.' 'With all this discussion about old people's homes,' said Jim 'we haven't looked at our nominations for people in broadcasting that we would prefer never to see or hear of again, having listened to you all and got your suggestions, and having had a long discussion with Vicky and Alice, I've drawn up a list of possibles for people to vote on.' 'Go on then,' said Bill 'let's hear your thoughts and we'll see if we agree.'

Jim cleared his throat, and said 'Well I've put them in alphabetical order so that it doesn't look as if I'm personally biased in any way, but these are the people most frequently nominated.' He then read out his list,

'Russell Brand, Jeremy Clarkson, Simon Cowell, Chris Evans, Piers Morgan, Jonathan Ross and Alan Sugar.' 'Not a bad list,' said Tom what about women though?' 'Well we did have Cheryl Cole down and Victoria Beckham nominated but then I thought that they're fairly harmless, their efforts at self promotion are just sad, whereas those men are really loud, grossly overpaid and without any discernible talent. Has anybody got any objections?' he said. 'Well not me,' said Beryl 'I only wish that we weren't losing people like Terry Wogan and Michael Parkinson, you never hear either of them using foul language and I could listen to people like John Humphries and Jim Naughtie all day.' 'Well,' said Vicky 'I like the One Show and I think Matt and Alex are really nice but I never watch it on Fridays when that noisy egotistic chap is on.' 'And,' said Lenny 'look at how the idiots who make the decisions about broadcasting have started dumbing everything down. The Archers and Eastenders are good examples. But times seem to be changing and the so-called powers that be, particularly in the BBC and slightly less so in the ITV, seem to like noisy, rude, unpleasant people. They don't seem to appreciate that older people have different tastes and different standards.' 'And they don't damn well care,' added Jim. 'Does any one think my list is unfair?' 'No,' said Alice 'they would all certainly be high on my list but there must be some we have overlooked.'

Tom said 'I am not sure we should tar them all with the same brush. Brand and Ross are the only ones who use foul or smutty language; the others are just too full of their own self-importance with the possible exception of Piers Morgan, who can at least laugh at himself and that is definitely a saving grace. For my part, I think the changes in comedy are the really sad loss. Comedians used to be nice people like

Morecambe and Wise or Les Dawson but now most comedians seem to have a spiteful edge, poking fun at people like the less able.' 'And,' said Alice 'they all seem to use foul language, even the female comics.'

'OK,' said Bill 'I think we all agree that Jim's done a good job and probably nominated the ones on which we would all be unanimous. Let us concentrate on the old people's homes and see where we go from there.' Beryl brought in the usual heavily loaded tea trolley and the day finished on a comfortable note.

Chapter Nine

The following afternoon Tom would have described himself as being in a bit of a dither, what was he going to wear for his evening out. Should he be very casual or go for the semi casual approach? He certainly didn't want to be too formal, a lot of young men didn't bother wearing collars and ties any more but then he wasn't a young man, so there was no use pretending he was. He decided in the end that he would wear his sports coat and a shirt with a tie and a pair of khaki linen trousers. He didn't think he would be over dressed for the bistro. He arrived there a few minutes before seven thirty and managed to secure a table in a discreet corner. Fran came through the door exactly at seven thirty and as he stood up to greet her he thought how very attractive she looked. She was wearing a crisp white blouse and a dark skirt down to her knees, her beautiful red hair was tied back and more than one man turned to look at her as she walked down the Bistro. 'Hi Tom,' she said, holding out her hand. 'Hello Fran,' he said 'thank you for coming.' They shook hands and sat down studying the menu.

At first the conversation was a little stilted because both of them were obviously unsure about what form the discussion should take. 'I know you're interested in boxing,' said Fran 'but what other activities do you like?' 'Well,' said Tom 'I used to play some tennis and some cricket and I've always been interested in hill walking.' 'Ah,' she said 'now you're talking, there's nothing I like more than wandering across hills unless it's doing a bit of rock climbing. Have you ever done any rock climbing she asked?' 'Oh a bit,' he said, 'but not for quite a long time now. I used to like pottering about in high mountains but obviously I had to give that up as I got older.' 'Burton,' she said thoughtfully, 'I don't suppose you're any relation to Monty Burton?' 'Well as a matter of fact,' he said rather quietly 'I am Monty Burton.' She threw back her head and laughed out loud, so loudly that everyone in the bistro turned to look. 'I'm actually on a date with a world famous mountaineer,' she said. Then she paused and looked embarrassed 'I'm sorry perhaps I shouldn't have said on a date,' and she blushed. 'You look even more beautiful when you blush,' Tom said kindly and I think the expression on a date is very flattering to me.' ,They lapsed into silence and Fran said 'I've read about you in magazines and alpine journals but I never thought I would meet you. You've climbed mountains like Nanga Parbat and you also put up some amazing routes in the Andes. But if your name is Tom where did Monty come from?' 'Well it started when I was a naval cadet, the petty officer in charge of our group said 'Burton, no relation to Montague Burton I suppose? That's where I buy my civvies.' 'After that some of my mates started calling me Montague and then it was shortened to Monty. When I started climbing it just stuck.'

After a few minutes, she said 'Why have you kept it so quiet, you must come and talk to the members at the club.' 'It was a long time ago and to be honest I try not to think about it too much. You will have heard the expression that there are bold climbers and old climbers but there are very few old, bold climbers. Most of us in our hearts were in denial and never really wanted to be among the old climbers.' 'That's nonsense,' she said 'in all the things I've read there were none any bolder than you and you have every reason to be proud. That route you and Geoff Mason put up on K2 will probably never be repeated. What happened to him by the way?' she asked. 'Would you believe he was guiding a beginner up a simple route above Chamonix, the beginner fell and somehow Geoff fell with him. They were both killed, such a stupid waste to go in such a miserable way.'

They ordered their food and as far as Tom was concerned the evening passed far too quickly. 'I know,' she said 'I'm taking a small group to Hathersage to climb on Stanage Edge, why don't you come with us? You won't have to do anything too strenuous but I could do with the moral support.' 'I'd like that,' said Tom 'where are you staying?' 'There's a little bed and breakfast outside Hathersage, it's run by a lady called Mrs. Castle and I'm sure you would like it.' They agreed that Fran would let him know the exact date which was in about three weeks time. 'We'd only be away a couple of nights,' she said 'as the kids don't like being away from the bright lights for too long.' They got up to leave the bistro and as they passed one table the man sitting there said 'Lucky old bastard,' and his wife said 'Shush, it's probably his daughter.' Tom felt like stopping and punching the man on the nose but Fran must have read his thoughts and taking his hand she pulled him through the door. She had travelled to the bistro on the bus so they walked to Tom's car and he drove her home. Just as she was getting out of the car she leaned over and kissed him gently on the lips. 'Thank you so much that was a lovely evening.' 'Thank you,' said Tom 'you've made an old man very happy.' 'Pooh,' she said 'you're definitely not an old man. Goodnight Monty,' she said with a little chuckle. He watched her walk gracefully up to her front door and then drove thoughtfully home.

Chapter Ten

Tom and Vicky had agreed to use Monday and Tuesday as their days for visiting the retirement homes, or homes for the elderly, or old people's homes, because every home seemed to have a different designation. They assumed the other pairs would also arrange to use these two days. However, when Tom telephoned the two homes he discovered that neither home would take visitors on a Monday so he arranged to visit the The Limes Retirement Home on Tuesday morning and The White House Home for the Elderly on Tuesday afternoon.

Vicky arranged with Alice that she would do Tom's makeup after breakfast on Tuesday morning so Tom drove them round there just after nine o'clock. He still had mostly dark hair with a few small streaks of grey so she added more white and produced a pair of tinted glasses. Then she showed him how to lean on a stick and shuffle slowly along. She had a long mirror in her hall and when Tom shuffled towards it, he said 'Oh dear I really do look about ninety.' Unfortunately, Vicky didn't drive and they agreed that it would look rather odd if Tom drove up to the homes in his own car. Consequently they had arranged for a taxi to pick them up at Alice's house. When they arrived at The Limes Vicky very carefully helped Tom to climb out of the taxi and then she rang the doorbell. A young woman opened the door, she was wearing a cream coloured uniform and had the name tag Jenny pinned on it. Vicky said that she was with Mr. Burton and the girl replied that Mrs. Jenkins was expecting them. She led them to her office door and then said 'Wait here,' while she knocked and went in. They could hear a brief conversation because the door had not shut properly.

'They're here now,' said the young woman to Mrs. Jenkins. 'She's black.' Mrs.Jenkins said 'Well it's not her that's coming is it? He's not black I hope? You know we don't take such people.'

Tom thought 'Well that's a good start anyway,' just as Mrs. Jenkins came out of the door. 'Mr. Burton is it?' she said. 'Good morning, please come in.' They went into the office and she asked them both to sit down. 'I gather you're looking for somewhere to live,' she said to Tom. 'Yes, well I will be shortly,' he replied because my carer Vicky is leaving. 'Well,' she said 'we can show you round but you don't look very mobile,' commenting on the way that he had shuffled in and lowered himself very carefully into the chair. 'I have good days and bad days,' said Tom 'and today my rheumatism is playing me up.' 'Oh well,' said Mrs. Jenkins 'I'm sure we can manage to look after you.' She then asked Jenny, who was still waiting, to show them round the home. It was certainly a very well kept home, the furnishings were bright and everywhere smelled clean. As Jenny showed them round she introduced them to some of the residents, most of who were sitting in chairs either looking at newspapers or staring into space. 'We're not very lively first thing in the morning,' said Jenny 'but we do activities in the afternoons. Will you be able to manage the stairs, Mr. Burton?' she said. 'So that I can show you the bedrooms.' 'Oh yes I think so,' said Tom 'if you give me time.'

They went upstairs and Jenny opened two or three of the bedroom doors without knocking. In one room a care assistant was helping an elderly lady to get dressed but Jenny did not apologise and just carried on as if there was no one there. The bedrooms were fairly small and rather bleak, in contrast to the rooms on the ground floor. 'Downstairs for show and upstairs for living,' muttered Vicky to Tom. Having looked in several rooms and two of the bathrooms they went back down to the office. Mrs. Jenkins wasn't there but another of the care assistants told Jenny that she unexpectedly had to go out. It was quite clear that Tom was not going to be welcomed with open arms. They asked Jenny about the charges but she told them that only Mrs. Jenkins could discuss that, she wasn't even prepared to discuss mealtimes and menus and it was quite obvious that Mrs. Jenkins was very authoritarian and the staff were trained to do as they were told. They went outside where the taxi had returned, as they drove away Vicky said 'Well I certainly wouldn't give that more than a C.' 'Oh well better luck this afternoon,' said Tom.

They picked up Tom's car and he drove them to a nearby pub for a simple lunch. Vicky was in high spirits and regaled Tom with fascinating and highly amusing stories about her childhood in Barbados. After lunch Tom said 'Never mind about the taxi I'll drive us to the White House and they can think what they like.' The White House was up a long winding drive and the house itself looked more like a fortress than a house. As they got out of the car a man in a white jacket appeared on the steps and said that his name was Carter and Mr. Warren was expecting them. They went into Mr. Warren's office where he was seated behind a desk, almost as large as a table tennis table. He got up when they went in and boomed a welcome to them, then he asked them if they would like tea or coffee and Tom said, 'Perhaps we can look round first.' 'Certainly, said Mr. Warren, 'I'll show you round myself.' All the downstairs rooms were large and airy and most of the residents seemed to be having a nap. They always like a rest after lunch,' Mr. Warren explained but I can assure you they're very lively in the evenings.' 'What time is lights out?' asked Vicky. 'Well we do try to get most people upstairs by ten o'clock or ten thirty at the latest but if they are watching a television programme it may be later,' said Mr. Warren. This was in contrast to The Limes where Jenny had told them that they liked residents to be in bed by half past nine.

There was no problem getting upstairs to see the bedrooms because there was a small lift just big enough for the three of them to cram in, particularly as Mr. Warren was a very large man. The bedrooms upstairs were also relatively large and well decorated, many of them had en suite facilities and Tom murmured to Vicky 'This is much more like it.' Mr. Warren asked Tom if he was on any medication and when Tom replied in the negative he said 'That's good, we try very hard not to use unnecessary medicines and we would never resort to the chemical cosh.' 'Oh, what's that?' said Vicky.' Mr. Warren explained that in some of the homes he'd worked in the staff used sedatives and sleeping tablets to keep the residents quiet. 'I decided that when I could open a home of my own I would make it as resident friendly as possible. I opened the White House about five years ago and I do believe we offer a high standard of care.'

After they had finished their tour they had tea in the large conservatory at the back of the house and then Tom and Vicky made their farewells. As they got in the car Tom said 'Well, it just goes to show how careful you have to be with first impressions. The outside of this home put me off at first but I think I would be happy to give it an A.' Vicky agreed and when Tom dropped her off at home she said 'See you tomorrow, I've quite enjoyed myself and if ever you do need a carer,' she said with a laugh 'I'm your woman.' 'Thanks,' said Tom dryly, 'but hopefully not for a long time yet.'

Chapter Eleven

The following afternoon they all met as usual and Bill suggested that they compare notes on what they had seen. He and Beryl had had sharply contrasting visits. 'The first home we went to in Barton Road was absolutely awful, it was dingy and depressing and when you walked through the front door there was a cloying smell of urine and stew.' 'The first thing I would have had to do,' said Beryl 'was open all the windows. The atmosphere seemed to depress the staff because without exception we didn't see a single smile. The residents were mainly watching television in their own rooms and these rooms were equally depressing.' 'Beryl and I would have to give it an E,' said Bill. 'Then in the afternoon,' said Beryl 'it was the total opposite, the Chestnuts was a purpose built home and humming with activity. The staff were pleasant and welcoming and all the residents we spoke to said that they were very happy. There were apparently joint managers, Sue and Margaret, and they too made us feel very welcome. I hope we never have to live in a home,' said Beryl 'but if we did then the Chestnuts would do for me. We would give it between A and B as a mark.'

Alice and Jim then took over. Alice regarded both the homes they had visited as rather mediocre 'But certainly better than the one where my aunt lives,' she said. They awarded both their homes as C and finally Tom and Vicky made their report. 'Well,' said Bill 'it seems as if it was a very useful exercise although at this stage I'm not sure what we do with the information we've gathered.' 'I think we ought to compile a report,' said Tom 'and at least let the local authorities see it, I would be prepared to do that.' 'Oh yes, said Jim 'and they will probably tell us to mind our own business.' It was time for tea and Alice said 'I don't know what will happen to our report but I for one felt that we were doing something useful.' There was general agreement and Mr. Wong nodded sagely. 'The real issue,' said Tom 'is whether people who have worked hard all their lives should finish up in places which are second or third class. Worse than that, most of them have to pay for the privilege. The social services apply a means test without telling them that if they have a medical problem the NHS will pay their fees.' 'That is disgraceful,' Alice almost shouted. 'My aunt had to sell her home to stay in that dump and she is severely diabetic and arthritic.' 'Well,' said Bill 'all the more reason for us to produce a really cogent report.'

Tom started work on the report as soon as he got home, he had arranged with Bill that he would draft it out and then Bill would type it out on his word processor and send it off. He finished it over the weekend and took it round to Bill on Monday morning. When he rang the doorbell, Beryl answered and greeted him with a broad smile. 'Oh Tom how nice to see you, please come in.' Bill joined them in the sitting room and Beryl went off to get some coffee. 'Including the home where Alice's aunt lives we have one A, one B, three C's, one D and one E. Apart from the first two the other five are just not good enough; in fact,' he added 'I would say far from good enough. I will send a copy of your excellent report to the head of social services and the councillor who chairs that committee.'

Beryl came in with coffee and some sponge cake which Tom described as mouth watering and delicious. Beryl blushed with pleasure and said 'You know Tom flattery will get you anywhere, have another slice.' Tom did so and then said to Bill 'I hope we are not wasting our time.' Shortly afterwards he made his farewell. When he got home, he found that the postman had been and delivered a cream coloured envelope which smelled of a familiar perfume. It contained a note from Fran thanking him for a lovely evening and telling him that their trip would be the Sunday after next and they would be back on the Tuesday. Two nights is about all that my brave outdoor warriors can cope with. She promised to be in touch nearer the time and signed the note 'Love Frances'. Tom found himself reading the note a second and then a third time, it was as if he didn't want to put it down and he was experiencing a feeling he had never known before. 'Now Tom,' he heard Evelyn's voice saying 'it's just a polite note.' He knew she was right but he couldn't help holding the note to his lips and breathing in the faint but delicate perfume. Silly old devil, he thought and went to get out the vacuum cleaner.

On Wednesday, Bill reported that he had taken the letters into town on Monday afternoon, delivering them personally. He had not as yet received any response from the councillor but on Tuesday, he received a visit from Mrs. Brooks. She was delivering a message from her boss, the head of social services. In effect, the message was for Bill and his friends to kindly mind their own business. She had apparently told Bill that she knew there would be trouble when she learned about their little group being formed. She went so far as to suggest that their group should be disbanded. 'The WRVS group is going very well,' she said, and I could probably arrange for you all to be readmitted if you apologise.' When Bill reported this last comment, the group exploded into a mixture of outraged gasps and hoots of laughter. 'Damned impertinence,' said Tom. 'Bloody cheek if you ask me,' said Alice. This led on to a general discussion about bureaucrats and politicians. 'Useless, the lot of them,' said Alice. 'Aye,' said Jim backing her up, 'we're supposed to live in a free country but it's no such thing.' 'No,' continued Beryl 'and look at the amount of council tax we all pay for the privilege of Mrs. Brooks telling us to mind our own business. I'll go and get the tea.'

The discussion continued over tea and there was general agreement that not only would they not mind their own business but depending on the response from the councillor they may try to take the matter a lot further, although at this stage no one was quite sure how. As they were leaving Tom noted with a quiet smile of approval that Jim opened his car door for Alice on the passenger side and Lenny and Vicky climbed in the back on the driver's side. He then adjusted Alice's seat belt and she gave him a warm smile of thanks. 'The cinema visit must have gone well,' thought Tom.

Chapter Twelve

On Friday morning, Fran telephoned and asked if she could call in on her way to the club to discuss the details of the climbing trip. 'Why don't you come earlier,' said Tom 'about five o'clock and I'll cook us some tea.' 'Oh, that would be nice,' she replied, 'see you at five.' Later that morning he walked round to Lenny's to get some fresh bread and a newspaper. They stood and chatted for a while because there were no other customers. Lenny pointed to a story in the local newspaper about two councillors, one from the north side of the city and one from their own constituency. It transpired that the councillors, both male, had been having an affair and had left their wives. They had decided to move down to the south coast together and in consequence had resigned their seats on the council. 'The world gets ever more complex,' Tom said to Lenny and headed for home.

About quarter to five, his doorbell rang and he found Frances standing on the steps clutching a large bunch of flowers. 'For you,' she said. 'Good Lord, talk about role reversal,' 'I know,' she laughed, 'makes life more interesting, but I thought tea was too early to have wine and you don't seem a box of chocolates type of man.' 'Well, you'd better come in and I'll find a vase and perhaps you'll be kind enough to arrange them for me.' He had decided on grilled bacon, fried eggs and some of his own speciality potato cakes. Fran said 'That sounds good but I will have to pass on the bacon.' 'Oh yes, I'd forgotten you were vegetarian,' said Tom. She spent some time looking through his voluminous collection of books while he prepared the simple but tasty meal.

'I see you've got the poems of Geoffrey Winthrop

Young,' she said. 'Yes, I met him once when I was temping at the Eskdale outward bound school; he was one of the great men of British mountaineering before the First World War. Unfortunately, he was injured by a shell in Italy in 1917 and lost one of his legs. Some people don't rate his poetry but I like it.' 'What other poets do you like?' 'Well I suppose I would choose Dylan Thomas and WB Yeats as my favourite poets. What about you?' 'Oh I'm a Wordsworth fan and I like Christina Rossetti.' 'I'm not sure I know her poetry,' Tom replied. 'There's a poem of hers I particularly like called Remember, it is sad but also hopeful.' 'I know what you mean; Thomas wrote one poem called 'Do not go gentle into that good night'. I particularly like the verse

Wild men who caught and sang the sun in flight
And learned too late they grieved it on its way
Do not go gentle into that good night.

I think it is probably very relevant to mountaineers but come, tea is served madam.'

While they were eating their tea, which Fran said was delicious, 'And where did you learn to make these potato cakes,' she added. 'It was a recipe of my mother's,' he told her 'and one of my favourite foods as a boy.' When they finished she told him of the plans for Hathersage. 'We will be taking two boys and two girls,' she said 'leaving on Sunday morning, staying overnight on Sunday, climbing on Monday, then travelling back on Tuesday. We will probably call in at one of the mines in Castleton on the way home.' 'Sounds good,' said Tom 'I'm really looking forward to it.'

She suddenly looked at her watch and said 'oh gosh, it's half past seven, I'd better get to the club, although I expect Harry will have opened it.' 'It is surprising how

quickly time goes when you're in enjoyable company.'
'Yes indeed,' said Tom, 'it's been another lovely
occasion. And as I said earlier I'm really looking
forward to the trip to Hathersage. Mind you most of my
equipment is pretty tatty now but I'll do my best not to
let you down.' 'I don't think there's any fear of that,'
she said with a smile. As she was leaving she again
gave him a light kiss on the lips.

Tom couldn't wait until Wednesday to see if they
had a response from the Chairman of the social services
department so he rang Bill on Tuesday morning and
asked if he had received a letter. Bill said 'Yes I have,
it's a very long, detailed letter and it would be better if
we all read it tomorrow.' The following day was really
wet and miserable and this was in keeping not only
with their discussion about the council but with some
rather disturbing news that Mr. Wong brought to the
meeting.

It seemed that in the last three or four weeks a group
of louts had decided to make themselves a nuisance in
Mr. Wong's fish and chip shop, ordering food and then
leaving without paying and intimidating his staff. On
the last occasion, the ringleader had told Mr. Wong that
unless he paid them they would probably go as far as
wrecking his shop and frightening away his customers.
'That's outrageous,' said Tom who at least on one
evening a week walked round to the shop and bought
his supper. Bill asked if Mr. Wong had reported the
matter to the police. He said he had but obviously they
could not mount a regular watch and they could only
take action if the louts were caught in the act. 'Well we
ought to do something,' said Alice, 'we can't let one of
our members be intimidated and do nothing about it.'
They discussed the various options and although they
agreed that they would like to help it was difficult to
know what they could achieve. 'Do they come in at the

same time every night?' Bill asked. 'Well, it's usually just before or just after ten o'clock.' 'And are there any specific nights?' Bill went on.' 'Yes, it's usually Friday or Saturday,' he was told. They decided to think about the problem during the afternoon and if anyone could come up with a plan, they should mention it at the end of the meeting.

Bill suggested they should have an early break for tea and then discuss the letter from Councillor James. Bill had made some enquiries, discovered that he was a long serving councillor and had rather a poor reputation for being pompous and overbearing. 'You can certainly tell this,' Bill went on 'from the tone of the letter.' And he proceeded to read it out to the group. The letter started by saying how surprised the councillor had been to receive a letter from a group that he had never heard of. He said that the questions raised by their letter were matters which were entirely the business of the homes and the council and he did not believe that the brief visits the group had made could possibly have given them a realistic picture. Furthermore, the homes were all privately owned and the charges were agreed between the proprietors and the local authorities. There was absolutely no way he was prepared to discuss financial matters with a group who had no business getting involved. The letter ended with a veiled warning that if the council felt that their group was interfering in some way they may well have to resort to some form of legal action.

This letter was greeted with dismay by some of the members and indignation by the others. 'These homes are part of the community,' Tom said, 'and surely anybody is entitled to be concerned about the welfare of the residents.' 'Obviously not'' said Bill 'we have been quite clearly told to mind our own business.' 'And are we going to?' asked Vicky 'just take it lying down?' 'Well, let's take a vote said Bill 'and see how many of us are not prepared to take it lying down. Hands up those people who think we should continue with some form of action.' The vote was unanimous, every hand went up and Tom was pleased to see that perhaps the Windmill Club was not made of straw.

He had been giving the matter a lot of thought in the expectation of a negative reply from the council. 'How many of you saw the article in the local newspaper about the two councillors who have just resigned?' Obviously, Lenny had and Bill and Beryl had also seen it but none of the others had read the article. Tom briefly outlined the story and drew a giggle from Vicky, although most of the others were not sure of his point. 'You don't expect us to do something about that?' Jim asked. 'No of course not,' said Tom 'the reason I mention it is because there is now a vacancy in our constituency, why don't we nominate somebody to be a councillor.' 'O, I don't know,' said Bill 'that's a bit complicated surely.' 'I'm not so sure,' said Alice 'if we had somebody on the inside of the council we could exert a lot more influence.'

'Well, said Tom 'apparently there is to be a by-election in a few weeks and if we wanted to do something about it we would have to get cracking fairly quickly.' 'Right,' said Bill 'I have a contact in the town hall and I'll find out the procedure. The question is who would we nominate? Do you fancy it Tom?' 'No, I think I'm probably too old to be accepted by the voters, it will have to be one of our younger members.' They all looked at each other and then Vicky said 'I think Alice would be ideal, she's always got a lot to say for herself.' 'Well thank you very much for that backhanded compliment,' said Alice 'but to be honest I wouldn't mind giving it a go if you are all in agreement.' 'Great,' said Tom 'I think you would be perfect,' and Jim said 'So do I, I think she would make a super councillor.' They decided that the plan would be put into action at the next meeting, providing there would be enough time.

They then went on to the question of Mr. Wong's problem. Jim said that he had an idea. 'We could wait in Lenny's shop on Friday evening and if the trouble makers started Mr. Wong could let us know and we could all go round and meet in the shop en masse, that would intimidate the bullies anyway.' 'Well, we haven't got time to make a more sophisticated plan,' said Bill 'but we don't want anyone getting hurt.' 'There are really only two things to consider,' said Tom 'how Mr. Wong signals and what we should do when we got in there.' 'The first one is easy,' said Bill we could put a bell push under Mr. Wong's counter and a bell in Lenny's shop, you don't need wires nowadays.' 'The second's easy too,' said Alice, 'we just give em what for.' 'Well I'm not sure it's that easy,' said Bill 'there's all sorts of questions about assaults and self defence.' They agreed that Bill and Tom would rig up the bell the following day and then any of the members who wanted to, could meet in Lenny's shop on Friday evening. As they made their farewells and headed for home, Tom thought 'We will have to see how this develops, but it looks as if the Windmill Club could be more useful than I first imagined!'

Chapter Thirteen

On Friday evening, about nine o'clock, they met round at Lenny's shop. Lenny led them all through to his living accommodation, where he served them coffee. Tom had been thinking about the problem and if they went round to Mr. Wong's he felt that Lenny should not go with them as they might start on his shop next. Beryl hadn't come with Bill, who explained that she had a migraine and he felt she should stay at home. That left them with Bill, Jim, Vicky, Alice, Tom, and Harry Baines from the youth club had also volunteered to join them. They knew that Mr. Wong would be alone in his shop apart from a young female assistant. About ten fifteen, just as they were deciding that it was no show and they were preparing to go home, the buzzer, which Bill had installed, went off in the shop. 'Right,' said Bill 'it looks as if we're in business.' And they all trooped next door to the fish and chip shop.

Bill led the way in to the brightly lit shop; apart from the counter, there were three tables and chairs for those customers who wanted to eat in. As they went in a middle aged couple, who looked frightened, pushed past them on their way out and there were two platefuls of half finished meals on one of the tables. Mr. Wong and his assistant were standing behind the counter looking very anxious. On this side of the counter, there were three large youths and an older, smaller man with what Tom described later as 'rat like' features. One youth was saying 'Right we'll have four large fish suppers pronto,' and the older man added 'You can pay us fifty pounds for the privilege of eating them.' With that, he picked up a large saltcellar and emptied the contents onto the counter and the floor.

'That wasn't very nice,' said Bill quietly. The man

and the youths looked around, becoming aware for the first time that there was a fairly large group standing behind them. The first youth glared at Bill and said 'What's it got to do with you, old man?' Tom intervened and said 'Well, this is a very nice fish and chip shop and the customers like it to be clean and tidy.' 'Oh, you can sod off and all granddad,' said a red headed youth, and went to push Tom in the chest. As he did so another hand shot out, grabbed his arm and he found himself lying on the floor with Alice kneeling beside him. 'We don't need any rough stuff,' she said 'people might get hurt,' and she gave his arm a vicious twist. 'Oh, you cow, get off me,' he moaned. One of his mates tried to go to his aid and found himself blocked by a very burly Harry Baines who said 'I know you Jimmy, you used to be in the club.' At this, the youth looked rather shamefaced and stepped back.

In the meantime Bill had pinned the ringleader against the counter and said 'Who the hell do you think you are, some small time Mr. Big I suppose. I've dealt with your kind before.' Mr. Wong and his assistant were still standing rather open mouthed behind the counter. The fourth youth went to kick Alice, who was holding her opponent down, but before he could connect, a hard punch in the solar plexus left him gasping on the floor and Tom looking rather pleased with himself. 'You're just a bunch of cowards and bullies,' shouted Vicky. 'You should know better,' she said pointing at the older man, 'your wife comes to my church.' Bill addressed the older man, 'Right,' he said, 'we have two choices, either you leave quietly and promise not to come into Mr. Wong's shop again or I phone one of my mates down at the nick and ask them to send a black maria. You will all be arrested for assault and demanding money with menaces.' 'There's no need for that,' said the older man, 'we don't want any truck with the "old bill", and if you let us go we won't come in here again.' Bill turned to Tom and the others and said 'What do you think?' Tom replied 'Well, we could let them go but next time, if they were stupid to have a next time, we would definitely call in the police.'

The youth who had been blocked by Harry Baines said 'Look lads, two of these are ex coppers so they mean what they say.' 'Right,' said the ringleader 'if you let us go we won't come in here again.' Bill nodded to Jim, who opened the door and the four louts walked rather shamefacedly out. Mr. Wong thanked them profusely and insisted that they all had a fish and chip supper on him.

At the next meeting all the early conversation was about Friday night at Mr. Wong's. He said that he was very grateful and so far there had been no sign of the four bullies. He fervently hoped that he would not see them again. Everyone congratulated Alice on her speedy response and Jim said 'Well it was a warning for me not to upset her when we start living together.' 'Oh,' said Beryl 'is that the plan, are you what people call an item now then?' Alice said 'We've been out a few times and Jim has been round tidying my garden for me and we quite like each other's company. We have discussed getting married but as yet we haven't made any firm plans.' The look she gave Jim was definitely not affectionate.

Bill said 'Well in any case it will have to wait until we get this council election out of the way, you're still happy about standing for election are you Alice?' 'Definitely,' she said 'I think I would enjoy the experience.' Bill had found the necessary details and it was agreed that he and Tom would be joint campaign managers. 'Of course there's a lot to do,' Tom said 'and first of all we must get leaflets printed and circulated. 'I've had a word with Harry Baines,' said Bill 'and he is sure that most of his members will persuade their parents to vote for Alice and they will also help with the circulation of the leaflets.' 'Everyone will help with the circulation of the leaflets,' said Vicky 'it will be such fun to have a councillor in our club.' 'It may be fun,' said Tom 'but I think it will also be quite onerous and Alice will need lots of support.' It was decided that they would have a small meeting with Alice, Bill and Tom to draw up the leaflet and Beryl said 'I have a friend who is a printer and I'm sure he will help with anything we need.'

Just before tea, Tom told them that he was going to Hathersage on the following weekend with some members of the local youth club. 'Ah,' said Bill 'Harry was very grateful because otherwise he would have had to go and he's not very keen on rock climbing. He tells me that you're a famous mountaineer. A bit of a dark horse because you've never said anything to us.' 'Oh, I wouldn't say famous,' said Tom 'I was well known in the climbing world, but not many people outside of that rather narrow fraternity would have heard of me.' 'Cor,' said Vicky 'an international wrestler, a famous mountaineer, I wonder what other secrets we're all hiding? It's funny,' she went on 'when Alice asked me to join I almost refused because I thought it would be just a bunch of old fogies waiting to die.' 'It doesn't have to be that way,' Tom commented 'just because we're old it doesn't mean that we're no longer interested in life, or that we have nothing to offer society.' 'That's largely the trouble,' said Bill 'once you retire the rest of the world forgets you and moves on.' 'Well it doesn't sound as if the world is going to forget the Windmill Club,' said Jim. 'Perhaps there ought to be a lot more Windmill Clubs up and down the country.'

Beryl brought in the tea trolley and the conversation turned to the bye-election and led on to discussion of politics in general. There was nobody in the group who had much time for politicians. 'It seems to me they're all crooks,' said Vicky. 'Well that's a bit of an unfair generalisation,' said Tom, 'but I do believe that many people have become disillusioned by greedy MPs and the comic figures in the House of Lords.' 'It may be that you will find, Alice, some of the councillors are decent people, I think local government may be a little less corrupt than the people in Westminster.' 'Well if there is any corruption,' said Alice 'you can be sure you'll all know about it. But listen to me I've not even got elected yet so we'll just have to wait and see.'

As they were leaving, Beryl said to Tom, 'Now, you make sure you stay safe this week-end. I'm not sure that you should be climbing at your age.' 'Don't worry; it's a bit like riding a bicycle you never forget.' 'Yes,' said Beryl 'but falling off a bicycle is not as dangerous as falling off a lump of rock,' and she patted him on the shoulder. It was clear that Beryl had a soft spot for Tom and her concern was genuine, so he promised that he would be very careful.

Chapter Fourteen

On Saturday morning, Tom searched out his boots and a few bits and pieces like carabiners and pitons and wondered whether his ropes were still usable. The telephone rang and it was Fran saying that she would pick him up about ten o'clock on Sunday morning, after she had collected her club members. Tom asked her about ropes, but she said not to worry about that as the club had purchased new ropes and slings about six months before. 'You're still good to come then?' she asked. 'Of course, I'm really looking forward to it.' On Sunday morning a very new looking mini bus, which Fran later explained she had hired for the occasion, pulled up at his gate. He took his rucksack and a small bag and making sure that his front door was firmly locked, loaded them into the back of the mini bus. It was most peculiar, he felt more excited than he had done for a long time. Whether it was the thought of climbing again or spending a few days with Fran he didn't really want to speculate.

Whilst the back doors were open, she introduced him to the four club members. Susie was a small, dark haired girl, who looked about eleven or twelve years old, although Fran assured him that she was fifteen. In total contrast, Chloe was a large, fair-haired girl, who in Tom's eyes, seemed to be wearing far too much makeup for a trip into the country and looked about twenty-five. Pete, his erstwhile opponent in the boxing ring, greeted Tom warmly leaning back to shake his hand and said 'Glad to see you.' The fourth member was called Robby and he apparently had been playing football the day before and hurt his ankle. Fran explained that, under normal circumstances she would not have taken him, as he was limping badly, but he would have been very disappointed to have been left out. 'I'm not sure how much climbing we will get out of this lot,' she said with a smile, as Tom climbed into the front passenger seat.

As they drove along Tom could hear the boys discussing football, Robby was a very keen blues supporter whereas Pete seemed to favour the reds. The girls were chatting about a DVD that Chloe had seen and brought with her because she thought it was very good. 'Has this place we're staying got a DVD player,' she said. 'Yes, I'm sure it has,' said Fran and Chloe passed the DVD to Tom and said what do you think about this Tom?' The cover was very lurid and Tom noticed that it was for 18 +. 'Very nice,' he said passing it back and fervently hoping that he would not have to watch it. Fran had decided that they would stop in Buxton for lunch and she knew a very nice café there where they all had toasted sandwiches and drinks according to their individual taste. Tom and Fran settled for a pot of tea but the younger group had soft drinks. They set off after lunch and Fran said 'I want to stop off in Castleton to check which mines will be available on Tuesday.' They did this, there were three to choose from and the group decided that they would like to go in the mine where they travelled by boat. They then moved on to Hathersage, arriving there about five o'clock.

The bed and breakfast establishment that Fran had booked was a large, white house above Hathersage and with a view of Stanage Edge. They were greeted warmly by Mrs. Castle and it was obvious that she and Fran were old friends. There were just four available bedrooms so the boys would share one and the girls would also share. Tom's room was a small but cosy room with a view of Stanage. They settled in and Mrs. Castle provided high tea at about six thirty, this was very nice egg and chips followed by apple pie and custard. After tea, Fran suggested that they should stroll up to look at the rock face and it was obvious that Robby was in some pain. They walked slowly back to the house and the youngsters settled down in the large sitting room to watch the DVD that Chloe had brought. Tom and Frances sat in the small sitting room where they could watch the last of the sun lighting up the rocks with an orange glow.

As they gazed out of the window, Tom remarked how much he had missed the hills. He said 'In the early days of our marriage I persuaded Evelyn to spend holidays in the Lake District and North Wales but we did very little walking. After a few years she preferred to go to the seaside, Devon and Cornwall being her favourites. I didn't mind the sea, after all I had twelve years in the Navy, but once I was bitten by the mountain bug the hills seemed to be the only place to be. Winthrop Young wrote in his collected poems,'

There is a great easing of the heart
And cumulance of comfort on high hills.

He looked up and realised that Fran was not looking out of the window but gazing at him with an affectionate smile. 'Sorry,' he said, 'here I am in the company of a beautiful young woman rambling on like a melancholy old man.' 'I've told you before, you're not old and we're all entitled to be melancholy sometimes.'

In so many ways you remind me of Craig,' 'Oh, who is Craig, you have never mentioned him before?' 'Craig is, or rather was, my fiancé. He was killed three years ago in Afghanistan and I haven't talked about him for a long time. We met on a youth leader's course where he was instructing canoeing while he was on leave. He was in the Para's and just a few months later, he was posted abroad. We were only together for less than a year but we planned to get married when his tour was over. Unfortunately, the Taliban altered our arrangements.' 'Oh, I'm so sorry,' he said, taking her hand. The wars in Iraq and Afghanistan are good examples of the stupidity of politicians and military top brass. Some wars are inevitable and necessary, such as the Falklands and the first Gulf War but others are merely a futile waste of life. Sorry to go on but I know quite a lot about Afghanistan, having climbed in the Hindu Kush and Afghans will never tolerate westerners on their soil. But that's of no help to you so I'll shut up., 'I'm over the worst now, I moved to the club two years ago and I've never told anyone about Craig, not even Harry Baines.' 'Well I feel very privileged and obviously I will respect your privacy.' 'Thank you,' she said quietly. 'I arranged with Mrs. Castle that we would get our own supper; that ghastly DVD should be over by now.' She paused at the door and said 'Do you really think that I'm a beautiful young woman?' 'That and more,' he said with a smile.

They went into the kitchen, all the young people had opted for cocoa except for Chloe who wanted coffee. Mrs. Castle had left out a plate of biscuits and a plate of very tasty rock buns. They sat round the dining room table and Chloe told Tom and Fran that they had missed a real treat not seeing the DVD. Tom thought to himself, how much more of a treat he'd had talking companionably to Frances. All the bedrooms were en suite, so Fran asked the four young people to go upstairs quietly so as not to disturb Mrs. Castle. As they went upstairs Fran said quietly to Tom, 'There is no danger of any "to-ing and fro-ing", Chloe has a steady, and very jealous, much older boyfriend. She's an only child and her parents let her get away with murder.

Susie shows no interest in the opposite sex as yet.' 'It is nice when they retain their innocence,' Tom remarked 'many young people today are so eager to try sex that they have lost the art of courtship and romance.' 'Love seems to have been replaced by lust in so many young relationships,' agreed Fran. She said she was going up to her room and she would see him in the morning. Tom said he would stay down and read for a while so she kissed him lightly on the lips and went upstairs.

The girls' door was slightly ajar as she looked in to say goodnight and saw that Susie was talking to Chloe. 'On your own Fran?' Chloe giggled, but Susie said reprovingly 'don't be silly,' goodnight Fran.' 'Night girls, sweet dreams,' said Fran, and gently closed the door. It depends on what one means by on your own she thought as she climbed into bed.

Chapter Fifteen

The following morning was bright and sunny and as Tom opened his curtains, he was relieved to see the good weather. 'Less likely to make a fool of myself, if the rocks are warm and dry,' he thought. As they all ate a hearty breakfast Robby announced that his ankle was worse, so he would not be able to climb. 'Oh good,' said Chloe 'I'll sit and look after you; I don't want to climb either.' 'I knew you were just coming for the ride, madam,' Fran said to Chloe. 'But it must be disappointing for Robby.' 'Never mind there will be other opportunities,' he said 'and it's nice to get away from home for a bit.' Robby had five sisters and a mother who doted on him as her only son. He was obviously over smothered by his family; his dad wanted him to become a professional footballer and put him under some pressure so Tom could see why he wanted a short break.

Pete on the other hand was an only child and wanted to be a professional boxer. This was an ambition, which did not please his parents who wanted him to go to university. After breakfast, they made their way up to the rock face, walking slowly for Robby's benefit. Tom was pleased to see that the area they were heading for was completely deserted. At the weekend, the Edge could attract hundreds of climbers and there were even queues for some of the more popular climbs. Fran suggested that she would climb with Pete and Tom would climb with Susie. It was obvious to Tom that she thought Pete would be more demanding, but in the event, she proved to be wrong. He suggested that they started in the Black Hawk area, so called because a hawk had attacked one of the early pioneers. Most of the early climbers came from the two industrial areas of

Manchester and Sheffield.

Tom had brought a number of pieces of equipment, such as carabiners and pitons and he explained how they could be used for abseiling. 'Many people nowadays use an elaborate harness but the club has not acquired any of these so far.' He also showed them a small hammer with which to knock in the metal pitons. They can be hammered into cracks in the rock to make a belay.' 'What's that?' asked Susie. 'It's a safety method used on harder climbs, you clip the rope in to give security.' 'We will not need them today though as we're sticking to easier climbs.' Somewhere, one of the mountain gods chuckled. 'Right,' said Fran, 'let's get busy.' They started off by doing a couple of simple abseils and Chloe was persuaded to follow Tom up a very simple route and try abseiling. With much giggling and squealing, they eventually got her down once and then she announced that that was her finished for the day.

Tom and Fran chose routes fairly close to each other and again he suspected that she wanted to keep an eye on him. He was relieved to discover that his arms and hands were very responsive, although his knees seemed less enthusiastic. However, he and Susie managed two climbs rated difficult before they stopped for coffee, which Mrs. Castle had kindly provided in flasks. Pete said he was really enjoying himself and Robby looked envious. Tom had been surprised and pleased to see how gracefully Susie climbed. 'She almost floats up the rock face,' he said to Fran, and Susie looked very pleased. 'Can we do something a bit harder next?' she asked. Fran looked anxiously at Tom, and he replied 'We can but try,' and after coffee he and Susie climbed two routes classed very difficult while Fran and Pete followed them up one of them.

When they stopped for lunch, Pete started to talk to

Tom about his boxing career. 'Will I make a pro boxer?' he asked. 'Well, I was only an amateur and the pro game is much harder, but I think you might make it if you're prepared to work really hard.' Fran then steered the conversation on to climbing, she asked Tom what the hardest climb was that he had ever done. He said 'If we're talking about high mountains then it would have to be Anna Purna or K2 in the Himalaya, but of course high mountaineering is quite different from rock climbing. I would describe rock climbing as a combination of ballet and chess, although I wouldn't have dared say so in front of my erstwhile companions.' 'It is a good description though,' said Fran 'what do you think Susie?' 'Could we do something a bit harder then please Tom?' she was off again. 'Well, it's obvious that you're a natural but you mustn't push Tom too hard,' said Fran. 'Oh I think I can manage a severe route,' he said with a smile and off they went a little further down the crag.

The sun was shining and apart from creaking knees he was thoroughly enjoying himself. 'We'll just try one more,' he said to Susie after they had been up a climb with a narrow crack which was graded severe. He knew that one of the problems was that he couldn't really use runners and belays because he couldn't expect Susie to hold on to the rope if he came off, but he was so enjoying himself that he said to Susie, 'How would you like to try a very severe climb?' 'Oh yes,' she said eagerly, then I would really have something to boast about to my sisters.' She had two sisters, one who was academically very clever and at university and one who played tennis for the county. Susie was regarded as the quiet one, without any particular skills, until today that is.

Tom stopped in front of a climb and said 'This one is called narrow buttress and is the first very severe I ever climbed although it was a long time ago.' He tied Susie on again and set off up the climb. It was definitely a very severe graded climb and he realised that towards the end of the day he was beginning to tire. At one point he had to stride across a wide gap and his left knee felt very painful, he got across without mishap and moved diagonally up to the overhang, here he paused to get his breath back then he was over the crux and quickly climbed the last fifteen feet. He sighed with relief and tied on to a belay. He brought Susie up and although she too found the gap rather wide and struggled on the crux, she floated up the final few feet and they sat on the top in the sunshine. After a few minutes, they heard voices below and when Tom looked down he could see Fran climbing up the same route he had just finished. Tom called down to ask what she was doing. He knew from what she had told him that she had never led a very severe route. 'Just following you up this severe,' she said. He decided to say nothing but continued sorting out his rope. Suddenly Fran gave a small, frightened shout, she had reached the crux of the climb on the overhang and found that she could not go forward or back. 'I think I'm going to come off Tom,' she shouted. 'Hold on,' he said 'I'm coming.' He placed his abseil rope round a suitable belay and told Susie to stay exactly where she was, then he abseiled down until he was level with Fran and on the small ledge she was trying to reach. She was shaking, almost uncontrollably and there was a look close to terror on her face. 'Give me your hand,' he said and as she did so he pulled her unceremoniously onto the ledge. She clung to him fiercely and a small tear rolled gently down her cheek.

'I'm so sorry,' she said. 'Don't worry,' he replied 'let's just get you down.' Luckily, there was a spike for a belay and he fastened himself to this and helped her onto the abseil rope. It was only about forty feet to the ground and she slowly abseiled down where Pete helped her off the rope. Tom attached himself back to the abseil rope again and followed her down. 'My hero,' she said and gave him a kiss while Pete, Chloe and Robby all cheered. Then she shouted up to Susie 'Walk carefully along the path to the end of the crag and we'll meet you there.' They pulled the abseil rope through and collected up the equipment. Susie walked to the end of the crag where they met up. She too threw her arms around Tom and kissed him. 'Thank you so much, I was very frightened for you and Fran but I did enjoy my climbing.' 'Blooming battleships,' said Tom 'kissed by two lovely ladies on one day, aren't I the lucky one.' Chloe said 'I would kiss you as well but my boyfriend wouldn't like it.' 'And you'd smudge your lipstick,' said Susie with a laugh. They made their way back to Mrs. Castle's where she had another of her high teas waiting for them.

After tea, the young people went to watch television and Fran and Tom again sat in the small sitting room. She wanted to talk about her fiancé Craig and Tom was a sympathetic listener. 'He was my first real boyfriend, I'd had a few short friendships but I went to an all girl's school and was much more comfortable with my own gender. I'm not even sure that Craig and I were ideally suited. He was very macho and not at all sensitive. Still, now I will never know if he was the right man for me.' 'I don't think I'm a lesbian but I did find sex rather uncomfortable and Craig was quite demanding, very much what you would call a "wham bam thank you mam" when it came to sex but he was very kind and considerate in other ways.' Tom murmured sympathetically and patted her shoulder. 'I had the opposite problem with Evelyn,' he said. 'We'd only been married a few months when she told me that she was now a little old for sex, she had two children and that was more than enough. I don't wish to sound unkind but I felt as if I had been lured into a marriage of convenience. We were affectionate and cared for each other but that was as far as we went.' 'Life is so very complicated,' sighed Fran and kissing him on the forehead she went to organise supper.

After supper the young people went up to bed, Susie and Pete were very tired after their strenuous day. 'Learning to climb is not just physical effort,' Tom remarked 'there's a lot going on in the brain as well.' He and Fran washed up the supper dishes and then went upstairs together. At the top of the stairs, he said goodnight but Fran held his hand and whispered 'Don't lock your door.' He brushed his teeth and had a shower wondering just what she meant but not daring to hope what he thought she might have meant. He got into bed and started reading his book, the door opened quietly and Fran came in wearing pale blue cotton pyjamas. She put her finger to her lips and pulling back the duvet climbed in beside him. He leaned across and fumbled clumsily in his efforts to switch off the bedside lamp. 'I just want you to hold me,' she whispered. 'Sometimes I feel so lonely and scared about the future.' 'I know what you mean,' he whispered back. 'One day we will go to the Alps, Zermatt or Chamonix and I will show you some of the climbs I have done.' He put his arms around her and drew her warm slender body close to him. They lay together, each drawing comfort from the other. From time to time she would kiss him tenderly and whisper sweet nothings and he would draw his hand down her spine and pull her close. 'This can't be happening,' he thought but he knew it was and he also knew that it would probably never happen again. 'Early summer and late winter are not a good combination,' he thought 'and do not have much of a future. Still,' he mused, 'now was now and it was wonderful.' He could smell the fragrance of her hair and feel her leg wrapped round his and he was more than content. Could there possibly be a nicer sound than affectionate whispers at midnight. After a while Fran fell asleep her gentle breathing was soothing and shortly afterwards he too fell asleep. He woke to see her climbing out of his bed; the first streaks of dawn were creeping through the gap in the curtains. 'I had better go to my own room now,' she said quietly. 'Thank you so much.' 'It's me who should be thanking you,' he replied 'you darling girl.'

At breakfast, he couldn't stop smiling and Susie asked him why he was so happy. 'Well, it's not everyday one has the privilege of climbing with a truly natural climber. It took me years to climb as well as you did on your first attempt.' Susie blushed with pleasure. 'Oh we will never hear the end of it now,' said Chloe. 'Fran and Pete were pretty good too,' said Tom 'and I'm sure Robby would have been as well if it wasn't for his ankle, because he's a natural athlete.' There was clearly a good feeling within the group and when they said goodbye to Mrs. Castle she said 'And you lot can come again anytime, it's been a pleasure to look after you.'

Fran drove down through Hathersage and along the valley to the pleasant village of Castleton. She first took them to see the castle and they had coffee at a nearby café, then she drove through the village into the area where the Blue John Mine and others were situated. The youngsters had chosen one of the mines where they could travel in a boat and they all enjoyed their trip. I wish we could stay longer said Susie wistfully but Chloe said 'No we've got to get home my Jack will be waiting.' Fran drove them home, stopping off at Bakewell where they sampled the delicious Bakewell tarts. When she dropped Tom off at his gate she said 'Thanks for your help Tom, see you soon,' in a bright, cheerful voice but he could see a small tear in the corner of her eye. He opened his front door and for once, there was no comment from Evelyn. Despite the fact that it was a warm day, the house seemed cold and very empty. Tom wasn't much of a drinker but he desperately felt the need to help himself to a large single malt and slump into his favourite armchair. 'Where does one go from paradise,' he asked himself.

Chapter Sixteen

He soon found the answer to his own question when Beryl met him at the door the following afternoon. She put her finger to her lips, which was reminiscent of Fran two nights before in Hathersage. However, Beryl had less happy news to impart, 'Alice and Jim have had a row and they're not speaking to each other or much to anyone else for that matter.' Tom was still fuelled by a mixture of joy and despair; he had hardly slept the night before trying to work out how the relationship between Fran and himself could possibly work out. 'Well, at least they have still come to the meeting,' said Tom following Beryl into the sitting room. 'Here he comes' said Bill jovially 'the bold climbing Lothario.' 'Not so loud,' said Tom with a smile, 'someone might hear you.' Then he smiled at Vicky and Alice and said, 'How are you lovely ladies?'

'I'm fine' said Vicky 'but Alice is not so good.' He had just been forewarned by Beryl but he feigned ignorance. 'What's wrong with Alice that the Windmill Club can't fix?' he said. Jim leaned forward and said 'I'm afraid it's all my fault, my mum always said that I'm like a bull in a china shop.' 'Well you weren't very subtle,' said Vicky 'us ladies like to be gently wooed not taken for granted.' 'I know,' said Jim contritely 'I am very sorry.' Tom said 'I'm sure Alice has a forgiving nature, it would be a shame for you two to split up.' 'We don't need to split up,' said Alice 'he just needs to take things a little more slowly.' 'I should never have announced we were an item,' said Jim 'please forgive me Alice.' She tried to hide a small smile, 'Very well you big lump, we'll tell our friends that we are almost an item.' Tom led the applause 'Bravo Alice, he's a very lucky man.' 'Hear, hear,' said

Mr. Wong solemnly and everyone laughed.

'Right,' said Bill 'now that's sorted perhaps we can continue making plans for the bye election.' They spent the next hour discussing their strategy, Bill said 'The leaflets with Alice's photo on should be here tomorrow and Tom and I could take some to the youth club on Friday.' As Beryl was bringing in the tea trolley she heard Bill's words and she said 'Yes my friend has done them at cost price just to help us. Alice takes a lovely photograph. We also have a few posters which could go up in Lenny's and Mr. Wong's shops.' Lenny said 'In all four shops, because I've spoken to the other shopkeepers and they are also willing to help.' 'Well my campaign managers will have to help me prepare myself mentally,' said Alice 'you know it's all new to me.' 'Ah, but you have got the gift of the gab,' said Vicky. 'That's a case of pot and kettle if ever I've heard one,' said Bill with a smile. Tom thought, not for the first time, how well the group had jelled. A few weeks ago we barely knew each other and now we can indulge in badinage without any ill feeling. 'The important thing,' said Bill 'is that our campaign is genuine, no lies or empty promises such as we usually hear from politicians.' 'That may be part of the problem,' said Alice 'I just cannot think of myself as a politician.' 'Good thing too,' Tom added 'we are just a group of ordinary citizens hoping to influence things for the better. Now let's do justice to Beryl's wonderful baking.'

During tea they were just talking among themselves, Beryl asked Tom if he had enjoyed his trip to Derbyshire. 'Yes I did and as you can see I have arrived back still in one piece.' 'I expect Frances is good company,' said Beryl a little wistfully. Tom realised that Beryl seemed to be interested in him personally it was obvious that although Bill was a nice capable fellow he was not sentimental or romantic and Beryl was giving the impression that she was a little neglected in emotional terms. 'Well yes, she is good company and she is very good with her club members, we get on well but of course she's more like a daughter or even a grand daughter to me.' Beryl seemed relieved and said 'Yes, it isn't wise to stray too far from ones own age group. When Bill had his fling with the constable he was almost fifty and she was in her early twenties. It was all quite silly really.' 'I couldn't imagine any man leaving you, with your charming smile and your wonderful cooking.' 'You flatterer you,' she said with a smile and started stacking the tea trolley. As Tom was leaving he and Bill arranged to go to the youth club with the leaflets on Friday evening and Tom said he would contact Fran to let her know they were going.

On Thursday morning he rang Fran and asked if it was convenient for Bill and him to drop off some leaflets. 'Of course you can,' she replied. 'I was going to contact you because I haven't had chance to thank you for all your help at the weekend. Susie in particular couldn't stop talking about you. I wondered if we could meet but I can't invite you to my flat it's pokey and not very nice.' 'Well, why don't you come here on Saturday; if it makes you feel better you can cook the tea.' 'Right,' she said 'that's an offer I can't refuse but in the meantime I will see you on Friday evening.' As Tom put the phone down, he once again felt the glow of excitement he had felt on the previous weekend.

When Bill called to pick him up on Friday evening, he was surprised to see that Beryl was sitting in the car. 'She insisted on coming,' said Bill 'even though she will be missing her favourite soaps.' 'Good evening Tom,' she said 'I've got a machine that records programmes anyway and I wanted to meet Frances again.' They got to the youth club just after it had opened so it was relatively quiet. Harry Baines greeted them enthusiastically and he and one of the boys helped them in to the hall with the boxes of leaflets. 'Most of the members have already started persuading their parents to vote for Alice,' he told them. 'They were most impressed by her arm wrestling skills.' 'Is it true she was a proper wrestler?' said the boy who was helping them stack the boxes. 'Yes indeed,' replied Beryl 'and she has travelled all over the world.' The boy looked impressed. 'Well that won't do her street cred any harm,' said Bill.

Just then Fran arrived, beaming when she saw Bill and Tom. Beryl thrust out her hand and said 'Good evening how lovely to meet you again Frances.' If Fran was a little surprised by Beryl's rather regal manner she managed not to show it. 'How nice to see you all,' she replied 'when more members arrive perhaps you will explain the bye election project to them.' 'Bill can do that,' said Beryl quickly 'he's our chairman you know.' She followed Fran into the little room where the refreshments were prepared. 'Tom tells me he enjoyed his trip to Derbyshire,' she said. 'Oh we all did and Tom was a great help with the climbing.' 'Yes I'm sure he was, but he is a little vulnerable you know, it's not long since he lost his wife.' Fran was puzzled by the line the conversation was taking. 'Oh yes, he told me,' she said 'but I assure you he was in no danger of getting hurt.' 'Well I do hope not because he's a good friend of mine.' Just then they heard Harry Baines clap his hands and ask for silence so that Bill could explain why the Windmill Club was getting involved in politics. After he had spoken, the members all promised their support in delivering leaflets and persuading their elders to vote for Alice. A few minutes later Susie shyly went up to Tom and said, 'Thank you for the climbing Tom.' 'Oh thank you,' he replied and gave her a large brown envelope. He had got Bill to help him draw up a certificate which stated that Miss Susie Kale had successfully completed six climbs on Stanage Edge, Derbyshire including one severe and one very severe climb. He had signed it Monty Burton international mountaineer. When she read it she said 'Oh Tom,' and burst into tears. 'I'll treasure this all my life. Why have you signed it Monty Burton?' 'Oh you'd better ask Fran to explain that later,' he said 'it's a bit complicated.' Chloe who had taken the certificate to read said, 'Oh you lucky thing I ought to have had one for my abseiling.' Shortly afterwards they made their farewells and Tom very politely refused Beryl's offer of coffee and cakes pleading that he had a headache. There was no way he could cope with any more probing questions about his relationship with Fran.

On Saturday morning it was raining and Tom got soaked when he went for his morning paper. After he had dried himself and made a cup of coffee he sat trying to read the newspaper but he could not concentrate. 'What time will she come?' he wondered 'or will she change her mind because of the weather.' He need not have worried, about three o'clock his doorbell rang and Fran stood on the doorstep carrying two shopping bags, she was soaked to the skin. 'My dear girl you had better come in and get out of those wet clothes.' 'Steady on Monty' she said 'I haven't got anything else to wear.' It was now his turn to be embarrassed, 'Well I'm sure I can find something.' He took her upstairs to the bathroom and produced a blue tracksuit some thick climbing socks and a fluffy white towel. 'There you are,' he said 'I'm sure you can sort yourself out.' A little while later she appeared at the sitting room door with her hair tied back and making the tracksuit look like it had never looked on him. 'She really is very beautiful,' he thought.

He showed Fran into the kitchen and said 'Everything you will need should be here but if you can't find anything please ask.' 'I'll make a cup of tea first for both of us,' she said 'and then I'll get down to cooking our meal.' Tom sat in his favourite chair with a cup of tea and the newspaper which still wasn't making much of an impression on him. He could hear her moving around in the kitchen and it sounded as if she was having no difficulty in finding what she needed. There were delicious smells wafting through the door and he felt quite hungry. She came in and said 'I do hope you like fish because as you know I personally do not eat any kind of meat and I'm afraid I'm foisting my own tastes upon you. Everything is on its way now so we can sit down and relax.' It wasn't possible to go into the garden because of the rain so Tom asked her whether she played chess. 'Actually, I love chess,' she said 'I was in the university chess club funnily enough I thought about it when you were comparing climbing to a mixture of ballet and chess because I used to have ballet lessons when I was a little girl.'

Tom got out his precious chess set, it was a nineteenth century set and the figures were based on the battle of Waterloo. 'Would you like to be the French or the British army?' he said. 'Oh I don't mind,' said Fran picking up one of the ivory pieces and admiring it. They decided to play the best of three games but it was no contest. Tom was quite useful but after he lost the first two games, he decided that he was definitely out of his class so they started talking about climbing. The only snow and ice climbing that Fran had done was in Scotland and they compared notes about climbs they had both done in Glen Coe and on Ben Nevis. 'I have not been on snow and ice for years now,' said Tom 'and although I miss it I am realistic enough to know that my high climbing days are over. There was another piece from a poem by Winthrop Young

Shattered my glass ere half the sands had run
I hold the heights; I hold the heights I won

Mind you I did complete far more than half a glass, poor Winthrop Young was much less fortunate.' 'I must get back into the kitchen,' said Fran 'before anything burns or goes awry.' Off she went and he could hear the clatter of pots and pans. 'Right, it's almost ready,' she called and he went in to help her move the food into the dining room. The main course was a delicious kedgeree and then she said they had baked apples to follow. 'You can come again,' said Tom 'this is absolutely delicious.' After their meal, Fran said that she had something to tell him. His heart sank because he could tell from her expression that it would not be good news. She had been negotiating to complete a PhD and had been accepted at Exeter University. 'Oh blimey,' thought Tom 'that is a long way away.' 'But when are you going,' he said, sounding as cheerful as he could.' 'Not until October,' she said 'but I have a problem with my flat. The landlord wants to refurbish the whole block and he wants us to move out at the end of this month which means I've either got to find somewhere for August and September here or move down to Exeter early. My other problem is that as my job is only part time it is not very well paid and I need to save as much as I can before October.' 'Well,' said Tom 'there is a very simple solution.' Fran looked puzzled, 'I'm not sure what you mean by simple,' she said. 'Well there's lots of room here, you could easily have a room and I wouldn't want any rent.' 'Just two problems,' she said

'I couldn't sponge off you and what would people like Beryl say?'

'You would not be sponging; I would love some company, even if it's only for a couple of months. This is not a large house but it is much too big for one person and I have been thinking about moving to somewhere smaller. Secondly, why should Beryl or anyone else have anything to say? We are both free adults and we know that our relationship is innocent.' 'Just good friends you mean.' 'Of course, so the devil take any gossips or trouble makers.' They sat in silence for a minute or two then Fran said 'Right you're on, but we share the day-to-day living expenses. When can I move in?' 'Why not tomorrow, I'll bring my car round in the morning and help you move. You can show me where you live when I take you home later.' Fran stood up and coming over to his chair she took his hand in both of hers, 'You are such a wonderful man,' she said and gently kissed him. Later he took her home and that night he slept very soundly.

Chapter Seventeen

About ten o'clock on Sunday morning Tom drove to Fran's flat. As she showed him in he thought, 'Yes, it is rather pokey.' She had done her best to brighten it up with some watercolours and photographs, mostly of mountains, but the furniture came with the flat and it was dreadfully shabby and well used. 'I have been in touch with my landlord,' she said 'and he is so pleased that I am moving out without a fuss he has waived the months notice.' By the time they had loaded her suitcases, rucksack, pictures and books the car was full. 'We won't get much more in,' said Tom. 'Oh I don't think I want to take anything else, let's go.' They went back to Tom's home and very quickly installed Fran into the larger of the two spare rooms. 'I use the smallest room as an office,' he explained 'and your room looks out over the back garden.' 'It's perfect,' Fran said 'and I can't tell you how grateful I am.' They decided to go out for a pub lunch to celebrate the new arrangement.

Tom was just tucking into a traditional Sunday roast beef lunch; Fran had opted for an omelette and salad, when he heard a laugh he could not fail to recognise. He looked up from his meal and there was Alice, Vicky and Jim who had also decided on a pub lunch. 'Well, who's a dark horse,' said Vicky. Tom stood up and said 'You all remember Frances from the youth club.' Jim and Alice shook hands with Fran but Vicky said with a grin and a wink 'What's a nice girl like you doing with an old reprobate like Tom?' 'Well, the quick answer is that we were both hungry,' said Frances with a smile. They were sitting at a small table, so the other three sat at a nearby table and ordered their meal. 'Well that's just put the cat among the pigeons,' said Fran quietly.

'Oh they would have to know sometime, the Windmill Club is small and friendly.' As they left they stopped at Jim's table and Tom said 'See you all on Wednesday.' Vicky said 'Will Fran be coming?' 'Oh, I'm afraid she doesn't qualify by about forty years,' said Tom with a smile.

When they got back to the house Fran spent the afternoon settling in. 'Is it alright if I put up some pictures and photographs, although perhaps it isn't worth it for such a short time?' 'Nonsense,' Tom said 'it will be your room and you can use it during vacations if you want.' With that, he found his toolbox. 'There are a number of hooks in there,' he said 'if you need anything else just shout.' That evening they played backgammon instead of chess. Fran told him a little more about herself, she was an only child and had a very sheltered childhood. Her mother had been unable to have children so her parents adopted her when they were in their fifties. This was older than usual for adoption but her biological mother died when giving birth to her. She apparently had no relatives and no one knew who the father was. She went on 'My father was a friend of one of the hospital administrators and somehow they managed to cut a few corners and I was lucky enough to be taken home rather than go through the care system. It probably couldn't happen now with all the nonsense about political correctness and health and safety but I'm very glad it did.' 'So am I,' said Tom 'had you gone another route you would not be sitting here now. It is strange how life twists and turns and how we are so often faced with crossroads. Sorry for interrupting, please go on.'

'My father was killed in a car crash when I was a teenager, I left school at eighteen but because my mother could not afford for me to go straight to university I spent almost three years as a nanny in

Canada. When I came back I was accepted to read history at Durham University and after getting a first class degree then spent three years at a university settlement in the East End of London. It was while I was training to be a youth worker that I met Craig. My mother is now living in Bournemouth with her older sister; this is why I have chosen Exeter. It will be easy to visit her' she said 'so here I am spinster of this parish, thirty two years old and fancy free.' 'And if I may say so,' said Tom quietly 'very beautiful.'

They then sat companionably drinking a final cup of tea. 'You have the bathroom first,' he said 'I'll just read for a little while. There's no lock on the bathroom door but I promise to respect your privacy.' 'Of that I have no doubt,' she aid with a smile. 'Perhaps you are almost too much of a gentleman.' She gave him a kiss and went upstairs. He didn't read, instead he sat wondering if for the first time in his life he was truly falling in love, 'whatever that is,' he mused. 'Loving someone and falling in love with them are two different emotions. The former one can do for oneself, but the latter needs reciprocation from a second person.' 'Oh stop it,' he said to himself 'you're much too old to fall in love.' He waited for a comment from Evelyn but he heard not a word, when he went upstairs Frances had her light out and was probably asleep and he too was soon sleeping soundly. In the morning, they had breakfast together and then she went off to the library and he tackled his usual collection of trivial chores.

He was a little late arriving at the Harris's on Wednesday afternoon; Bill let him in and said quietly, 'I imagine your ears have been burning.' 'I wouldn't be at all surprised,' Tom replied 'let's go in and face the music.' When he went into the sitting room all chatter ceased and there was complete silence. 'Hello everybody, I'm Tom and no I'm not living in sin.' 'We never thought you were,' said Alice quickly 'but we were a little surprised to hear that Beryl saw Frances leaving your house on Monday morning.' 'It's quite simple' Tom said 'we spent the night together, but no not in the way you might think. Fran had to move out of her flat and I have a spare room. It's only until September until she goes back to university.' Everyone seemed to relax and soon the talk turned to the forthcoming bye-election. 'All the leaflets have been delivered,' said Bill and Lenny added that he and Mr. Wong had been inundated with enquiries about Alice. 'Of course we could not tell the truth,' said Mr. Wong with a secretive smile, 'so we tell everyone she is quite nice.' For a moment there was a shocked silence and then everyone realised that it was one of Mr. Wong's little jokes and the group erupted into laughter.

'Well,' said Bill 'it looks as if we have a very good chance of getting her elected.' Alice stood up and made a small bow. 'Ladies and gentlemen you can count on me,' and they all clapped enthusiastically. Tom said quietly 'It will be our own version of Alice in blunderland unless I'm very much mistaken.' Beryl brought in the tea trolley, in addition to the usual collection of cakes and scones there was a large cake with pink icing. 'A celebration of mine and Bill's birthday,' she said. They all sang happy birthday and Jim produced a garden centre voucher. 'A small present from us all,' he said. Beryl burst into tears 'How very kind you all are,' she said blowing her nose loudly and Bill patted her gently on the shoulder. 'By the way,' he said 'Harry Baines has asked me if he can join the Windmill Club, I know he is only in his middle sixties but he is a widower and a very nice chap.' 'There would certainly be no objections from me,' said Tom 'he has already been helpful on a number of occasions.' 'Does anyone else have any objections?' asked Bill.

But everyone was perfectly happy about the idea. 'Good I will invite him to the next meeting.' As the meeting was breaking up Jim quietly approached Tom and asked if he could call and talk to him, as he needed some advice. 'Certainly,' Tom replied 'why don't you come round for coffee in the morning.' 'Great,' replied Jim 'I don't work on Thursdays.'

He walked down the road with Lenny and Mr. Wong and Lenny remarked that he was having much less trouble with the local children since they had linked up with the youth club. Mr. Wong said that he had not been troubled by the bullies since their confrontation. Tom said 'Perhaps we can do something for the youth club during the holidays.' 'What did you have in mind?' Lenny asked. 'Well, supposing we hired a coach and took them on a day trip somewhere like Blackpool or the North Wales coast.' The other two were enthusiastic and Tom said he would discuss it with Fran and the other members of the club next week. He realised that they had walked well past his gate so he decided to continue as far as Lenny's shop and buy an evening paper. They said goodbye to Mr. Wong and went into Lenny's shop. Whilst he was there, he decided to buy Fran a box of chocolates. He realised that he did not even know if she liked chocolates and what her preference would be. I really know very little about her he thought, apart that is that she is beautiful and young. He decided on chocolate brazils, said farewell to Lenny and walked briskly home. As he opened the gate, he could see Fran in the garden planting a small group of geraniums. The scarlet flowers made a brave splash of colour and he said how nice they looked. She stood up with a smile and said 'I'm afraid they will only last until the first frosts.' They went into the house and while she washed her hands he made a pot of tea. It was a warm evening so they took it into the back garden and sat in the evening sunshine on a couple of old-fashioned deckchairs. 'I'm afraid I have never got round to buying some of the modern garden furniture, which is so popular nowadays,' he said apologetically. 'This is lovely,' she replied, 'there was no garden attached to the flat, so this is a real novelty.'

He went back into the house and brought out the chocolate brazils, 'For you mademoiselle,' he said formally. 'How on earth did you know they are my favourites,' she explained. 'Oh, I think we have some sort of telepathic link,' he replied. As they sat and drank their tea and munched chocolates he told her of his idea about the coach trip. 'That's a great idea, but not Blackpool I took some of the club members there in a mini bus about two years ago and it took ages to round them all up, we didn't get back until midnight. There are some nice places on the North Wales coast.' Tom said he would contact some coach firms and Fran said she would put up a list in the club so that members could put their names down. 'Another example of your kindness,' she said, and put her hand on his knee. It's just a friendly gesture, he told himself but why does it seem like an electric shock. 'Well it's your turn to cook dinner,' he said 'so I will just sit and laze in the sunshine.' 'Not a problem,' she replied 'there's a flan in the oven and I've just got to toss the salad.'

Chapter Eighteen

The following morning Fran went to the library and at about ten thirty Jim arrived at the front door; Tom invited him in and made some coffee. 'You must try a slice of Fran's fruit cake,' he told him. 'Yes please,' was the eager reply, 'I haven't had much breakfast.' 'You and Fran seem very settled,' he said, as he devoured a second slice of fruitcake. 'We are settled, but it is not the same as it will be with you and Alice because our relationship is just platonic.' 'You know, a few months ago,' said Jim 'I could never have imagined me sitting here in your house with you.' 'What do you mean?' asked Tom. 'Well, you're obviously a well educated, middle class sort of chap and I'm just a part time labourer.' 'That's just the trouble with this Country said Tom 'artificial class barriers, which are really meaningless as far as I'm concerned. We are all equal; it is the so-called establishment which is completely wrong. I was just a Chief Petty Officer not a Vice Admiral and of course, in the services one has to acknowledge rank as a matter of discipline. In civilian life we are all entitled to mutual respect. Anyway, I know that's not what you came to talk about.'

'No,' said Jim slowly 'it's a bit embarrassing really. At some point soon Alice and me, well ....we're going to move in together and I'm not sure what to do.' 'I assume you will be moving into her bungalow.' 'Crikey, yes I wouldn't want her to move into my council house.' 'Well, I suppose the first thing to remember is that it is her house and many of her possessions will be important to her. Secondly, you will both need some space.' 'How do you mean?' 'Well you should not expect to do everything together, she has her friendship with Vicky and you have your mates at the pub, they should continue.' 'Yes, I see what you mean,' said Jim thoughtfully. 'Then I suppose you're used to helping with the household chores and I know you're keen on working in the garden, so that should help. Just play it by ear and don't be afraid to ask Alice what she wants and whether the sharing is acceptable to her.' There was a silence, and then Jim said 'Er, you will think it strange but I've never slept with a woman.' 'Oh Lord,' Tom thought, 'a sixty nine year old virgin. I wonder what the odds against that are nowadays. I suppose the way young people regard sex there won't be many virgins over the age of sixteen in this city. Well I'm sure Alice will understand, tell her and discuss it with her. She is rather more experienced than you, but she is also a very kind person so I'm sure she will understand. You are obviously very fond of Alice and only time will show whether you are in love or you will learn to love each other. In any case it seems to me that love is an over used word which means different things to different people'

'Thank you,' said Jim, 'I will take your advice and talk to Alice. Is there anything else I should be aware of?' 'Well, personal hygiene is very important; you know, regular baths and leaving the bath and the loo clean.' Oh dear, I must be careful not to hurt his feelings Tom thought but he had no need to worry. 'Yes, my old mum always drummed that sort of thing into me; she was very keen on hygiene.' 'It seems to me that you will fit in fine, but just remember the need for personal space and I am sure you will both be very happy together.' Jim stood up with a relieved smile, 'Thanks Tom,' he said 'and thank you for the coffee and cake. Please tell Fran it is delicious.' Tom walked with Jim to the gate thinking, I don't know if I have been much help but they are both nice people. So, late in life it may be but I'm sure they'll make a go of it. Later that evening he told Fran about his discussion with Jim and his anxiety about whether he had been of any help. 'It sounds as if you said all you reasonably could say,' she said with a smile, 'perhaps I'd better ask your advice, because I'm presently living with this charming and attractive man, who seems to think he is a reincarnation of Don Quixote.' 'Well, it's probably a lot safer than if he thought he was a reincarnation of Casanova.' 'Oh I don't know,' she said with an enigmatic smile, anyone for chess?'

Chapter Nineteen

At the meeting on the following Wednesday, Harry Baines was introduced as their latest member, everyone knew him from their meeting at the youth club or in Mr. Wong's shop and they all murmured welcome noises. For his part, he made a very brief speech saying that everything he had heard about the Windmill Club made him look forward to being a member. 'And of course Beryl's cake,' said Vicky with a giggle. There was an air of tension in the group. The bye-election was now only two weeks away and Alice had been invited to a question and answer session with two other candidates. 'You will come with me?' she said anxiously to Bill and Tom. 'Of course,' Tom replied 'and I'm sure the others will be in the audience, along with people like Fran and Harry.' 'Supposing someone asks me a question and I don't know the answer?' she said. 'In my opinion the best thing to do is admit that you don't know the answer. There's nothing worse than to listen to politicians on the radio or television mumbling along and trying to admit that they didn't understand the question.' 'Will many people be there?' she asked. 'Well it's hard to say but the hall holds about eighty people sitting so there could be that many. Anyway, you will have lots of moral support.'

Tom then told the members of the Windmill Club about his idea for taking the youth club members on a day out. 'We've already hit one snag,' he said 'because Fran would like to tell her members that younger siblings would be welcome and she may get more than a coach load and that doesn't include any of us.' 'That's not really a problem,' said Bill 'we can have two coaches or two outings and make sure that nobody is disappointed.' They discussed where they should go and the unanimous feeling was in favour of the North Welsh coast. 'We can get the best of both worlds there,' said Alice, 'there are some nice seaside towns and there are some nice places to visit like Conway Castle.' They agreed that if there were to be two coaches then they would split up and half of them would go in each coach to help supervise the children. 'What do we do about the money?' said Bill. Tom said that he knew someone from his old firm who was in the Rotary Club and Jim said that he knew somebody in the Lions Club and they both thought they could get small grants from these.

'We could of course ask the Freemasons,' said Alice 'but nobody knows who they are, I think it's very sad that they are such a secretive organisation.' 'It's not just a question of being secretive,' said Bill 'but the way in which they operate could be described as very self serving. I was approached on a number of occasions while I was in the force and I was told quite adamantly that I would never make Chief Constable unless I joined.' Tom said 'It's common knowledge that the legal system is riddled with Freemasons, personally I have always found their peculiar ceremonies rather adolescent and although they claim to be a charitable organisation why do they need all the secrecy?' 'Well,' said Vicky 'I don't know if it was true but I read that the Duke of Edinburgh was supposed to be a Grand Master or whatever they're called and I'm surprised that the Queen allows it. I'm sure I would not allow my husband to be a freemason but then I can't imagine that any club of any kind would want my husband as a member.' She paused and then said, 'well perhaps gamblers anonymous.'

They all made a note of Alice's question and answer meeting on the following Monday and promised to attend. They also promised to do some last minute canvassing in the week before the election. Lenny asked how many other candidates there were. Bill replied that there was one each from the three main parties, one from UKIP and one from the English League. 'Blimey,' said Jim, 'it's a lot of opposition but I'm sure my Alice will defeat them.' Tom said that he thought the fact that all the main parties were fielding candidates would make it easier for Alice. 'They will divide a lot of votes between them and the fact that Alice is a local independent person will definitely count in her favour.' 'I should think that being a woman will also be in her favour' added Beryl. 'Anyway there are only a couple of weeks to go so we will soon know; I will bring in the tea.'

While they were eating and drinking, Harry Baines approached Tom and said, 'I hear Fran's moved in with you?' 'Yes,' replied Tom, 'I know she has known you a lot longer but it's only a very temporary move.' 'Oh I don't mind, my flat would not really be suitable and I am sure you and she will look after each other. I am just offering my good wishes.' 'Well thank you Harry, she has often said what a good friend you are. The move was thrust upon her rather suddenly by the landlord's decision to refurbish. You must come round and have a meal with us very soon.' 'Thank you, I will be glad to accept your invitation.'

Shortly after that conversation, the meeting broke up with promises to see each other next Monday. Bill and Tom arranged to meet with Alice on Sunday afternoon to go over her short speech. 'Come round to my house,' suggested Tom. 'Fran will be down in Bournemouth visiting her mother.' Over dinner that evening, he told Fran of his conversation with Harry. 'Yes, I did wonder if he would have expected me to stay with him but I knew his flat was as small as mine. He and his wife used to have a lovely house about five miles away but when she died it was too large for him and he moved to his present flat.' 'I'm sure he didn't mind,' Tom said 'he gave us his good wishes.' 'Yes, well in any case he and I had a different kind of relationship; I expect it's the mountain bond that has drawn us together.'

She confirmed that she would be going down to Bournemouth on Friday. 'Harry has promised to hold the fort but I will be back on Monday for Alice's meeting.' 'You must borrow my car,' said Tom 'I won't be needing it and trains are so expensive and unreliable.' Fran protested that she could not take yet another advantage as she put it but Tom insisted so she reluctantly agreed. 'It will certainly make the travelling a lot easier,' she said 'and if you don't mind I can take my mother and Auntie out.' 'That's agreed then,' said Tom with a smile. 'We'll do the washing up and I'll thrash you at backgammon.'

Chapter Twenty

Over breakfast, Tom remembered to tell Fran that he had suggested Harry came round for a meal. 'That's a good idea,' she said 'the coming week will be a bit hectic but perhaps we could have him over on the following weekend, either Saturday or Sunday, which ever suits him.' 'Good, I will tell him.' 'Also I have invited Bill and Alice here on Sunday to go over her speech.' Fran smiled mischievously and said 'What's the betting he brings Beryl with him and that she just happens to go to the bathroom and check out the bedrooms.' 'Oh you naughty girl, how could you think such a thing,' he said laughing.

About ten minutes after breakfast Fran said she was off to the library and Tom decided that this was a good opportunity for him to sort out the rest of Evelyn's clothes. After she died, he did not have the heart to dispose of them so he had put some into the spare room and left some in the drawers and wardrobes he and she had shared. When he knew Fran was moving in he had moved the clothes out of the spare room into the small room he used as an office. Much of the routine he had followed in the kitchen he had allowed to lapse once Fran had started sharing and now was the time to make the final break.

He rang Alice because he knew that she and Vicky worked as part time volunteers in a charity shop. Alice was pleased to hear from him and assured him that the shop was always happy to receive clothing. She told him to put everything into bags and she would ask Jim to give her a ride round to Tom's house in the afternoon and pick them up. He was relieved to think that the problem could be so easily solved, however, the process proved much harder than he anticipated. Many of the clothes were almost brand new, Evelyn had been a keen shopper before she became ill; she used to refer to it as her retail therapy. Everything was hung neatly on hangers or carefully folded in the drawers. She had been very fond of lavender water and many of the clothes smelled delicately of lavender.

He decided to use two of the suitcases which they used to use when they went on holiday. 'Won't be using them again now,' he thought, 'and they are very good quality so the charity shop might as well have them.' He took out the clothes and placed them on the bed, he could remember occasions when she had bought a particular dress or blouse, she would hold it in front of her and ask him to admire it but then quite often she would never wear it and he would never see it again. At first, she seemed happy to help him with the task; he could clearly hear her voice saying 'Well someone will enjoy wearing that.' Then inexplicably the atmosphere in the room seemed to change. Now he could hear her saying, 'Getting rid of me once and for all are you and replacing me with that pretty young girl, you should be ashamed of yourself.' He sat on the edge of the bed and heard himself saying 'No, I will never forget you and no, Fran is not a replacement for you.' He whispered 'I love you Evelyn and I always will.' This seemed to placate her and the atmosphere in the room lifted.

He carried on until both suitcases were full and he put the shoes and handbags into plastic bags. He kept one handbag, a beautiful leather one, which they had bought in Paris on one of their very rare trips abroad. In it was a collection of photographs which they had taken in the earlier, happier days of marriage. As he looked through them, he recalled the pleasure of sharing and caring. He put the photographs back in the bag and placed it on the wardrobe shelf. Then he made two journeys downstairs leaving the bags in the hall. He realised it was lunchtime and although he wasn't particularly hungry he made himself a cheese and chutney sandwich and a pot of tea. Fran must be working through at the library he thought.

About three o'clock his doorbell rang and when he opened the door he found Alice, Vicky and Jim standing on his step. 'What a nice surprise,' he said 'please come in and I will put the kettle on.' He showed them into the sitting room and went into the kitchen, he could hear Alice and Vicky exclaiming what a nice house it was and admiring the view of the garden through the French windows. He took the tray into the sitting room and Alice said 'Oh this is nice.' Vicky said 'You should have let me carry the tray Tom,' and turning to the others she said 'I'm booked to be his carer one day you know.' Tom smiled and said 'Yes, when I'm ninety five.' While they were drinking tea and eating some of Fran's cake Alice said 'Jim told me you and he had a nice chat, it was very kind of you.' Tom did not know what Jim had told her so he just murmured 'It was my pleasure.'

They were talking and Vicky was giggling as usual when Tom heard a key in the door. The front door closed and Fran poked her head round the sitting room door and said 'Is this a private party or may I come in?' 'Oh don't be silly dear,' said Tom 'come in and I'll make a fresh pot of tea.' 'And I'll help you,' said Vicky 'just to get the practice and find my way around.' After more tea and cake Alice said 'We'd better be going because the shop shuts at five and we don't have a key. Don't worry Tom we'll sort everything out.' They loaded the bags and suitcases into Jim's car and with a toot and a wave they disappeared down the road. Tom felt a momentary pang of loss; it was almost as if he was saying goodbye to Evelyn for a second time. He shook himself and went back indoors. Fran had guessed what the bags contained and with a rueful smile she said 'I hope I didn't force that on you?' 'Not at all my love, it had to be done.' What did Vicky mean about getting in practice? Or am I being too inquisitive?' 'No,' he laughed 'it's just a little joke about her becoming my carer when I'm ninety five.' 'Oh, I thought that would be my job,' she said with a gentle smile. 'I wish,' he murmured under his breath as he went into the kitchen to start preparing dinner.

He was very ambitious in his dinner attempt and Fran declared that it was one of the best meals she had ever eaten. The main course was a cheese soufflé and this was followed by a delicious crème brulee. 'This is fantastic,' she declared. 'I might have tackled one of these but to do both is very brave.' 'Well I thought we should have something special as you are going away for the weekend.' 'Yes, it will be odd to miss the club on Friday evening, I've only missed one before and that was because I had the flu. Would you mind if I set off early in the morning, I thought if I left about six thirty I will miss the workers heading into the city. 'Not at all, I am always awake just after six. I could cook you some breakfast.' 'No, I've got a better idea I will bring you a cup of tea in bed.'

Sure enough the following morning there was a tap on his door and Fran entered carrying a tray on which there was tea and toast. 'It's just after six o'clock and I'm off in a few minutes.' He sat up and said 'Thanks very much and please drive carefully.' 'Oh I won't bend your car,' she said. 'Never mind the car, just look after yourself.' She kissed him lightly on the forehead and quickly left the room. He waited for a comment from Evelyn but there was no sound. Never mind, he told himself, it's only three nights and then she'll be back. He munched his toast and drank his tea then lay back on the pillows and allowed himself to dream.

He got up just after seven o'clock and as he had already had some toast, he settled for a bowl of cereal and some coffee. He thought about going shopping for some new shoes but remembered that he had not got a car. He decided to walk round to Lenny Patel's for a morning paper. Lenny wasn't there; his son was looking after the shop and said his father had gone to the wholesalers. He told Tom how much his father enjoyed being a member of the Windmill Club. 'He says it's one of the best things that has ever happened to him.' As Tom walked home, he decided to have a purge and clean all the windows inside because after the window cleaner had been a couple of weeks ago it had made him aware that he had not cleaned them for some time. In fact, he could not remember the last time they had been properly cleaned inside and out. He spent the rest of the morning and half the afternoon before he had completed them all and he was glad to sit down and read his paper.

He did not feel like cooking so he decided on fish and chips from Mr. Wong's. There was a small queue but he waited patiently and when he got to the counter Mr. Wong was delighted to see him. Unfortunately, he would not take payment for Tom's supper which made Tom feel slightly embarrassed but grateful. He walked quickly home with his warm parcel and he was just sitting down to enjoy the crisp battered fish and chips when the telephone rang. 'Damn,' he said but his annoyance was immediately dissipated when he heard Fran's voice. 'I just wanted to tell you I arrived here safely,' she said 'and although I am pleased to see mummy and auntie I am missing you.' He was sure his heart missed a beat and he replied that he was missing her too. 'The house seems quite empty,' he told her, 'I've just collected my supper from Mr. Wong's.' 'Well

I won't keep you now,' she said 'but I will call you tomorrow night.' They said their goodbyes and he thought, is it conceivable that we could really be missing each other after a few weeks friendship. Perhaps it was the time in Hathersage, which somehow speeded up and strengthened our relationship. My feelings are genuine but perhaps Fran was just being kind. He then finished his now slightly cooler supper.

A little later, the telephone rang again. Did she forget something he thought, but it wasn't Fran it was Alice. 'First of all,' she said 'I want to thank you for those super clothes, they will make the charity a lot of money, secondly my lump, Jim has asked me to speak to you because he's a bit shy.' 'How can I help?' said Tom. 'Well one of his mates from the pub has gone on holiday and he has left two season tickets with Jim. He wondered if you would like to see Lancashire play in a one day, forty over, cricket match tomorrow.' 'I'd be delighted,' said Tom 'but wouldn't you like to go?' 'Not likely,' she said 'Vicky and I are going to bingo, much more fun to me. Cricket is like watching paint dry. Jim said he will pick you up about ten o'clock in the morning.' Tom was pleased, he knew Lancashire was playing a neighbouring county and it should be a good game and of course it will fill another day. He stayed up rather late reading because the house seemed too quiet and too empty and he knew he would have difficulty in getting to sleep. I just hope Jim won't be looking for more advice he thought. Just before he fell asleep he heard Evelyn saying, "Are you missing her more than you miss me?" 'Of course not, in any case it's quite different, Fran will be coming back on Monday and you will never come back. You know how much I grieved when I lost you.' There was a silence and then he said 'I thought you had left me forever.' "Oh no, this is our house and as long as you live here I will be around. Good night dear." He waited but there was no more and he fell asleep.

Promptly at ten o'clock the following morning he heard Jim sounding his horn outside. He was ready to go so picking up his coat he went out. Jim wound his window down and said 'Morning Tom, jump in.' Tom climbed in the passenger side and said This is very kind of you Jim, I haven't been to a cricket match for about three years.' 'My pleasure, a mate was going on holiday and he didn't want the tickets wasted.' They chatted in a casual way until they reached the ground and Jim found a place in the car park. They found their seats and settled down. Lancashire won the toss and put their opponents in to bat. Their bowling was sharp and controlled and at the end of the first forty overs their opponents had scored 213 runs for the loss of 8 wickets. Jim produced a flask and some sandwiches out of a plastic bag. 'Alice thought you wouldn't want to queue up,' he said. 'That's very thoughtful of her.' 'Yes, well my Alice is a very thoughtful lady.' She had provided three different kinds of sandwiches and cake to follow and as they ate Jim said 'I need some more advice Tom.' Oh dear,' thought Tom, 'they say there's no such thing as a free lunch.'

'Fire away Jim, although I may not be much help.' 'Well, Alice said it would be nice to have your opinion.' 'About what exactly' said Tom. 'Oh dear it sounds silly really, but we can't make up our minds about whether to get married or just live together.' 'Do you love Alice and do you believe she loves you?' 'I certainly do and I'm fairly sure she loves me.' 'Do you hope to stay together for the rest of your lives?' 'Yes, we both do.' 'Well then, why not get married? It will make you both feel more secure and you will have a tidier financial situation.' Just then the cricketers came out of the pavilion, saved by the bell, Tom thought. 'Oh good,' said Jim 'I was hoping you would say that. Will you be my best man?' 'Oh, that's a bit of a surprise, but yes I will be honoured.' They watched the rest of the cricket and were pleased when the home team reached their target of 214 runs for the loss of 5 wickets. Jim drove them home and when he stopped at his gate Tom said 'Thank you very much Jim I really enjoyed that.' 'No, thank you, I am so glad you have agreed to be my best man and I know Alice will be delighted. We hope to arrange something for early October.'

Chapter Twenty One

When Tom got in he did not feel like slaving over a hot stove so he settled for beans on toast. About nine o'clock the telephone rang and he knew exactly who it was from the way his heart jumped. He was not disappointed; Fran was warm in her enquiries about him and his day and enthusiastic in telling him about her outing with her mother and aunt. He was sure that she was sincere when she said again that she was missing him and he was fervent in his response. After they said their goodbyes he sat wondering how he could feel so drawn to someone he had known for only a short time. He could understand the relationship between Alice and Jim, they were both in their late sixties and both had been living alone for some time, but he and Fran were forty years apart in age and he had spent most of his life as a loner, in the Navy and on the mountains. He recalled something he had once read written by a French soldier and poet in the seventeenth century.

Absence is to love what wind is to fire.
It extinguishes the small and kindles the great.

During his time in the Navy, there were many hours of tedium and he had filled them by becoming an avid reader.

It was true that he had a loving relationship with Evelyn, but he remembered that during her visits to stay with her daughters in London, sometimes for as long as two weeks, he had enjoyed the peace and quiet. He had never known feelings like those he was experiencing now. 'It can't work you silly old fool,' he told himself, 'but just suppose it could,' said a little voice. I could live another ten or fifteen years but what then for Fran? He had another of his splitting headaches, so he decided to stop fretting and go to bed early.

When he got up the following morning, his first thoughts were that she will be back tomorrow. While he was eating a simple breakfast he decided that he would go to the cemetery and visit Evelyn's grave. He personally preferred cremation but Evelyn's father had been killed in the Second World War and he was buried somewhere abroad. Her mother had been buried in the local cemetery and Evelyn had wanted to be buried in the same plot. As he cleared the breakfast dishes away, he thought with some shame that he hadn't visited her grave since February. The cemetery was only about a mile away so he had no excuse for the neglect, on the other hand she wasn't really there, just her remains, so was there much point? As it was only a mile away and Fran had his car he enjoyed the walk, he bought some flowers from a woman who had a stall at the cemetery gates and placed them in a vase on her grave. He noticed with dismay how many of the gravestones were knocked over and defaced and recalled Jim complaining about vandalism. 'I am so sorry Evelyn,' he murmured.

He did not feel like cooking lunch so he decided to stop at the local pub on his way home. He was going to order the Sunday roast but it was a warm day so he decided to settle for a ploughman's and a pint of shandy. After this simple meal he headed for home to get ready for his visitors. At first, he thought about using the garden for the meeting but, as he had neighbours on both sides and there was an element of confidentiality about the meeting, he decided to use the sitting room with the French windows open. He did speak occasionally to his neighbours but as they were both relatively young and so far childless couples who went out to work, he did not often see them and in any case he didn't have much in common with them. He wondered whether there would be two visitors or three, including Beryl, or even four including Vicky. His instincts told him there would be four because Jim would not come; he would not want to embarrass Alice.

Sure enough, at three o'clock the doorbell rang and on his step were the four visitors he had expected. Bill said 'Beryl and Vicky wanted to come along so I made them promise not to interfere.' 'We'll sit as quiet as two mice,' said Vicky with a chuckle. 'Squeak, squeak' said Beryl. Tom asked if they wanted tea before or after the discussion. 'Oh, after please,' said Alice, 'I'm nervous enough and I would like to get it over first.' She had prepared some notes and Tom suggested she read them slowly and either he or Bill would make comments if necessary. Each candidate in the question and answer session would begin by giving a brief resume of their lives. Alice had decided that she would begin at the end. 'I retired six years ago from my job as a school secretary, I worked at a large comprehensive school and I was there for fourteen years. I came to this City after my husband died; I hadn't any real roots because my parents moved around a lot as my father was in the Royal Air Force; anyway, they are both dead now. My husband and I were both professional wrestlers, attached to a circus and travelled round the world. He died in Canada but his solicitor was here so I came back to see him and thought, this is a nice City, why not stay here. I have lived here for over twenty years and believe I now know it well.'

'Bravo,' said Bill 'now go on about why you should be elected.' 'I think you should elect me as a councillor because I am honest, hard working and care about the welfare of the people in this City. I would hold regular surgeries every Tuesday evening and Saturday morning. I would be happy to see anybody living in this district and help with their problems if I can. I will attend all council meetings and ensure that our district is properly represented on the council.' Tom intervened, 'What if someone in the audience suggested you were too old?' 'I would point out that my life has been extremely varied and given me plenty of experience. I would say that good wine matures into better wine as it gets older. I would also point out that it is likely that half the people that turn out to vote will be over sixty.' 'Very good,' Tom said. 'I do not think that you have anything to worry about. Either Bill or I will sit behind you and prompt if really necessary, although I do not think it will be.' 'Any questions, Alice?' asked Bill. 'No, I just hope I'm not too nervous on the night.' 'Well,' said Vicky 'if any of the other candidates get too rude or cocky you can always challenge them to arm wrestling.'

Beryl said 'Well if we can now talk, can I help you with the tea Tom; I brought a cake as I knew Frances was away.' Fran had left a Bakewell tart and with Beryl's cake there was more than enough to go round. After tea Vicky said she would help with the washing up and Beryl said 'If you don't mind Tom, I'll just pop up to the loo?' 'No I don't mind, help yourself.' And he smiled as she made her way upstairs. When they all left just after five o'clock the house once again descended into silence. There were no comments from Evelyn and Tom wondered if his disposal of her clothes had caused her to finally leave him. He made a ham sandwich and ate some of the leftover cake. 'Oh dear,' he thought, 'I'm reverting to my old, lazy eating habits.' At nine o'clock the telephone rang and his spirits lifted when he heard Fran's voice. She told him about her day, visiting a National Trust House. 'All rather slow but then mummy is almost eighty seven and auntie is a few years older. How did your meeting with Alice go?' 'Very well,' he told her, 'and I'm sure Alice will do very well tomorrow night'. 'Did I win my bet?' she asked. 'I'm afraid you did, and Beryl looked a bit disappointed when she came down.' Fran told him that she would leave Bournemouth early and hoped to join him for lunch. 'Must go now,' she said 'I've got this handsome hunk waiting at the bar.' And then she laughed. He swallowed, 'Well enjoy your evening then,' he said, 'see you tomorrow.' 'Bye Tom dear, mummy's got the cocoa ready.' As he got ready for bed, he wondered which version was the truth. If it was the handsome hunk, what right had he to mind? I don't know he told himself, but I would much rather it was mummy with the cocoa.

Chapter Twenty Two

The following morning he was awake early, in sharp contrast to his waking a few months ago, he felt alive and eager to start the day. Of course, she was coming back today and somehow that made the world seem to be a brighter and happier place. He spent the morning cleaning and tidying an already clean house and he found himself constantly looking at the clock. Just before twelve o'clock he heard a car entering the drive and he peered out of the window to check that it was indeed his own car. Then he went to the front door and opened it just in time to greet Fran who was walking from the car. 'Hello, you're early,' he said. 'Oh, shall I go and drive around the block a few times?' 'Don't be daft, I just meant that you must have left Bournemouth early.' 'Indeed I did and I'm dying for a cup of tea. Let's put the kettle on.'

Later, while they were eating a simple salad with prawns for lunch Fran told him of her adventures. 'Not that it was very adventurous, mummy and auntie both suffer from severe arthritis and they are very slow moving. Unfortunately, they are both very independent and insist that they do not need any help from social workers or nurses. However, if you saw them you would understand why I have great difficulty in thinking of you as old.' There was a pause and then Tom said, 'I believe that old age is relative to ones state of mind and physical well being. I don't see myself as old but the last few weeks have taken years off me.' Fran smiled mischievously 'I wonder why that is,' she murmured. 'Anyway, tell me about the meeting this evening. I assume we are both going?' 'Oh definitely, we must support Alice, although I'm sure she will do very well. By the way you have not yet told me about

this handsome hunk you were having a drink with.'
'Just a little fantasy of mine, actually I was listening to
two elderly ladies reminiscing about their wartime
experiences. Mum was in the ATS and auntie was in
the land army; they had some pretty exciting social
times too.' 'Yes, I was only a small boy but I know that
there was an atmosphere of live for the moment
because tomorrow may never come. This applied to all
service men but especially those who were flying
regularly, having said that, I feel that I have adopted
that philosophy myself.' 'Oh Sartre and his
existentialism theory,' said Fran thoughtfully. 'It's not
a bad way to live your life, are you afraid of dying?'
Tom thought very carefully before replying. 'No, I do
not believe that I am afraid of dying, indeed there have
been a few times in my life when I would have
welcomed the thought, but at the present time I think I
would prefer to stick around.' 'Good,' she said 'now if
you'll excuse me I've got to attend to some laundry.'

About six forty five they set off in Tom's car for the
hall where the meeting was to be held. The meeting
was scheduled for seven o'clock but there were very
few cars in the car park. Tom parked next to Bill's car
and when they went into the hall he was disappointed
to see only about thirty people in the audience. He and
Bill had agreed that he would sit on the platform with
Alice and leaving Fran to sit with the other members of
the Windmill Club; he made his way to the front where
Alice greeted him with a relieved smile. 'Thank
goodness,' she said 'I did not want to sit up here on my
own.' There were three other candidates present, one
man for the Liberal Democrats, one man for the Labour
Party and a woman representing the Green Party. Alice
told him that the Conservative candidate was ill and
could not attend. The chairman was a councillor from a
nearby constituency and he greeted Tom and Alice with

a slightly bemused smile. 'You're the grey party I gather.' 'Indeed not,' said Tom 'Mrs. Jackson is an Independent candidate, but she is also a member of the Windmill Club.' 'Oh yes' the chairman replied 'I've heard a bit about you lot, a group of Bolshie's I'm told.' Just at that moment, and before Tom could reply, the Labour candidate said 'Excuse me Mr. Chairman, but could we get on with the meeting?'

The chairman hastily called the audience to order. As there were two male and two female candidates the chairman suggested that they should go alternatively with the woman from the Green party starting the ball rolling. They each gave a short speech and Alice, who was third, delivered hers perfectly after a small hesitation. Then the chairman told the audience they could now ask questions. The numbers had grown to about forty people and several hands shot up. After a few of the inevitable ordinary questions about such things as buses and dustbin collection, there was a slight moment of silence. Then a stout, red faced man got to his feet and announced that he was Councillor Tutt. He directed his question specifically at Alice. 'All the other candidates have had experience over the years with such things as committees and party meetings; they all represent well established political parties. You have apparently had no experience and don't represent any party. What makes you think you would do better than them?' His tone was aggressive and Alice coloured slightly. Tom leaned towards her and whispered, 'Familiarity,' this was a trigger for something they had already discussed. 'Pardon me,' said Alice 'but I don't remember saying that I would be better than the other candidates. What I do know is that a lot of politicians become comfortable in their seats and familiarity breeds contempt. They become much more interested in their own future and ambitions and the people that voted for them become unimportant. Most people in Parliament, either the Commons or the Lords, are concerned with increasing their status or in some cases their wealth. Many councillors become puffed up with their own self importance but I just want to serve my fellow citizens' 'Hear, hear,' shouted a voice loudly from the hall, and Tom recognised the voice as Bill's. After that the audience seemed to lose interest and the chairman decided it would be better to draw the meeting to a close. As he did so he reminded them that the election would be held a week on Thursday and he hoped that they would all turn out and vote.

'That went well,' said Fran as they drove home. 'Yes, I think Alice played a blinder, she will make a very good councillor, of course, if she gets in.' 'Oh, I'm fairly sure she will,' said Fran 'we've done a lot of canvassing on her behalf and tonight will not have done her any harm.' 'Incidentally,' replied Tom 'I came across that chap Tutt a few years ago and he has not improved with time.' 'Once a prat, always a prat,' said Fran with a laugh. Over supper they discussed the youth club outing. 'It looks as if we will need two coaches, but I think we should all go on the same day.' 'I agree,' said Tom 'much less hassle for the adults and better for the kids because they will definitely be with their friends or siblings.'

Chapter Twenty Three

When Tom arrived at the Windmill Club meeting, there was a definite air of excitement and optimism. Alice was in particularly high spirits. 'Well Tom' she shouted across the room 'how did I do?' 'You did very, very well, I'm sure we are all proud of you.' 'Yes' added Vicky 'you coped with that red faced bully very successfully.' They settled down and the talk turned to the election day the following week. 'We will all turn up at the polling station at different times and encourage any one we know to vote for Alice' said Bill, 'and Beryl has had a very good idea.' 'Well,' said Beryl 'we don't all want to wear those silly rosettes such as the big parties wear, so I've persuaded Bill to part with some of his large, red roses and we can all wear those.' 'What was that,' said Jim 'large red noses?' 'Shh,' said Alice. 'That is a good idea,' said Tom 'it will certainly make us stand out from the rest.' 'And,' said Vicky practically bubbling over 'we can say afterwards that we all rose to the occasion,' there were groans all round. They also made arrangements to be at the town hall for the count which would be held on the morning after the election day.

Tom then put up his hand and addressed Bill, 'We now need to talk about the youth club outing Mr. Chairman and find out how many volunteers we have. Fran has been in touch with the coach firm and we can have two of their small thirty-two seater coaches for half their usual price. 'We will have to avoid the bank holiday weekend, how about the third week in August?' Beryl suggested. 'Bill and I are going away in September and in August all the younger members will be off school.' 'We may as well do it on our club day,' said Tom 'how about the third Wednesday in August?'

Everyone said that they would be available with the exception of Mr. Wong who said he was very sorry but he was going to Hong Kong to see his ancient and revered mother this coming weekend. 'I will not be back until the beginning of September,' he said. 'Very well,' Tom said 'that leaves four of us in each coach. I assume Harry will be in charge of one and Fran the other.' It was decided to put Bill, Beryl and Vicky in Harry's coach and Alice, Jim, Lenny and Tom in the other. 'That will mean about twenty seven youth club members in each coach,' said Harry 'and at the last count there were fifty names on the list so that will be perfect. We will have one or two spare places for any late additions.' The plans were agreed and Harry said he would pass the information on to Fran. Then Bill announced that the Rotary Club and the Lions had each agreed to give two hundred and fifty pounds and with the coach owners concession there should be plenty of money left over for ice creams.

The ladies said they would pool their resources and produce hampers of sandwiches, cakes and other edible goodies. The men said they would be responsible for several crates of drinks. 'Which will be non alcoholic of course,' said Beryl. 'Of course dear,' replied Bill. Mr. Wong produced fifty pounds and said it was his contribution to the refreshments and Bill thanked him. He then reminded the group that it was only five weeks away. Beryl wheeled in the tea trolley and they got down to the serious business of savouring her cakes. Just before they left Harry asked Tom if he would join Fran and himself in interviewing candidates for her job. 'The interviews are next week but Fran does not like to ask you herself because she thought you would be pressured into saying yes, even if you didn't want to take the task on.' 'I would be delighted,' said Tom 'it should be very interesting.'

When he got home, he told Fran of his conversation with Harry. 'Oh good,' she said 'I did want to involve you but I was afraid you would feel obliged to say yes.' 'It's not a problem,' said Tom 'I would be glad to help, not that we will find anyone as good as you.' That evening as they played chess Fran moved her queen and said 'Check mate, will you miss me when I move to Exeter?' Tom was not sure how to reply 'Of course, I will miss you enormously, but I understand why you have got to go.' 'Well, it will not be a permanent good bye; I can come and visit you. In fact, I could come up and stay after Christmas. I will have to spend Christmas with mummy and auntie but then I could come here for the New Year. If you wanted me to,' she added hastily. 'My dear girl that would be splendid, nothing could please me more.' 'Good, then that's a date.'

Chapter Twenty Four

Fran had arranged the interviews for a replacement for her job on Monday afternoon; she told Tom that apart from him and Harry she also had to have a representative from the education department. 'I just hope it won't be that creepy little man Terry, every time I meet him I shudder to think of his involvement with children.' There were four candidates, two men and two women, and Fran had asked them to come for forty five minute periods between two and five o'clock. She and Tom met Harry at one thirty in order to discuss the CVs. They would use the small room used by the music group to hold the interviews. About one forty five the door was thrust open and Tom could tell from Fran's face that it was indeed the man she had hoped would not attend. She introduced him to Tom and Harry and he said 'Well I'm the official representative of the education department so I will take the chair and in the case of a tied decision I will have the casting vote.' Tom took an immediate dislike to the man, partly because of Fran's comments but also because of the man's manner. He was a small man, almost bald but with a few strands of hair placed carefully over his pink scalp. He had small beady eyes and a thin moustache and he was wearing a brown suit with a purple spotted tie and black shoes. 'Oh Lord,' Tom thought 'this could be fun.'

Tom knew that Fran had the youth club on Friday evenings and a junior group for seven to ten year olds on a Tuesday evening. In addition, she had to liaise with the local schools and visit parents in their homes. It was a more demanding job than he had realised. 'Right Miss Summers bring the first candidate in,' said Terry in a pompous manner. The first candidate was a thin, nervous young woman called Mavis Jones. She had been a teacher for two years, when Fran asked her why she wanted to leave teaching she said that she had difficulty controlling the children and thought she might do better in a less structured setting. After some other questions the Chairman said 'Thank you very much Miss Jones, we will write and let you know our decision.' The second candidate was a tall, thin young man who had a science degree but no experience with children and he too got the thumbs down.

The next candidate seemed to blow into the room like a breath of fresh air. She was a tall, athletic looking girl with her blonde hair tied back in a pony tail and her name was Jenny Porter. She had been working at an outdoor centre in the Lake District but had to return to the area because her mother had died and she was looking after her father and two younger brothers. She and Fran seemed to establish a rapport immediately and it was obvious to Tom that she would be suitable. However, there was one more candidate, he was a slightly rotund man, a bit older that the other candidates. Tom noted that he was thirty-three and had a varied number of jobs on his CV. He was skilled with computers and his last job had been as a deputy manager in a shop which sold electrical goods. Mr. Terry warmed to him immediately and addressed him as Marcus whereas he had called the other candidates by their surnames. Fran asked if he had any experience with children and he said that he used to be in the boys brigade and still helped out sometimes.

After he went out Mr. Terry said, 'Well he's our man, used to responsibility and meeting people.' 'Ah yes,' said Tom 'but meeting people as shop customers isn't quite the same as in Fran's job.' 'Look here,' Terry replied 'he comes from a good family, I play golf with his father and he's the man for me.' 'Well,' said

Fran 'we have to be democratic so we had better take a vote.' 'Yes, well remember I have the casting vote, I'm in the chair.' In the event a casting vote was irrelevant because Fran, Harry and Tom all voted for Jenny Porter. 'Easily the best candidate,' said Harry and I could work with her.' Terry spluttered and said 'Well I think you're making a mistake.' 'And what will you tell his father,' murmured Tom quietly to Fran. 'I knew it was a mistake to have amateurs on the panel. I just hope it doesn't blow up in our faces.' 'I'm sure Miss Porter will do a splendid job,' said Fran quietly and so the interviews were over.

Later that evening, while they were having supper Fran suddenly slapped her forehead with her hand and said 'What have I done!' 'What do you mean?' asked Tom. 'Well, we have appointed someone who is probably a climber and when she knows who you are she will want to climb with you.' Tom laughed and said 'Relax girl when I saw one of her references was the Keswick outdoor school I rang the warden who was an old friend of mine. Jenny's boyfriend is the chief instructor there and they climb together all the time. She certainly will not want to climb with an old has been like me.' 'There you go again,' said Fran 'selling yourself short; still I'm glad I will not have competition.'

Chapter Twenty Five

The club meeting on the day before the election was rather subdued; Alice was very tense and said that she dreaded letting them all down. Tom smiled at her and said that whatever the outcome she had done a splendid job, he personally was sure she would get elected. Bill reminded everyone that the coach outing was only two weeks away and he hoped everyone was still willing to go. 'Definitely,' said Vicky, 'I have a new bucket and spade and I will organise the sandcastle competition.' 'Well, that is if you can persuade modern kids to make sandcastles,' Bill replied. 'Oh I can be very persuasive,' said Vicky with a chuckle. They then worked out who would be at the polling station the following day. Jim, Alice and Vicky would be there in the morning Beryl, Bill and Lenny would cover the afternoon and Tom and Harry would be there in the evening. Mr Wong was going to be away from tomorrow for a month. 'Then we could all meet here after ten o'clock,' said Beryl 'when the polling station has closed. That is if you want to of course.' 'That's a good idea,' said Jim 'then we can either cheer Alice up or try to hold her down.' 'Yes, I'm sure we will have a good idea of how she's done by then,' said Tom.

Polling day was bright and sunny; Tom said to Fran over breakfast that it should mean a good turn out for the election. Fran asked whether he thought that would be to Alice's advantage and he replied that he thought so because the big parties would split each other's vote. 'Is it alright if I join you and Harry this evening,' said Fran. 'It certainly is, because some of the parents will recognise you and may be influenced in favour of Alice. Furthermore, with someone like you wearing a red rose there is no danger of anyone seeing us as the grey party.' 'Good, well I'm working in the library today so I'll see you at tea time.' After Tom had washed up the breakfast dishes and tidied up around the house he decided to stroll around to the polling station to see how Alice and her companions were getting on. They told him that things had been fairly quiet since polling opened but a number of voters had greeted Alice and wished her good luck. One man had gone so far as to say that it was about time that they had a councillor who represented the people rather than the party. Tom said that he had read that there was a group in Herefordshire who called themselves *"It's our County"* and it seemed to be doing very well. He then suggested that when the three of them had finished their morning stint they should meet him at the local pub for lunch. 'My treat,' he said. That was more than an hour away so he decided to walk on to the cemetery and tidy up Evelyn's grave. When he got to the graveside, there was no one about, well no one living he thought, so he sat by the grave and told her about the election. 'I know a lot of people would think that I'm mad, or going gaga talking to a grave,' he thought 'but it is simply a version of thinking out loud and that sometimes helps to clear the mind.' It certainly helps me to remember Evelyn he told himself and it's good and necessary to remember people that you love.

He looked at his watch and realised that he had been sitting there for more than half an hour so he got to his feet and made his way slowly to the pub. He was greeted warmly by the landlord with whom he was on first name terms. 'Afternoon Tom, what can I get you?' 'Hello George, half a pint of cider please, I'm expecting Jim and his two lady friends so can you do lunch for four?' 'Not a problem,' replied George 'sit in the corner by the window and I'll bring your drink over.' About ten minutes later Alice arrived and to

Tom's surprise, she put her arms around him and gave him a big kiss. 'That's for relief as much as anything,' she said, 'but it's also to thank you for your friendship.' Just then, Jim and Vicky came in and they decided that they all wanted the pub special, which proved to be a delicious lasagne. Alice and Vicky asked for salad with theirs while Tom and Jim plumped for chips. While they were eating their lunch, Tom was regaled with stories about the morning's activities. 'If people were telling the truth,' said Jim 'about half of them were voting for Alice.' 'I'm sure that was a true picture,' said Vicky 'and we can be very optimistic.' After lunch, the morning three went home for a rest and Tom decided to go into town to make final arrangements for the outing with the coach firm. They had decided that they would go to the North Wales coast, leaving the youth club at nine o'clock in the morning and arriving back at approximately nine thirty in the evening and the coach proprietor said this was fine. Afterwards he called at the library to give Fran a lift home.

During their evening meal they discussed the by election and the likelihood of Alice winning. Tom said that he was fairly optimistic and if she became a councillor it would give the Windmill Club more information about what was happening in the city. Fran suggested that the Windmill Club might not stop at just one councillor in future elections but Tom thought that there was little likelihood of any of the others taking on the responsibility. 'I certainly would not like to be a councillor,' he told her. 'All this political stuff leaves me cold.' Afterwards they went to the polling station and Harry Baines was already there. It was clear that the type of voters was now changing because there were far more men, many of them had been at work all day and were either calling on their way home or calling after they had had their evening meal. One man said to Fran 'Now if you were standing for election I'd definitely vote for you.' But two or three others commented that there was no way they would vote for a woman. Despite comments such as these Tom and Harry still felt that there was a bias in Alice's favour. After eight o'clock there were very few voters, most people were now at home settling down in front of their televisions and the last two hours before the polling station closed saw less than a two dozen voters. At ten o'clock they went round to Bill and Beryl's house and found that the others were already assembled there. 'Here we go again,' said Tom to Beryl, 'you providing the catering and looking after us all.' 'But I've told you before, Tom dear, I really enjoy doing it.'

The general consensus was that Alice had had a good day and with the exception of Lenny, who would be working in the shop, they decided that they would all gather at the town hall at ten o'clock the following morning for the count. 'How long will that take?' Alice asked. 'Oh, we're only talking about two by-elections,' said Tom so I wouldn't think it would be more than an hour or so.' About eleven thirty many of the members were looking rather tired and after drinking Alice's health in champagne they all wended their way home. As he and Fran went through the front door she yawned and said 'gosh it's been a long day I'm off to bed.' Tom watched her climb the stairs and said 'I'll see you in the morning, probably.' She paused and said 'Oh surely you mean definitely.' 'Of course,' he replied, and then as he went into the kitchen he thought to himself, such is the arrogance of youth, at my age it has to be probably.

After breakfast, Tom got the car out and they drove round to collect Harry Baines. Bill and Beryl had arranged to pick up Alice, Vicky and Jim and they all arrived at the town hall within five minutes of each other. The large room in which the count was to take place had two long tables, one for their constituency and one for the by-election in the north of the city. The staff that had been recruited to count were all sitting at the tables and promptly at ten o'clock two porters brought in the ballot boxes. The Lord Mayor, who would be announcing the result, asked all the visitors to stand behind the tasselled cords which separated them from the counters. The members of the Windmill Club watched their table very carefully and they saw that there were two very large piles developing, one slightly smaller pile and two very small piles. 'I do hope one of those small piles isn't us,' Vicky said. It was strange because up until this point none of the members of the Windmill Club had been very concerned with politics and it now seemed as if they were all up for election. There were a number of arguments on the table for the north city count because there appeared to be quite a lot of spoiled ballot papers. There had been a representative of the English League standing for election in that constituency, but no candidate in the ward which Alice hoped to represent. At eleven fifteen, it seemed as if decisions had been made and the Lord Mayor stood on the platform at the far end of the hall and asked the candidates to join him. He said that he would first of all announce the result in the northern constituency followed by the result from the south constituency. As he read out the votes from the first ballot, it was clear that the winner was the person representing the Labour Party. On the other hand, the southern ward usually elected a Conservative candidate and their representative was wearing a confident smile. 'Oh dear,' thought Alice 'he obviously thinks he's won.' She hadn't seen him before because he had been ill when the candidates had their question and answer meeting.

The Mayor read out the figures for the Green and Liberal democrat candidates who had both received less than two hundred votes. The Labour candidate received three hundred and forty votes and then it was Alice's turn. She grew very tense and the members of the Windmill Club smiled encouragingly at her as the Mayor announced that the Independent candidate had received five hundred and seventy two votes. Finally, there was the vote for the Conservative candidate. As the Mayor said five hundred, Alice stopped breathing 'five hundred and what,' she thought 'and fifty nine votes' he completed. Alice nearly fainted, 'Seventy two is more than fifty nine isn't it,' she thought and she heard the members of the Windmill Club giving a loud cheer. 'I declare that Alice Jackson is the duly elected councillor for the Wilton Ward.' The Windmill Club surrounded Alice hugging and kissing her, and she still stood there as if in a daze. Then the Mayor came up and congratulated her and she knew that she had actually won.

They decided to reassemble at their local pub and George the landlord congratulated all of them and said the first round was on him. He joined two tables so that they could all have lunch together. It was a happy and excitable occasion and as other customers came in Alice continued to receive congratulations. 'This is fun,' she whispered to Tom, 'I've not been so excited since I won my first wrestling match.' Tom proposed a toast to Alice and they all stood and congratulated her. 'The next thing we must plan then is our celebratory outing he said. You remember that we did talk about visiting a Casino, so why don't we kill two birds with one stone and have our celebration there. If you'd like to leave it to me I will arrange it.' On the way home he said to Fran 'I thought we could arrange it for the evening before you went down to Exeter.' 'What a lovely, but weird, idea' said Fran 'a celebration party for Alice and a going away wake for me.' 'Now Fran,' he murmured 'that isn't quite what I meant.'

Chapter Twenty Six

As far as Tom was concerned the next two weeks went all too quickly, he and Fran did manage to get out to the Peak District for the day on one occasion. They went to some climbs known as the Roches. While they were eating their lunch, after completing a couple of climbs, they watched a climber on a route known as Bloodstone. When Fran half seriously wondered if they could attempt that Tom laughed and said 'Only in our dreams, there's no protection on the slab and it's bloody dangerous.' They were silent for a few minutes and Tom remembered an occasion in the Alps when he and a companion were on a climb ahead of a young girl and a much older man. The man got into difficulties and Tom's companion had to drop him a top rope. The girl looked none too impressed and a few days later they encountered her again climbing with a much younger man. 'You're looking very thoughtful,' said Fran. 'Oh it's nothing, just dwelling on the passage of time. Let's try a couple more and then call it a day.'

Fran was very busy with her preparations for Exeter, so Tom spent some time with Alice and Bill looking at some of the issues which would affect the council in the next few months. Tom was particularly concerned having read about the planned cutbacks in the welfare of the elderly and the disabled. Suddenly the day of the outing dawned, the coaches were due to pick the group up at the youth club hall. Tom and Fran arrived there about eight forty five having collected Lenny on the way. The car park was already crowded with young people. The under twelves, who were mainly siblings of the older club members were excited and noisy. The older teenagers were standing in small groups trying to look as if the whole thing was something of a bore. The coaches pulled into the car park but Fran asked the drivers to keep the doors closed until the other adults arrived. Shortly before nine o'clock Bill and Jim drove their cars into the car park, a few moments later Harry cycled in and locked his bike away in the hall. Fran then called the group to order and Tom was impressed to see how quickly they quietened down. She then read out two lists and the two groups headed for their allocated coaches. Fran said quietly to Tom that she would sit with Lenny for the outward journey, as he was obviously a bit shy and out of his depth. 'In any case,' she said 'I have had a request from a young lady who wants to talk climbing with you.' 'That will of course be Susie,' said Tom 'we've already exchanged good mornings, won't she want to sit with her friend Chloe?' 'Oh, Chloe is not coming; apparently her boyfriend has told her that she cannot come. He does not like her associating with Pete but as it happens Pete is not here either. He's gone to Sheffield for a boxing tournament.' As Tom got in the coach he saw Susie waving to him, so exchanging a rueful smile with Fran he went and sat next to the excited young lady. She was clutching a book on Anna Purna which one of his friends had written and in which his name appeared several times. She showed it to Tom and said 'Please Tom will you autograph it for me?' 'Of course I will,' he replied 'but we had better wait until we are off the coach with somewhere steady for writing.'

Fran and Harry had agreed that the coaches would not travel in tandem but meet up in Llandudno below the Great Orme. They bypassed Chester and Flint and Fran asked the driver to stop off near the white church at Bodelwyddan near St. Asaph. She told them of the row of graves belonging to Canadian soldiers who had travelled over during the First World War. They were intended to join the Allied Army in France but died before they got there. 'Very sad don't you think,' she said to the youngsters and Tom was again surprised at how carefully they listened to her and showed an interest in the subject. Fran had been the club leader for three years and had obviously gained their respect and admiration. 'A tough act to follow,' he murmured to himself.

They then drove on through Abergele and Colwyn Bay until they reached Conway. Tom was very conscious of Susie's presence; she had obviously taken care about her appearance and was wearing a very strong perfume. From time to time she would clutch his arm and even put her head on his shoulder. He could not help thinking of Nabakov's book 'Lolita' but told himself there was no danger of him getting carried away as his Lolita had red hair and was sitting further down the bus. In Conway Fran gave the group a choice, they could either look round the castle or go down to the harbour and eat ice cream. All the younger children voted for the latter course of action and Alice, Jim and Lenny agreed to accompany the larger group. 'The ice creams are on me,' announced Lenny. The smaller group went with Fran and Tom around the castle. She told them that it was more than eight hundred years old and had been built by King Edward I to control the Welsh. Susie clutched Tom's hand and said 'Oh it's a bit spooky'. After the tour, the two groups boarded the coach and travelled quickly on to Llandudno where the other coach was waiting. They found an area on the beach which was big enough for them all to gather for a picnic, the baskets of food and boxes of drinks were unloaded and everybody sat around in the sunshine, eating and drinking until they were all satisfied, then once again the young people were given a choice. Either join Vicky's sand castle competition or walking up the Great Orme. The more affluent could of course ride up on the cable car. At first there was not a great deal of enthusiasm for the sand castle competition but when Vicky announced that they could work individually or in groups and there would be prizes of £20, two £10 and two £5 then more than half the group volunteered. 'Who is putting up the money?' Tom asked and Fran told him that it was the money that Mr. Wong had kindly donated. It was agreed that the judging would take place at four o'clock and the judges would be Vicky assisted by Bill and Beryl.

Most of the adults decided they would sit in the sun and watch the castle builders but Fran and Tom, inevitably accompanied by Susie and another girl would walk up the Great Orme. 'I need some exercise after all those goodies,' said Fran. They ascended very slowly and sat on a bench at the top admiring the view while Susie and her friend Kate chattered non-stop about everything and nothing. At half past three Fran said 'We had better get down for the judging.' There were six entries in all and Tom quietly gave Vicky another five pounds. 'There will have to be three third prizes,' he said 'it would be unkind just to leave one out.' Vicky and her two fellow judges walked solemnly round the entries there was one outstanding sandcastle, two of the older girls assisted by two young siblings had tried to create something similar to Conway Castle only in addition they had put a moat all round. Two castles created by some of the boys were rather sad little affairs, as the boys had soon lost interest and started paddling. The judges announced the results, the big castle won first prize and every other entry received a prize. There was applause and laughter and then some of the younger boys charged around kicking the castles down.

Harry had arranged for them to have tea and cakes in a very large tearoom in Abergele so they all trooped back to the coaches. There were a few minutes of panic when two boys were missing from Harry's coach, the adults had just agreed to split up and go looking for them when they appeared eating very large ice creams, which they had purchased with their prize money. Susie asked Tom whether he minded if she sat with her new friend Kate and he assured her that he was not at all offended. Lenny was sitting on the back seat with Jim and Alice so Tom was very grateful to see that he could sit next to Fran. Tea in Abergele was a great success and then it was a question of heading for home. Some of the children were tired so it was a much more subdued journey back. Tom was very aware of Fran's presence by his side. Like Susie, she too was wearing perfume but it was much lighter and more subtle. Many of the children were met by their parents when they arrived back at the hall. Susie brought her mum over to meet Tom and she seemed a little surprised at the object of her daughter's hero worship. She was even more surprised when Susie threw her arms around his neck and gave him a kiss. Tom smiled apologetically at Susie's mother and said 'She is just grateful because I taught her to climb.' 'I know,' replied the mother 'it's been Tom this and Tom that for weeks although I get a bit confused when she also talks about Monty.' 'Very nice to have met you,' said Tom tactfully 'you have got a very talented daughter.'

Fran came up and rescued him and on the journey home she said 'I don't know if I should be jealous or just admire your ability to relate to the opposite sex.' 'Well I quite like the idea of you being jealous, but I assure you I am not some kind of predator.' I know that she said 'and I will try to keep my jealous streak under control.' 'By the way,' she said 'I thought your group were splendid today, a real help I wish I had known them sooner.' 'Well that would have been impossible;

141

we have only been in existence a few weeks.' 'Perhaps there ought to be more Windmill Clubs around the country, she said 'they could do a lot of good, certainly liaising with young people for a start.' 'And don't forget keeping an eye on local authorities, Tom added. When they got in Tom proposed a night cap and he got out a bottle of his favourite brandy. 'Claret is the liquor for boys; Port, for men; but he who aspires to be a hero must drink brandy;' 'Ah now he's quoting Samuel Johnson at me,' she said. They clinked glasses and sat in comfortable silence, then Fran got to her feet kissed him lightly on the lips and said, 'See you in the morning.' He forced down the urge to hold her and kiss her again but contented himself with saying 'Night love,' and poured himself a second brandy.

Chapter Twenty Seven

The following Wednesday Harry repeated the thanks from Fran and himself, 'It was a great day,' he said 'and you were really good sports. We have had a lot of feedback from the youngsters and their parents.' Lenny said how gratifying it was that so many people came into his shop and said how much they appreciated the Windmill Club. 'Right,' said Bill 'now we must discuss our own outing, over to you Tom.' 'Well I thought it should be in three weeks time when Mr. Wong will be back and it will also be before our new councillor takes her seat and Fran moves down to Exeter for her studies.' 'Will you miss her terribly Tom?' asked Beryl. 'Well I would be lying if I said I would not miss her, it has been nice to have company in the house, but she is young and must get on with her own life.' 'Well Tom my man,' said Vicky 'don't forget if you need a carer I'm your girl.' 'Thank you Vicky, I am definitely bearing that in mind. Anyway, back to the outing, I have been to a couple of casinos and I think the Tudor Sporting Club.' 'Not the Lucky Horseshoe then,' said Vicky. 'No, I think the Tudor is much nicer. Incidentally, they have a red rose theme which ties in with Beryl's lovely suggestion for the election.'

Beryl beamed with pleasure 'don't forget Bill and I will be away next week, we're going to Scotland for ten days but we will be back for the following Wednesday.' 'It won't do the club any harm to miss one week,' said Tom 'again, back to the casinos. The Restaurant at the Tudor is on a mezzanine floor and overlooks the main gaming room. The manager will organise a table for ten, which includes Fran if nobody minds.' 'Nobody will mind,' said Alice 'she's practically one of us. Please go on.' 'Well, we can sit down for dinner at seven thirty and then afterwards sit in the lounge area and have coffee or go to the bar, or, some of us may even have a little gamble. Roulette is fairly simple and blackjack is not too complicated.' 'Oh I don't know about that,' said Beryl 'Bill and I have never been gamblers.' 'Well,' said Vicky 'my good for nothing husband used to say "a man who is afraid to gamble is afraid of life". Although it must have been a quote from someone else as he wasn't bright enough to think it up for himself. In fact he wasn't bright enough to know when to stop.' 'Yes,' said Tom 'that's the secret of successful gambling. Set yourself a figure you can afford to lose and if you lose it then stop. On my way back from South America I stopped off in Las Vegas and actually won enough money to pay my fare home but there were some very sad sights among the addicted gamblers. The car lots were full of good cars being sold at bargain prices, a lot of people drove to Vegas and sold their cars when they lost, most of them went home on the bus. But have no fear Beryl it won't happen to us. I have arranged for a mini bus to pick us up here and bring us back so that we can all have a drink. All I need to do now is confirm the date with the casino and the mini bus driver.' 'Sounds great,' said Alice 'will it be very expensive?' 'No, they like to attract customers so the meal will cost us thirty pounds a head including a couple of glasses of champagne each.' 'Smashing,' said Jim 'I can't wait.' 'You just remember you're a councillor's partner,' said Alice in a mock threatening manner. 'Not to mention an accomplished wrestler,' said Vicky. Lenny then asked about dress code. 'Oh well, the Tudor is one of the more formal casinos,' said Tom. 'Jackets, collars and ties are compulsory. DJ's, dinner jackets, are optional and dresses or smart trouser suits for the ladies.' 'Well, I will enjoy dressing up for once,' said Alice, 'let's make it formal, dinner jackets and dresses.' 'I'll hire one for Jim and I'll bet the rest of you men have already got dinner jackets.' They all nodded meekly. 'Yes councillor,' said Tom 'good idea.' 'It should be a night to remember,' said Beryl and she went out for the tea trolley. Before the meeting broke up they confirmed that there would not be a meeting the following week.

Chapter Twenty Eight

When Tom got home, he told Fran about the Casino party. She asked if he was sure that they definitely wanted her to attend. 'They don't mind?' she said. 'On the contrary, they were delighted and everyone is looking forward to the evening.' He told her that there would be no Windmill Club meeting the next week. 'Oh good,' she said 'I haven't got a junior club next week so we could go away on Tuesday and come back on Friday. I have to be there on Friday evening as it's my penultimate meeting. I've got a shrewd suspicion that they are planning something for my last night with them.'

So on Tuesday morning Fran and Tom loaded his car and set off for North Wales. Tom had an old climbing friend who owned a small cottage near Beddgellert and he had said they could use it. When Tom telephoned him he had immediately responded, 'Going with someone nice?' he asked. If only you knew, thought Tom but he said 'just a climbing companion.' They drove in a leisurely manner along the route they had travelled on the coach trip and stopped off in Bangor for lunch. They arrived at the cottage about half past three and the first thing that Tom did was to light a fire. The two bed roomed cottage felt cold and damp, as his friend had not been there since Easter. 'This is nice,' said Fran. 'Yes,' said Tom 'we'll have it warm and cosy in no time. We won't bother cooking tonight; instead we'll go to one of the pubs in the village to eat.' They had brought breakfast supplies with them. At six o'clock they went for a walk around the village, Fran hadn't been to Beddgelert before so Tom took her to Gelert's grave and told her the story of the faithful dog who had been mistakenly killed by his owner, Prince Llewellyn.

'All very sad,' said Fran 'but I'm starving.' 'Have you no soul woman,' Tom asked with mock severity, 'still, you are right, I'm starving too.' So they went to the Prince Llewellyn hotel and had a very nice meal of battered haddock and French fries followed by fruit salad and ice cream. They then sampled the hotel's wide collection of single malt whiskies. When they got back to the cottage Tom started to revive the fire while Fran went upstairs to sort out the beds. He heard a mixture of bumps groans and curses as something came thumping down the stairs. 'Give me a hand with this Tom' she called. He went to the foot of the stairs and found Fran wedged behind the larger mattress from upstairs. 'It is still damp and musty up there' she said, so I thought we could put the mattress in front of the fire.' We've got our own sleeping bags so it will be quite respectable to share the mattress.' 'We can always top and tail if you're embarrassed,' she said. 'Oh I think I will cope,' he replied, 'I've slept in some very strange places with some very strange companions.' 'Oh thank you very much,' said Fran 'I'm trying to look after you and you're calling me strange.' 'Not at all, you will definitely be the nicest person I have ever slept with. In a manner of speaking,' he added hastily. They put the mattress in front of the fire and sat on it. 'I will make us a nice cup of cocoa,' said Fran. 'Cocoa?' he queried. 'Oh yes, we mountaineers always drink cocoa at bedtime,' she said with a smile. They drank it in companiable silence then Fran went off to the tiny bathroom to get ready for bed. When she came back she rolled out her sleeping bag and made a pillow with some of her spare clothes. Then Tom went to the bathroom and soon they were lying side by side in the flickering firelight.

'This is nice,' she murmured 'finding one of his

hands with one of hers. 'This is much better than nice,' he told her. They chatted for a while and then as she became drowsy she leaned over and kissed him firmly on the lips. This time he did hold on to her and kissed her firmly. 'That too was nice,' she said 'I am so grateful that you are being patient.' The following morning Tom woke about six o'clock and scrambling out of his bag he made some coffee. Although it was not quite September, there was a definite chill in the air and he told himself that it was going to be a long winter. Later, while they were having breakfast, he told Fran that he wanted to go round to Cwm Silyn and climb a route called Jabberwocky. Fran said 'I have been meaning to ask you why so many climbs have strange names?' Tom told her that they were usually named by whoever put up the route first. 'Well obviously,' she said 'this one must have been put up by a Lewis Carroll fan.' 'Sometimes they're named after a person, for example tomorrow we will go round to Clogwyn Du'r Arddu, usually referred to as Cloggy. There we will do a route called Longlands climb which is one of the easier very severe routes and named, I presume, either by Jack Longland or one of his friends.'

By the time they got out of the car the world had warmed up and Tom said 'We'll go the shorter route by Rhyd Dhu and come back through Tremadoc and the Aberglaslyn Pass.' They got round to Cwm Silyn and the climb was every bit as interesting as Tom had promised. When they sat on top he said 'Oh Lord I had almost forgotten how wonderful the combination of warm sun and a challenging climb can be. It makes me realise why part of my life now seems missing.' They got down to the foot of the climb and sat by the lake, Fran said 'Let's go skinny dipping.' 'You just put your foot in first and see how cold it is,' said Tom. 'Bless me it's freezing,' she said 'let's have lunch instead.'

They sat munching rolls and drinking tea from a flask in the warm sunshine, then as Tom leaned back against a rock Fran put her head on his lap and closed her eyes. Tom played with her beautiful copper curls and thought this too is wonderful. As the man in the bistro said ,'I am a lucky old bastard'.

'Right,' he said 'off to Blackrock sands for a paddle.' As they drove down the lane they passed a white house called Tyn-y-Pwll which was an outdoor centre. 'I used to know a couple of chaps who ran that place in the early sixties. Quite mad, both of them, but very good with kids from Liverpool.' When they got to Tremadoc they made their way past Portmadoc and down to Blackrock sands. There, the long golden beach was sparsely scattered with a few people and the sun sparkled on the gently rippling sea. They took off their boots and socks and wandered along, hand in hand splashing in the gentle waves. 'This is what lovers do,' murmured Fran quietly. 'Are we lovers then?' asked Tom. 'Well, I'm certainly growing to love you,' she replied 'much more than is probably good for either of us.' 'Can one love too much?' Tom asked. 'Yes if it ends in tears.' 'Well in that case we will just have to ban tears,' and he kissed her on the cheek. After tea in Portmadoc they drove back through the beautiful Aberglaslyn Pass to the cottage. That evening they chose the Tanronen for their evening meal. Tom had a very large steak and chips and Fran settled for scampi and salad.

Afterwards on their return to the cottage they sat in the flickering firelight again. 'You know Tom, one of the things that really intrigues me, is that your eyes are typical of a mountaineer or a sailor.' 'What on earth do you mean?' he said. 'Well they always seem to be focussed on the middle distance, as if you are constantly searching for something.' 'Well tonight they are firmly focussed on you, I will never get tired of your beauty.' 'What, even when I'm old and wrinkled,' she said. 'For me you will always look as you do right now, and anyway I will not be around when you are old and grey.' 'You know, I love that poem by Yeats, *"when you are old and grey and full of sleep"*. 'Actually it's one of my favourites too,' said Tom 'we do seem to have a lot in common. It's a pity we are so far apart in age.' 'I don't feel as if we are,' said Fran 'I am more comfortable with you than I have been with any man.' 'Maybe so,' he said 'but in ten years time the gulf will be even wider.' 'Well then, let us just enjoy now, live for the moment, be real existentialists.' 'Suits me,' said Tom. They got ready for bed, then they lay side by side in their sleeping bags. The flickering firelight seemed to have a hypnotic effect and they both became drowsy. After kissing gently, they fell asleep holding hands. Tom woke in the morning and patted Fran's sleeping bag, she was not there and for a horrible moment he had a feeling of déjàvu, remembering his search for Evelyn, this was soon dispelled by the sound of clinking crockery in the kitchen. Fran came in carrying mugs of coffee. 'An angel in pyjamas,' he said. 'Well master, Cloggy today is it?' 'What's the weather like?' he asked. 'Misty and slightly damp,' she replied. 'Oh well, let's hope the sun comes out, bits of the climb can be tricky if they are wet.'

After breakfast, they set off for Llanberis and leaving the car on the outskirts of the popular village they headed up to Clogwyn Du'r Arddu. The sun had burnt the mist off and Fran said 'There you are the sun shines on the righteous.' 'Well that must be you,' rejoined Tom, 'because most of the times I've been on Cloggy it has rained.' She looked up at the massive rock face in awe. 'Where are we climbing?' she asked.

'Well if you look to the right of centre that's the west buttress and our climb is the second from the left; a nice mixed climb with some tricky bits. If you want to lead any pitch just say so. 'No, after our experience on Stanage I will be more than happy climbing second.' They roped up and Tom started off up a wet groove. The first pitch was the one Fran disliked most, but from there on she really appreciated the climbing. There were a couple of occasions when she felt nervous, but by the time they scrambled up the short chimney near the top she was thoroughly enjoying herself. Tom too had cursed quietly to himself when his suspect knee gave him some difficulty. After they finished the climb he asked Fran if she would like to do something else. 'Yes please, have lunch in Llanberis,' she replied. 'No I meant another climb, but I think your idea sounds very good.'

They made their way down to the village and found a café that served toasted sandwiches with pots of tea. 'Well, did you enjoy Cloggy?' he asked. 'Very much so,' she answered enthusiastically. 'I feel quite a proficient climber now after yesterday and this morning.' After lunch, they went for a stroll round the village including the ritual visit to Joe Brown's shop. Tom said 'For my money Joe was one of the best climbers ever. Some of the pioneering routes he put up with equipment that modern day climbers would laugh at were superb. Did you know that on a lot of his first routes his seconds were unable to follow him, in some cases they had to use knotted ropes; despite that he has always been modest and self effacing. 'You sound like an admirer,' said Fran. 'Yes I suppose I am, for me the most interesting days of rock climbing were the nineteen fifties, with Joe, Don Whillans and the rock and ice club; tough working lads who paved the way for modern climbers. After their stroll, they drove up the Llanberis Pass and had a drink in the Pen-y-Gwrd Inn. 'This is where the 1953 Everest Expedition was planned,' Tom told her 'another group of great mountaineers.' They then headed for the cottage, Fran stopped off in the village to do some shopping. She said 'I thought we could eat in tonight, if that's alright with you.' 'No problem,' he said 'something simple and delicious.' 'Well simple anyway, I can't promise delicious in that primitive kitchen.'

In the event, she produced some very tasty deep omelettes and followed it with tinned peaches and cream. They consumed a bottle of Rosé and Tom pronounced it the best meal he had ever eaten, 'Well apart from some goat stew I had in Nepal,' he said with a grin. 'Damn cheek,' she replied and poked him in the ribs. They got ready for bed for the last time in the cottage, but neither of them could sleep. They were still talking in whispers at midnight and Tom recalled the previous occasion in Derbyshire when he had thought how wonderful it was to lie with someone you loved and whisper about nothing in particular. Again Fran did not seem ready to take their love to the final stage and there was no way he was going to push her. Indeed, he wondered if he had any right to expect her to go further. Eventually he realised she had fallen asleep and he allowed himself to drift off also. The following morning Fran was awake first and as she handed him his coffee she said 'Idyllic holiday over, work tonight.' The drive back home was one in which neither of them wanted to talk very much and Tom drove quickly and efficiently until he pulled up outside his gate. As they went through the front door, they simultaneously dropped the bags they were carrying and hugged each other as if they had been apart for years.

Chapter Twenty Nine

On Tuesday morning, the day before the outing, Beryl rang to say she and Bill were back from Scotland and did the arrangements for the outing still stand. Tom assured her that indeed they did and he knew that Mr. Wong was also back. He enquired about their holiday and Beryl told him that they had really enjoyed themselves 'Apart from the horrible midges,' she added. Tom confirmed that the mini bus was collecting them all from her house at six forty five. Beryl said how much she was looking forward to it and said 'Goodbye Tom dear, do take care.' I don't think I'm in any immediate danger he thought to himself as he put the phone down. Although in truth he had another of his splitting headaches.

Fran went to the library as usual on Wednesday morning but came home at three o'clock to get ready for 'the doo' as she put it. 'Surely it's not going to take you three hours to get ready?' Tom asked with a smile. 'Oh we ladies can't be hurried when we are going out with a handsome man,' she told him. Later as Tom got dressed he stood in front of the wardrobe mirror admiring his dinner jacket, 'Had it for twenty years,' he said aloud 'and it still fits like a glove.' Fran, who was standing at his door, laughed and said 'Perhaps it would be better if it fitted like a dinner jacket?' He turned and his gasp was audible. Fran looked absolutely stunning; she was wearing a black dress which came down to just above her knees with black stockings and high heeled shoes. Her beautiful hair was loose and down to her shoulders and she had a simple chain with a locket round her lovely throat. She touched the locket and said 'This was the last present my father ever bought me.' 'You are absolutely beautiful,' he told her. 'Oh stop it,' she said, 'you will make me blush.'

They walked down to Bill and Beryl's and Tom was conscious of more than one curtain twitching as they passed the houses in between. It was a pleasant early autumn evening and everyone gathered at the Harris's house in high spirits. Tom thought that all the ladies looked beautiful and the men very smart; they arrived at the casino just before seven fifteen so they decided to go straight to their table. 'But this is lovely,' exclaimed Beryl 'so respectable.' 'Yes I bet there's not a crook in sight,' said Vicky with a big wink at Tom. They started with a complimentary glass of champagne and then everyone studied the menu and decided on their choices. They also ordered drinks to go with their meal and while Jim ordered a pint of beer and Beryl a small sherry the remainder decided they would share three bottles of wine, red, white and rosé. Below them, they could see most of the gaming tables, roulette, blackjack and dice. Tom explained that there were some side rooms for poker and chemin de fer. 'Have you been here often Tom,' asked Alice, 'No, just a couple of times with colleagues from work before I retired.' 'Are you going to tell us how to win?' asked Jim. 'I don't know about that, but you can have some fun and make your chips last longer if you go for the shorter odds such as black and red or odds and evens.' 'Not for me,' said Vicky 'I went to the Lucky Horsheshoe a few times with my old man and I go for the thirty five to one shots, single numbers. Mind you, this is a much posher place. My old man would have been uncomfortable in here'

After dinner, they went down to the very comfortable seating area and Tom pointed out where they could buy their chips. Anything from two pounds to a hundred pounds, he told them. 'Who on earth would buy a hundred pound chips?' Beryl asked.

'There are some pretty wealthy people around the city Beryl,' Tom said looking very serious, 'and some very poor people too. We do not live in a fair and equal society. Just for tonight let us rub shoulders with the wealthier members of society; tomorrow and the days after we can devote some of our energies to the less fortunate.' Fran said 'Mr. Wong is going to show me how to win at dice.' And they went off in the direction of the dice tables. Tom noticed how many men's eyes followed Fran as she strolled across the gaming room with Mr. Wong. 'They're probably thinking he's a lucky old bastard, but I know better.'

Vicky seized his arm and said 'Come on Tom let's go and win a fortune.' They went to the counter where the chips could be purchased and Tom bought a hundred pounds worth of five pound chips. 'You can be my lucky mascot,' he said to Vicky. They went to one of the roulette tables and he gave Vicky some chips. She put two down, one on thirteen, 'That's my old man's lucky number,' she said and one on twenty-seven, 'that's my birthday.' Tom put two chips on red and eighteen red came up, he then put the four chips he had been returned and put them on odds and thirty-three came up. 'Cor,' said Vicky 'you've got the touch.' She followed her birthday number three times more and on the third occasion, it came up. She let out such a shout of glee that Tom was sure that everyone in the casino was looking at them. After half an hour he had had enough of roulette. He was about thirty pounds in profit and Vicky had lost most of her winnings. They went over to the dice table where Mr. Wong had amassed a large pile of chips. 'He's very good at this,' Fran whispered to Tom.

By ten thirty most of them had reassembled in the lounge area and Tom asked a waiter to bring their second glass of complimentary champagne. He then proposed a toast to the Windmill Club. 'We cannot be responsible for the whole country but we must ensure that there are no neglected old people in the Wilton district.' 'Hear, hear,' said Jim rocking unsteadily on his feet. 'He spent most of the time at the bar,' said Alice with an indulgent smile. They eventually got everyone in the mini bus and Tom found himself sitting he s next to Jim. 'I've never been in a place like that before,' he said 'or worn one of these,' he said tugging at his dinner jacket. 'Well, you need the practice,' said Tom 'Alice may be the mayor one day.' When they arrived back at the Harris's Bill invited them in but they all declared that they would not impose on his hospitality but head for their own homes. The minibus driver agreed to take Jim and Alice with Vicky and Harry home as Jim was not really in a state to drive. 'We'll pick the car up in the morning,' said Alice. The others were walking home and Mr. Wong and Lenny walked with Fran and Tom to Tom's gate where they made their farewells. Mr. Wong kissed Fran's hand and thanked her for her delightful company, 'You helped me win,' he said. Lenny followed suit, kissing her hand and then shook hands with Tom. As Fran and Tom went into the house he said 'Now it is my turn to be jealous.' 'No need to be jealous,' said Fran 'you can kiss my hand any time you like.'

Chapter Thirty

While they were having breakfast on Friday morning Fran said 'Well, tonight is my last night at the club, I have asked Jenny to be there so that I can introduce her to the members and hand over formally.' 'Are you sad to be leaving?' asked Tom gently. 'Yes I am, three years is quite a long time and I have become quite attached to many of the members. Unfortunately, I will be even sadder tomorrow evening when it's our last night.' 'Ah, but hopefully that will only be au revoir and we will be meeting again won't we?' 'Of course we will,' she replied, 'but will it be the same? Can we possibly replicate the last few weeks?' 'Time will tell in that respect,' Tom said. 'But as for tomorrow night presumably we must celebrate in some sort of way?' 'Yes we must, but let's not go out; we should stay in and be just the two of us.' 'Good, that is just what I was hoping you'd say,' said Tom. 'I will run you down to the club this evening and pick you up afterwards, but I won't come in, it's your night with the members.'

When they were tidying up after breakfast Fran said 'I must check the train times for Sunday. I know there is one rather long winded journey via Birmingham and Bristol.' 'Oh you can't go on the train,' he said 'I was hoping to take you.' 'Nonsense, you don't want to drive to Exeter and back in one day.' 'Indeed I do,' Tom said. 'I have driven much greater distances in my time. Anyway, you can do the driving down if you want. Either way it will be much more convenient than a dreary train journey.' 'Right,' she said 'you have convinced me. It is a lovely idea and I suppose it is almost entirely motorway; should be reasonably quiet on a Sunday in September.' 'Good, that's settled then,' he said. 'Now I'm off to see Alice and Jim about their wedding arrangements.' Fran said 'Please give them my regards, I am sorry to be missing the wedding but I will only just have settled in at Exeter.' 'I understand,' said Tom 'and I'm sure Alice and Jim will also understand. Anyway, I will probably make a fool of myself as best man and I would not like you to see that!' 'There you go again,' said Fran 'selling yourself short. Well I'm off to the library for the last time.' She kissed him lightly and went out of the front door. Every time either of them referred to the last time, Tom felt a dull thud in his stomach. Must be my heart slipping, silly old fool that I am, he told himself.

When he got round to Alice's bungalow he said 'Good morning councillor,' in a serious voice. 'Oh that is something I will have to get used to, but not from you Tom. Please call me Alice.' She then shouted through to the kitchen 'Jim, Tom is here, please put the kettle on.' Jim appeared through the kitchen door, wiping his hands on what looked suspiciously like a tea towel. 'Oh Jim,' Alice said 'a hand towel is hanging next to the tea towel, and that is not for drying your hands.' 'Sorry love' Jim replied 'I must have grabbed it by mistake when you called that Tom was here. Just doing a bit of gardening,' he said to Tom. 'Well Jim, anytime you have to spare you can come and do my garden.' 'Oh I can always find time for gardening,' Jim said 'just give me a shout.' 'Only if I'm allowed to pay going rates,' said Tom with a smile. While this discussion was going on Alice was in the kitchen making coffee, 'Instant alright for you Tom,' she asked. 'If I'm honest, I must confess that I prefer instant, much easier both at sea or in the mountains, he replied.' They sat down for coffee and biscuits and discussed the wedding.

'We did talk about a church wedding,' said Alice, 'but we decided that we would both be more comfortable with a registry office ceremony, so that's what we've booked. After all I could hardly wear white,' she said with a smile. 'And I still can't believe I am getting married,' said Jim. 'My old mum used to say there was no woman on earth daft enough to take me on, so I was better off living with her at home.' Alice said 'Now you have found someone daft enough to take you on, I must be mad.' Tom thought he should join in at this point. 'It seems to me that you are a very well suited couple and Jim is a very lucky man.' 'Well, I won't argue with that,' said Jim. Tom continued 'If I am to be the best man and Vicky is to be the matron of honour, how many other guests are you inviting?' Alice said 'Of course there are the other members of the club and Lenny thought his wife would be well enough to accompany him. I don't suppose Fran will be able to come?' 'I'm afraid not,' said Tom 'she will be busy in Exeter but she does send you both her best wishes.' Jim said 'I would like my darts partner, Charlie Thomas, and his wife to come; I have known them for years.' Then Alice said 'And we'd better ask my next door neighbours, Mary from the left side, she's a widow, and Mr. and Mrs. Ward from the other side. After all, they will have to put up with Jim singing in the garden in the future.' Tom laughed, 'That is as good a reason as any, I suppose. George the landlord has said he can give us a reception upstairs in the pub, so I'll tell him between fifteen and twenty guests in case you think of any more.

As part of our wedding present Fran and I have arranged for a limousine to pick Alice and Vicky up here and take you to the registry office, then onto the pub afterwards. Of course, Jim won't travel with you to the registry office, so I will pick him up at his house and try to get him there on time. He can then travel in the limousine with his beautiful bride to the reception.' 'He'd better be on time,' said Alice 'or I might marry

Mr. Wong instead.' 'Right, that seems everything,' said Tom 'apart from the catering, and Bill and Beryl are arranging that with George. Then after the reception I will take you both home to pick up your suitcases and then on to the station. You will then be off on your honeymoon.' 'It is very good of you Tom,' said Alice, 'you seem to have thought of everything.' 'Apart from what the bride will wear,' said Tom with a smile 'and I imagine that is a secret.' 'Yes,' she said 'we bought Jim's suit but only Vicky and I know that I will be wearing a see through sequined little number.' 'Blimey,' said Jim 'that sounds exciting, I can't wait!'

At teatime, Tom told Fran about the wedding arrangements. 'It sounds as if you are being you're usual helpful self,' she said, 'I do wish I could be with you, but it would just be too difficult to arrange.' 'I completely understand,' he reassured her 'and it will make the end of term even more important.' 'That is, I am assuming you will be back up here at some point.' 'Oh yes, I plan to spend Christmas Eve and Christmas Day with Mummy and Auntie then come up to you on Boxing Day until early in the New Year. All subject to travel arrangements of course.' After tea, she got ready for her last night at the youth club. Harry had said that he would open up and she should arrive at about seven fifteen. Tom drove her to the club and watched her go through the door, almost certainly for the last time. As he was driving off he heard a tremendous noise of clapping and cheering as her members greeted her. The next three hours passed very quickly, as the time of Fran's departure to Exeter grew nearer time seemed to have speeded up.

He went back to the club just after ten o'clock. Fran and Harry were chatting to Jenny Porter on the doorstep. He got out of the car and Fran re introduced him to Jenny. All three of them said how successful the

160

evening had been. Harry had his bike and Jenny had a small sports car so Fran climbed into his car and he took her home. She talked about her evening in greater detail. The members had presented her with a very pretty watercolour of Striding Edge in the Lake District. There had been an enormous cake made by Beryl in secret consultation with Harry. 'She is probably looking forward to me moving on,' laughed Fran. Jenny had apparently been a great success with the club members. 'I feel happy that I'm leaving the club in good hands,' she said. When they got indoors, they both seemed rather quiet and Fran said that she felt a bit flat after her rather emotional evening. She told Tom that Susie had made her promise to tell him that he must keep in touch with the club. 'She is probably hoping that you will go on a climbing trip organised by Jenny.' 'I think that is very unlikely,' Tom said 'it just wouldn't be the same without you.' 'Right,' she said 'I will make us a cup of mountaineers' cocoa and we will have a lovely day together tomorrow.' Shortly afterwards they made their way to their own rooms.

Chapter Thirty One

On Saturday morning, just after seven o'clock Tom opened his curtains. Rain was pouring down from a dull grey sky. Very appropriate, he thought, even the gods are crying. He put his dressing gown on and went downstairs to make a cup of tea. Fran had beaten him to it and was already in the kitchen. 'Good morning,' he said kissing the top of her shoulder where her nightdress and flimsy dressing gown had slipped down. 'Morning Tom,' she replied as she poured the tea. They took their cups into the sitting room and sat watching the rain beat against the French windows. 'I was going to ask you how shall we spend the day,' Tom said 'but the weather rather limits our options.' Fran smiled and said 'Let's make the most of it anyway.' 'I need some shopping so we could drive into town and wander round the shopping mall. It's all under cover, so we won't get wet. The weather forecast claimed that it will dry up by lunch time and we could then go for a walk.' 'Good plan,' Tom said 'we will have breakfast in about an hour and go into town early before it gets too busy.'

It seemed as if the world and his wife had a similar idea and although it was only just after nine o'clock the mall was very busy. They bought salmon steaks and fresh fruit for dinner and while Fran was in a chemists buying toiletries Tom went into a wine store and asked for a bottle of champagne. On second thoughts he bought two bottles, one to save for the next time we meet he thought. In his heart he was not entirely convinced that they would ever see each other again once Fran had moved to Exeter.

When they had finished shopping, they had coffee in one of the numerous cafes and then headed for Tom's car. 'Phew, I'm glad to be out of that scrum,' said Fran. 'Me too,' he replied. When they got home, it had stopped raining and the sun was just peeping behind the clouds. Tom suggested they could drive down to the river and have a snack lunch in the Angler's Rest then a walk along the river bank. 'Sounds good to me,' said Fran. And that is exactly what they did. Several weeks later when Tom tried to remember how they spent the last Saturday, it was all blurred. All he seemed to think about was Monday when the dream would be over. In the evening, they shared the preparation of dinner, salmon steaks with fried, sliced potatoes and vegetables. Fran had bought some cream so she made a fresh fruit salad and Tom opened the champagne, which he had left in the fridge earlier.

When they sat down Fran proposed a toast. 'To us and the future,' she said. And Tom added 'to us and the past few months. There's no harm in looking to the future' he said 'but we can also remember and treasure the past. After dinner, Fran got the chess board out, 'One last thrashing,' she said with a smile. 'Blimey girl, you sound like some old dominatrix.' 'Not so much of the old,' she replied, 'anyway I can't remember where I left my whip.' The evening wore on and she did indeed thrash him at chess although they both knew that his mind was largely elsewhere. About ten o'clock Fran yawned theatrically and said I'm very tired I will have a quick bath and retire into my comfortable bed.' Tom was disappointed he really did not want the evening to end. 'Don't you want a supper drink?' he asked. 'No, I will take a last glass of champagne up with me.' She topped up her glass kissed him gently on the lips and went upstairs.

Tom sat sipping the last of the champagne and thinking back over the last few months, their first dinner at the bistro, the trip to Derbyshire and the wonderful break in North Wales. 'Of course I knew it was all too good to last,' he told himself. He heard Fran come out of the bathroom, there will be enough hot water for a quick dip, he told himself. He made his way upstairs and had a quick shallow bath. As he came out of the bathroom he heard Fran calling his name, he opened her bedroom door and said 'You called madam'. 'Indeed I did, you haven't kissed me properly goodnight.' He went over to the bed and sat rather gingerly on the side then he leaned over and kissed her tenderly.

'You need to come in to kiss me properly,' she said. 'He started to pull back the duvet when she stopped him by holding up her hand. 'I haven't got any pyjamas on,' she said 'and therefore you can't come in overdressed as you are.' Tom was momentarily taken aback, but he knew that she meant what she said, 'Because she always does,' he thought. He removed his pyjamas and climbed into bed. She was indeed naked and they clung together as if they were drowning. He could feel her warm, beautiful body pressed against him and she was kissing him passionately. 'I want you to make love to me,' she whispered. 'Are you really sure,' he said caressing her gently. 'Of course I'm sure, I have thought about it every night since we slept together in Derbyshire.' Tom went to switch off the bedside light. 'No, leave it on I want to see you and remember everything,' she whispered. 'This is madness,' he said 'but I really do love you.' 'And I love you too,' she replied. So he caressed her and made love to her slowly but with such longing they felt as if they were two souls encased in one body. Tom felt as if it was the most wonderful thing he had ever experienced and Fran whispered 'Thank you, I never dreamed that making love could be so beautiful.' Afterwards they lay in each other's arms whispering the same things that lovers have whispered to each other since time began. Just after midnight, Fran put her mouth to his ear and whispered 'Encore please Tom.' So they made love for the second time and then fell asleep in each other's arms.

The following morning Tom awoke first and crept out of bed, he retrieved his pyjamas from the floor and went downstairs to make coffee. They had agreed that they would leave by nine o'clock so that Tom could get back home in the daylight. He took coffee into Fran, she opened her eyes with a smile that lit up the whole room and said 'Good morning my darling Tom.' Clutching the duvet modestly around her and taking the proffered coffee, she said 'I know, let's forget about going to Exeter, we could stay in bed and make love all day.' 'If only,' he said 'but no, you'll have to go because I have a new, very attractive lodger moving in tomorrow.' She laughed and got out of bed, 'Me first in the shower' she said throwing her arms around him and kissing him, making no attempt to cover her naked beauty. He thought for the millionth time how lucky he was even if it had only been for a tiny fraction of his life.

While Tom was preparing breakfast, Fran completed her packing. 'I'm not taking everything,' she said 'your new lodger will have to use your wardrobe.' Shortly before nine o'clock, they loaded the car and set off up the avenue. As they passed the Harris's house Beryl, who must have been watching for them, waved from her front room window. Tom tooted on his horn and Fran waved, 'Glad to see the back of me,' she said with a chuckle. They were travelling on the M6 and the M5 and although they stopped twice at service stations, they arrived in Exeter at lunchtime, the journey having been uneventful. Fran had been given a room in a hall of residence in return for acting as deputy to the warden. The students would not arrive for two more weeks so the hall was quiet. They unloaded Fran's baggage and set off to find somewhere for lunch.

They found a pub by the river called The Mill on the Ex and Tom had a traditional Sunday lunch, while Fran settled for scampi and chips. The food was good but the atmosphere was strained and they both picked at their food. Although they were still metaphorically floating as a result of the night before, they were acutely aware that this was the moment of separation. They finished their lunch and went for a short walk along the river. They held hands and spoke in monosyllables, 'Oh come on,' said Fran 'take me back to the hall of residence, I don't want to burst into tears in the street.' Quickly they walked back to the car and drove to the place where Fran would spend the next few months. As he pulled up, she leaned across and kissed him passionately. 'Please, kiss me and go quickly, I can't bear protracted goodbyes.' Tom kissed her and said 'Thank you for everything.' Fran got out of the car, blew him a kiss and ran gracefully into the building. Tom started up his car and drove northward, his driving was as efficient as ever but his spirits had never been lower.

He arrived home just before seven o'clock. The house seemed deathly quiet. He went up to Fran's room and stood inhaling her perfume, there were two long strands of red hair on her pillow and he picked them up and rolled them round his finger. Then he went to his room and put them in a glass and silver box, which contained some, rarely worn, cufflinks. He half expected a comment from Evelyn but the house remained cold and silent, it seemed as if Evelyn had finally left him. He wasn't hungry and he had no desire to cook anything for his dinner so he made a cheese and pickle sandwich and poured a very large brandy. 'Must go and see Bill tomorrow and get on with the work of the Windmill Club,' he told himself.

The chess set was still on the coffee table. The night before Fran had played with the white pieces so he took the white queen and held it to his lips. Please come back for the New Year he whispered. About nine thirty the telephone rang and he heard Fran's voice saying, 'I just called to say goodnight and check that you were home safely.' They chatted for a few minutes but neither of them found it easy to converse in a nonchalant manner. 'I will ring you on Wednesday,' he promised, 'and tell you of the developments in the Windmill Club.' Fran made him promise not to forget and they said goodnight at least three times. After he had put the telephone down he made his way upstairs and eventually fell asleep.

Chapter Thirty Two

On Monday morning he woke with a throbbing headache. Did I stop at the one brandy?' he wondered. He did not feel like getting up but he had adhered to routines all his life and he was not going to change now. He had his breakfast, reflecting on how different it was not to have the beautiful Fran sitting opposite. He wondered again how he had fallen in love with her and even more astonishing, why she had fallen in love with him. I have often wondered, he mused, about the term serendipity and if I hadn't been involved in the formation of the Windmill Club and if we hadn't then forged links with the youth club, these past few months would have been fantasy instead of a wonderful reality.

He shook himself out of his reverie and said aloud, 'Serendipity or not I must get round to Bill's and start planning our Christmas project.' He rang the Harris's doorbell and Beryl opened the door. 'Tom,' she said 'how nice to see you, please come in.' He went in, Bill was in the sitting room and looked equally pleased to see him. Beryl bustled off to the kitchen to get coffee and biscuits and Tom outlined his ideas for the Christmas project. 'If you remember, we said at our casino party we did not want any neglected elderly people in our district.' 'Yes, and I'm sure we meant it,' said Bill 'despite the champagne,' Tom continued, 'I thought Christmas would be a good time to start, although we would have to continue afterwards if it was to mean anything. We need to find out all the people who will be alone at Christmas or the couples who are struggling to make ends meet. We could provide them with some company and extra rations.'

Bill looked thoughtful, 'It is a good idea in principle,' he said 'but how do we find out who we should be helping?' 'Ah, well that's where our alliance with the youth club will be helpful. I'm sure Harry Baines and the new club leader will help us to organise their members.' Beryl was just coming in with the coffee and biscuits, 'Oh yes,' she said, 'the new club leader, I gather she is very nice.' 'She certainly is,' said Tom 'and she seems to have lots of energy.' 'I suppose you will miss Frances a bit,' said Beryl 'well just remember, if you need anything such as cooking or ironing or just someone to talk to, I can easily pop round. Bill won't be jealous, will you dear?' 'Me jealous, no certainly not old girl, you must do whatever you want.' Beryl smiled at Tom with a slightly rueful look, 'He used to be jealous,' she said 'how times change.'

Tom steered the conversation back to Christmas, 'We will ask the youth club members to be our eyes and ears. If we take every road, street and avenue in the district and ask all those members who are willing to help to find out how many people there are in each that might be glad of a little help. Of course, we can use the electoral register as a starting point but that will only give us the bare details. There will be some old people who will not want any help or visitors, so a little human input is necessary. Then we will have to make up hampers and it will be up to our members to do the visits and deliver the hampers.' 'Yes,' said Bill 'we have to be careful not to offend or patronise.' Beryl added 'We have one advantage in that we are not official social workers or other "do gooders".' 'Our watch word must be sensitivity,' Tom added, 'the last thing we want to do is upset anybody.'

They decided that on Wednesday they would have to discuss the composition of the hampers and any other gifts they could manage. 'But,' said Bill 'we need to know just what sort of figures we are discussing.'

They continued their discussion until Tom looked at his watch and saw that it was almost lunchtime. 'Right,' he said 'I must get back.' He almost added, Fran will be back from the library, and stopped just in time as he remembered that of course she wouldn't. Beryl asked if the wedding arrangements were all in hand. 'I have almost finished decorating the wedding cake,' she added 'and George has some good ideas about the food, so the catering arrangements are fine.' 'Splendid,' said Tom 'I knew we could rely on you. See you both on Wednesday.' Beryl saw him to the door, 'Remember dear, if you need anything you only have to ask.' 'Thanks Beryl,' he said 'I will remember,' and he kissed her lightly on the cheek, leaving her looking flushed and bemused.

On Wednesday, there was a full turnout and everybody seemed to be in high spirits, 'With the exception of me,' thought Tom wryly. They first looked at the collection of notes and cards which Harry had brought from the club thanking them for the outing to North Wales. Some of these were from parents as well as the young people themselves. 'It does seem a long time ago now,' said Vicky a little wistfully. They then moved on to the Christmas project, as it was now officially called and everyone was very keen to be involved. Lenny said he had already had discussions with the two wholesalers who supplied him and one of them had introduced him to the manager of a large grocery wholesaler who had shown a lot of interest and said he would be able to help. Bill pointed out that an important side benefit would be if they got some publicity and interest then other areas may follow suit. Of course, there are these food banks springing up everywhere for people apparently in need but many elderly people would not go to them. What we are offering is a much more personal service with the addition of some friendly contact. It was agreed that Bill and Tom would go along to the youth club on Friday evening and Harry would ask the new leader, Jenny, if they could talk to the members. 'I am sure she will be glad to help,' said Harry, 'she is very similar in disposition to Fran.'

While they were enjoying their tea break, Alice told them about her first council meeting. She was a very good mimic and amused her companions with some stories and comments. 'Some of the other councillors are really pompous and full of their own self importance. But to be fair' she added 'some are very nice and obviously care about their fellow citizens while others seem more interested in the size of their allowances instead of having to get a proper job.' Alice had hoped to get on the welfare committee but her predecessor had been on the transport committee, so that was where she was for the moment. 'I can see some fireworks ahead,' she said 'when we start discussing the renewal of bus passes and car park permits.'

Beryl asked her if she and Jim had decided on their honeymoon destination. 'Yes,' she said with a naughty smile. 'Jim wanted to go abroad so we're going to the Isle of Man. No passports, and no language problems, we will be sailing from Liverpool.' 'Aye,' said Jim 'I am really looking forward to it, Alice has been all over the world but I've never been further than Blackpool or Morecambe with my mother.' 'Good choice,' said Harry 'I really like the Isle of Man and I'm sure you will love it.' There was only one more meeting before the wedding so they agreed to make final arrangements then.

Chapter Thirty Three

Tom went home to his empty, silent house, but he remembered that he had promised to telephone Fran that evening. He had a moment of panic when he thought he could not remember her mobile number but he found that she had written it in his little telephone memo notebook. He wasn't particularly hungry, he never was after sampling Beryl's cake and sandwiches so he settled for beans on toast and waited impatiently for nine o'clock when he had agreed to make the phone call. While he was waiting, he amused himself by reading Dylan Thomas's Under Milkwood aloud. He had read it so many times that he regarded the characters as old friends and he read his lines, changing voices with enthusiasm. Just before nine o'clock he got his little memo book out and nervously dialled Fran's number. He couldn't explain it but for some reason he felt rather apprehensive.

She answered on the second ring and told him that she had been waiting for his call. She said that the hall of residence was still very quiet but she had met some of the university staff and some of the people who would be doing postgraduate work. 'They seem to be a very nice group of people,' she told him. Tom told her about the afternoon meeting and assured her in response to her questions that he was eating properly and looking after himself. 'After all I was managing before we met,' he reminded her. 'Of course you were,' she replied 'but you know that for some reason you bring out my maternal instincts.' 'Oh no,' he said 'the last thing I want you for is to be a substitute mother.' 'Don't panic,' she replied 'when we are together I feel quite different emotions.' They eventually said their goodbyes; she told him that she would be spending the weekend with her mother and auntie but that she would ring him on Sunday evening. He put the telephone down and again felt a great sense of loss.

The next few days seemed to drag along very slowly; it was enlivened one evening when Jim came round to voice some of his anxieties. He had apparently given the council notice for relinquishing his house and was in the process of moving some of his belongings to Alice's bungalow. 'The trouble is,' he said 'where will I live if it doesn't work out?' Tom told him that he mustn't go into marriage fearing that it wouldn't work out. 'You have to make sure it does,' he said 'Alice is a very nice person and providing you make the effort to meet her half way there should not be any problems.' They then got on to the subject of Jim's stag night. 'I feel it is probably a bit unnecessary at my age,' he said 'but Alice and the other ladies are having a little hen party in the Harris's house.' 'Well in that case,' said Tom 'we will have your stag night here, but I promise you that we will not be tying you naked to the gatepost.'

The other highlight of the week was Fran's telephone call on Sunday evening. She said that she had enjoyed her weekend with her mother and that one of the other postgraduate students, Leo, had given her a lift down. 'Leo has a beautiful Harley Davidson,' she added 'and we were at Bournemouth in no time at all.' Tom did not like to ask any questions about Leo in case he sounded too anxious. 'Motor bikes can be pretty dangerous machines,' he said. But she reassured him that Leo was a very experienced rider and that there were no problems. 'I came back on the bus to Exeter,' she said. Tom told her about the wedding arrangements and Fran said 'Oh what a pity, I would love to have been at the hen party.' 'Don't tell porkies,' he told her

173

'you know you would rather be at the stag night.' They said their goodbyes and Tom promised to telephone on Wednesday.

When the Windmill Club assembled the following Wednesday all the wedding arrangements were agreed and everybody said how much they were looking forward to the event. There had been a number of small meetings in the meantime to try and decide what they should do about the wedding present. Vicky had told the other members of the group that Alice's television was rather ancient and as Jim was very fond of watching sport they agreed that they would club together and buy them a new flat screen television. Tom confirmed that Jim's stag party would be held at his house and Bill said that was a relief because he didn't want to be the only male at the hen party, which was to be held at his and Beryl's house. 'Why not,' said Harry, grinning broadly, 'you could have a lovely time.' Bill and Tom then reported on the meeting at the youth club the previous Friday. The new club leader, Jenny Porter, had been extremely helpful and most of the young people had been enthusiastic in their offers to help. Bill was busy producing a map, which covered the whole district. Alice said that she had discussed their idea with some of her fellow councillors and while one or two had pooh, poohed the idea, several others seemed to think it was the kind of thing they ought to encourage in their own areas.

Before the meeting broke up they agreed that once the wedding was over they would then get down to discussing all the elements of the Christmas project. Beryl suggested that the ladies would think about the hampers and the men would be responsible for the distribution arrangements. Tom asked if anyone had any ideas how to refer to the elderly people they hoped to help. Words such as client and customers were rejected immediately because 'We are not social services,' said Vicky firmly. 'Friends?' Beryl suggested. 'Well, no' said Tom 'they may not want us as friends, at least, not all of them.' 'Well, they are going to receive,' said Bill, 'we could call them recipients.' 'Or even victims,' laughed Harry. In the end they settled for associates. 'After all,' said Alice 'they will be temporary associate members of the Windmill Club.' They broke up saying that they would be meeting at the respective parties on the Friday evening and at the wedding on Saturday.

Chapter Thirty Four

Tom woke on Thursday morning with another of his excruciating headaches. 'I really should go and see a doctor' he thought but be took some painkillers and promptly dismissed the idea of going to see his GP. He had neglected Evelyn's garden in recent times so he spent most of the day weeding, trimming hedges and generally tidying up. If it did nothing else it made the garden look a bit more respectable and helped him to pass the day. In the evening Bill Harris telephoned and asked what they were doing about refreshments for Jim's stag party. Apparently Beryl had offered to do some savouries, such as sausage rolls and vol au vents and Bill said that he and Harry would provide a crate of beer. Tom said 'well in that case I will provide the wine and spirits.' Bill told him that the ladies were having some kind of fancy dress party. Alice and Vicky had invited some friends along so they would be about a dozen women in all, 'I can't wait to get out of here' he added.

Thus on Friday evening the men's group assembled at Tom's house. Bill and Harry arrived first with the promised beer and a box full of goodies from Beryl. 'She also sent you her love' said Bill, 'I don't know whether to shake your hand or knock you down.' 'I should choose the former' said Harry 'remember Tom's a boxer.' 'Ex boxer' murmured Tom, 'but I assure you I have no intention of running off with your wife.' 'I know' said Bill laughing 'and that's why I want to knock you down.' Just then Jim arrived and Tom said quietly, 'no anti matrimony comments, Jim is worried enough as it is.' The four of them moved into the sitting room and Tom had just poured the first drinks when Lenny and Mr. Wong arrived. Tom thought it slightly odd that they were still calling the latter by his surname but as he himself had not suggested otherwise the members of the Windmill Club had not pressed the matter. He asked the two newcomers what they would like to drink and served them accordingly. At first the little group was rather constrained, but after the second drink they started to relax. Tom had decided to limit his own drinking because he was going to drive Harry and Jim to their respective homes. Alice was apparently staying at Vicky's for the night in keeping with the custom of bride and groom staying apart the night before the wedding.

Lenny asked Jim if he was nervous and to everyone's amusement he confessed that he was bloody terrified. 'I am sure that you have no need to worry,' said Lenny kindly 'Alice will make you a lovely wife.' 'Ah yes,' said Harry 'they are all lovely at first but once the shine goes off the wedding ring so the bloom often goes off the romance.' 'That reminds me,' said Bill 'do you remember that old Irish sergeant we were supervised by when we were young, fresh faced and eager coppers?' 'Do I not,' said Harry, Paddy was a real old cynic. His favourite comment was "when I first got married I loved my wife so much I thought I could eat her. Now when she starts nagging I wish I had". They all laughed with the exception of Jim, 'There you are then and you say I have nothing to worry about.' Bill patted him on the back and said 'But you are not Paddy and Alice is a really lovely person.' Tom thought he had better change the subject. 'She is also very brave, look how she has gone into politics to represent us and talking of politics, what do you all think of the recent collection of party conferences?'

'If you ask me,' said Mr. Wong, suddenly looking animated, 'they are just talking shops, full of hot air and no wisdom. This is a very nice country with a majority of nice people but you allow the less nice people who are greedy for power and material possessions to take control.' 'Well I agree with most of that,' said Bill 'but how is that different from your own country.' 'Well, in China the nasty people seize control by force. In this country you actually invite them to take control in the name of democracy.' 'I know exactly what you mean,' said Tom, 'we delude ourselves that our elections are fair and voter friendly, but half of us are brainwashed into believing the different party manifestos and the other half don't bother to vote.' 'And,' interjected Harry 'the politician's will spout rubbish at their conferences and rubbish when seeking election, but the real crime is that most of them know its rubbish.' 'In fact,' added Tom 'it is the system that's wrong. You wouldn't go to a dentist or a doctor who hadn't been properly trained and yet we hand control of all the services to people who know nothing about it and rely on the civil servants to sort everything out.'

'And a right bloody mess they make of it,' said Jim, 'could we talk about something a bit more cheerful.' Tom thought that they had a useful if small cross section of the community sitting in his house and not one of them trusted or even liked politicians. 'We haven't mentioned the House of Lords,' said Mr. Wong 'to outsiders that seems to be the biggest farce of all.' 'Ah, but that's attached to the honours list,' said Lenny 'and speaking as another outsider that too is a ludicrous and hypocritical process.' 'Look,' said Tom 'I agree with you both but I don't know why you refer to yourselves as outsiders?' 'You ask the louts who use Paki as an insult,' said Lenny 'or Chinky,' added Mr. Wong.' 'I suppose I know what you mean, sometimes I am almost ashamed to be British,' said Tom, 'however, Jim has requested a change of subject and it is his stag night.' 'Right,' said Bill 'I'll just recite a little poem, which Paddy, our sergeant, used to recite when he'd had a few. It was actually written by a lady called Dinah Moethum, which I think is appropriate for the present gathering.'

Twas an evening in November as I very well remember
I was walking down the street in drunken pride
But my knees went all a flutter so I rested in the gutter
And a pig came round and laid down by my side.
Yes I laid there in the gutter thinking thoughts I could not utter
When a colleen passing by did softly say
"You can tell a man that boozes by the company he chooses."
And then the pig got up and walked away.

After he had finished Tom said 'As you say, that was quite appropriate, but to add a more serious note I would quote Oscar Wilde, just a line that would sum up the Windmill Club'

We are all in the gutter but some of us are looking up at the stars

'That sounds a bit too serious for me,' said Jim, 'even if I understood it.' I know,' he went on 'I will sing a song my mother used to love.' To everyone's surprise Jim had a pleasant baritone voice and they all listened intently while he sang a song about an old fashioned lady. When he finished they all clapped and applauded loudly.

Then the talk turned to sport, football and cricket in particular and then on to the recent Olympics; there was general agreement that modern soccer players were grossly overpaid and sadly under talented. 'There is no hope of England ever winning the world cup' said Harry 'too many foreign players in the premier league. Teams like City and Chelsea are a joke, they play one or two token Englishmen and the rest are foreigners including the managers and owners.' Tom said 'What about the women's teams, both the cricket and soccer teams have done extremely well lately and they seem to be a damn sight more sporting than their male counterparts. Furthermore, you don't get the nasty language and thuggish behaviour, which is so prevalent in the men's soccer world.'

'Speaking of women,' said Bill 'if you could take any woman in the world out for dinner who would you choose?' There was a thoughtful silence, and then Harry said 'Is that living or dead?' 'Either,' said Bill 'it's only a hypothetical discussion.' 'Well, in that case, I would choose Marilyn Monroe,' said Harry, 'I thought she was terrific.' Lenny and Mr. Wong both named women that the others had never heard of and Bill said 'I think Grace Kelly was the most beautiful woman I have ever seen and Beryl could not be jealous of her as she's dead.' 'What about you Tom?' 'Oh I've always been slightly in love with Anne Boleyn, she was apparently very beautiful and was badly treated by the oafish King Henry and his despicable henchman Thomas Cromwell, and she certainly did not deserve to be beheaded. I sometimes think that I was alive in those days.' 'Right,' said Bill 'now for the sixty four thousand dollar question, who would you, choose Jim?' Jim said 'Why, there is no argument, I would choose my Alice of course,' and the others clapped and cheered him.

Harry said 'You notice that none of us chose any of the modern day film stars or so called celebrity women.' Bill said 'That's hardly surprising, they're all plastered in make up and most of them have got plastic boobs and botox.' Oh be fair,' said Tom 'that's a sweeping generalisation, some of them are not that bad.' 'Right,' said Bill a bit truculently, 'just name one.' 'Well if you insist,' said Tom 'what about Gwyneth Paltrow? I think she is genuinely beautiful and I really enjoyed the film Shakespeare in Love.' Mr. Wong nodded sagely 'Me too and I have seen it four times.' They all laughed again. Tom wondered briefly about Bill's demeanour, 'That was the second time tonight he has challenged me, I wonder if he is slightly jealous about Beryl's attitude to me? He certainly has no need to worry.'

He glanced at the clock, it was almost eleven o'clock, 'How time flies,' he said, 'we had better do justice to Beryl's goodies or she would never forgive us.' They munched the sausage rolls and pronounced them and the vol au vents to be delicious. 'Beryl will be pleased,' said Bill. Tom then suggested a toast to Jim and they all wished him a very happy marriage. Jim was by now definitely the worse for wear, but he thanked them solemnly and said he felt much more confident now. He said he was glad that they were not going to tie him naked to the gateway, as it was rather cold. Lenny and Mr. Wong were rather puzzled by this comment and Tom explained that it was the kind of thing that sometimes happened on stag nights. 'But of course,' he added 'not with a mature group like ours.' 'You British are so barbaric,' said Mr. Wong with an inscrutable smile. 'We have a saying in my country "never judge a man until you have walked five miles in his shoes. Then you can forget him because he is five miles away and you have his shoes".' Most of the group laughed but Jim just looked puzzled. 'On that note,' said Tom 'we can bring the stag night to a close.'

Tom got Harry and Jim into his car and the other three set off to walk home. It was just before midnight when Tom got back, he spent half an hour washing the glasses and tidying up, although in truth there was not much mess. 'A bit of a contrast to my younger days in the navy,' he murmured to himself. I suppose wedding and stag nights are different when people have lived most of their allotted span, although Jim and Alice are very healthy and hopefully will have a happy few years ahead of them. Mustn't get morbid he told himself, thinking of when he and Evelyn got married and then he went back in time a couple of hours. When we were discussing beautiful women I almost mentioned Fran he thought, but it would not have been appropriate. 'Thoughts about her I will keep to myself' he said aloud as he went upstairs.

When Bill got home the hen party was just breaking up, Vicky had arranged for the same minibus that had taken them to the casino to take all the women home. It was just as well because most of them were a little more than merry. At least two were being held up by their companions. As they passed Bill, where he stood at the front door, he received a number of semi drunken kisses and one bold lady pinched his bottom. He was relieved when he and Beryl waved the minibus off. Beryl told him that they had all had a very pleasant evening and it was just as well that he had not been there as some of the ribald jokes would have made him blush and he would have been bored when they were talking about diets and swapping weight loss ideas. She told him that Alice had cried at one point, and said that she was very fond of Jim but no one could ever take the place of Jack, her first real love and she still missed him. She said she was not sure whether she was marrying Jim or adopting him. But then she said she had obviously drunk too much wine and they should just ignore her. They had all reassured her that they remembered their first real love although some had fonder memories than others and two of the ladies said they bitterly regretted ever falling in love. Then Beryl stood on her tiptoes and kissed him passionately, 'You were my first real love,' she told him, 'do you remember our wedding?' she asked. 'Of course I do darling, it was the happiest day of my life.' They tidied up in the kitchen and went upstairs hand in hand.

Chapter Thirty Five

On Saturday morning Tom woke before seven o'clock, when he opened the curtains the sun was just lighting up the world. 'Happy the bride the sun shines on,' he said aloud. He thought about Alice and Jim and fervently hoped that theirs would be a happy union. He had written his best man's speech a few days earlier and whilst he was having breakfast he glanced at it and made a couple of small adjustments. About nine thirty Bill called round and left the buttonhole flowers for Tom and Jim. He had volunteered to call at the florists and to collect the bouquets for the ladies and the buttonholes for the men. He had already been round to Vicky's and she had told him that Alice was calm and happy. He added that Vicky still looked a little the worse for wear. Tom knew that they had to be at the registry office for eleven fifteen and he did not know what state Jim would be in so he set off for the bungalow at ten o'clock. Jim looked a little hung over but Tom made them both coffee and helped Jim with his tie. Neither Alice nor Jim had wanted too much formality so the men would be wearing lounge suits and the ladies whatever they chose to wear.

'The see through dress was a joke wasn't it?' Jim anxiously asked Tom. 'I wouldn't want Alice to be too bold,' he said 'even though she is a very attractive woman.' Tom reassured him that Alice was very unlikely to be too bold, 'She is a councillor now,' he reminded Jim. As they were going out to the car Jim wondered if they could call at the pub and have a quick one on the way. 'You know,' he said 'a bit of Dutch courage.' Tom said he thought Alice might not appreciate the smell of alcohol at the ceremony so he drove straight to the registry office. Unfortunately, they were ten minutes early and this meant that Jim kept looking at his watch and saying perhaps she has changed her mind. However, two minutes after eleven fifteen the limousine pulled up outside the registry office and Alice, looking radiant in a blue suit with a cream blouse, stepped out and was followed by Vicky beaming from ear to ear and wearing a bright red floral dress.

The ceremony was brief and efficient and when the registrar said, "you may kiss the bride" Jim enthusiastically obeyed. 'Changed your mind about the see through dress with sequins,' he said rather too loudly and the guests burst into laughter. The guests all stood on the steps of the registry office and watched Alice, Jim and Vicky climb into the limousine. They then followed in their separate cars until they all assembled at the reception in the local pub. Lenny had said that his wife would attend but now said apologetically that she was not very well. Beryl and George had cooperated well and prepared a splendid meal and the cake, which was the centrepiece in the middle of the table, was magnificent. There were two little figures representing the bride and groom. After they had eaten Tom gave the traditional best man speech and regaled them with some very funny stories, then he proposed a toast to the bride and groom and the couple were loudly cheered. George came upstairs and joined in the toast and then he whispered something to Tom. The men then cleared the chairs and tables to one side of the room and a local DJ appeared and produced his equipment from behind a curtain. 'We have music,' said Tom 'a wedding present from George. I know there are only a few of us but we may as well enjoy ourselves in the traditional way.' The DJ had been briefed to play music from the sixties and seventies and Alice coaxed Jim onto the floor for the opening waltz, then Vicky grabbed Tom's hand and dragged him onto the small dance floor. Bill and Beryl then joined in and Harry danced with Alice's neighbour, Mary. The afternoon passed quickly and at five o'clock Tom announced that the DJ would play the last waltz especially for Alice and Jim, although the rest of them would presumably carry on dancing afterwards.

Tom then collected Jim and Alice and took them off to their bungalow to collect their suitcases. Jim had spent the afternoon telling everyone how lucky he was and Alice looked every inch the radiant bride. The train to Liverpool was six forty five and Tom got the happy pair to the station with a few minutes to spare. Jim shook him warmly by the hand and said 'Thanks a million mate,' and Alice gave him a kiss and a warm hug. He watched the train pull out and then made his way back to the pub, some of the regulars had moved upstairs to enjoy the music and the dancing was still in full swing. Bill congratulated Tom on the way he had organised the wedding and after a couple of hours Tom went to each of the members of the Windmill Club and explained that he was going home. In fact, he had another of his throbbing headaches and he had promised to telephone Fran at nine thirty. He got home just after nine forty five and his telephone was ringing.

It was Fran on the other end of the line and she said she had been worried when he hadn't rung her. 'Anyway, I've got you now,' she said 'how did the wedding go?' 'I think it was a great success,' he said 'but I missed you.' 'I know,' she replied 'I have spent all day wishing I had made an effort to get there, but my tutor started back yesterday and she's a real slave driver. I'm sharing her with Leo and we've already got mountains of work.' They talked a little while longer until Tom was overcome with the need to hold her, 'Must go,' he said 'I will phone you on Wednesday.

When he had put the phone down he said to himself, probably for the hundredth time, just what does she see in me? Is she just being very nice because she feels sorry for me or perhaps she sees me as a kind of father figure. That would make our lovemaking almost incestuous. He thought back to their last night together, their love had reached an intensity which he had never experienced before. He had been very fond of Annie, the girl in New Zealand, but looking back he could see that their relationship had been largely physical and they had behaved towards each other just as many young people, who are planning to get married, normally do. Then they had realised that they wished to live in different places and have different futures.

His relationship with Evelyn had bordered on the platonic. She made it clear soon after they were married that she regarded passion as something one read about or saw in films, it didn't apply to ordinary people. 'Anyway,' she once said 'we're both a bit old for that sort of thing.' Once she became ill, even the limited amount of intimacy they had shared became irrelevant and yet he had never at any time considered being unfaithful. Now he was hopelessly in the throes of love and longing that surely could not possibly have a realistic future. 'What about this chap Leo,' he thought, 'obviously he must be near her own age and is probably a dashing figure, with his Harley Davidson. How can someone as old as me compete with someone like him?' He did not sleep well that night, about three o'clock in the morning he was wondering whether he should drive down to Exeter but then what could he say when he got there. I will probably just look foolish. After tossing and turning for the rest of the night he was glad when the clock reached six o'clock and he could get up and start thinking about the Windmill Club and the Christmas project.

Chapter Thirty Six

Tom had taken on the role of coordinator for the Christmas project and he spent the next few days liaising with Mr. Wong, Lenny and their suppliers. Mr. Wong had already promised to supply all their associates with a fish and chip supper on Christmas Eve and Tom was busy arranging deliveries of these. The ones nearest to the fish and chip shop could be delivered by members of the youth club but those further afield would have to go by car and that meant Bill, Jim and himself. Then of course there was Harry on his bicycle. One of Mr. Wong's popular lines was sausages in batter and the butcher who supplied his sausages had agreed to give a pound of sausages for every associate. Lenny was acting as treasurer for the project, Tom himself had given him one hundred pounds but suggested that they kept the donations private so that the other members of the club would not feel any pressure to give more than they could afford.

Having sorted out the arrangements with Mr. Wong he then went with Lenny to his suppliers and negotiated a large quantity of groceries, chocolates etc. at half price. It really did begin to look as if they were going to provide very satisfying hampers. At the meeting on Wednesday Tom reported his progress and the ladies said that early in December they would start making Christmas puddings and mince pies. The technicalities of freezing some of these were a bit beyond some of the men and they were happy to leave the arrangements to the ladies. The next problem to overcome was how these hampers were going to be packed and it was agreed that Harry and Bill, who had a number of contacts, would scavenge round all the local shops to obtain cardboard boxes and these would then be decorated in Christmas wrapping paper.

Beryl wondered how Jim and Alice were getting along on their honeymoon and Tom said he was certain that it would be going well. Vicky then asked Tom about Frances, 'Will we be seeing her again? she said. 'Oh yes,' Tom replied 'she will be coming to stay with us over the New Year.' 'In that case,' said Beryl 'we must have a New Year's Eve party, we can hold it here.' Everyone agreed that this would be a good idea. Bill then asked whether they were going to follow up their visits to the various retirement homes. 'I know we had that letter from the council,' he said 'but everything now seems to have gone very quiet, is that it, or can we do something more?' Tom replied that if they did not do anything more the whole exercise would have been a waste of time and he proposed that they should all give it some thought and bring their thoughts to the next meeting. Beryl brought in the tea trolley and as she did so Tom felt a severe pain in his head. Vicky said 'Are you alright Tom, you have suddenly gone very pale?' 'It's nothing Vicky, just a headache, it will soon pass.'

They chatted during tea and Beryl asked Harry how the new club leader, Jenny Porter, was settling in. Harry said she was coping very well. 'Not as good as Frances though,' said Beryl with a quizzical look in Tom's direction. 'Oh, she will be in time, obviously she has to get to know the members,' Harry said with a smile and a wink at Tom. Vicky said that she would like to visit the casino again, 'Is anyone else interested?' she asked. Harry and Tom both said they would be happy to escort her and after some discussion they settled on the Thursday after next. Shortly after tea the group broke up and Tom was not sorry because his head was still throbbing. He walked back to his gate with Lenny and Mr. Wong, Lenny remarked that the nights were drawing in. 'We will be walking home in the dark in a few more weeks,' he said. After Tom had said goodnight to his friends he decided that he would definitely contact his doctor on the following day.

At nine thirty he telephoned Frances but her mobile was turned off, she is obviously busy he thought, I will try again at ten o'clock. This he did but again there was no reply. He started to worry, I do hope everything is alright, he thought. This was the first time they had missed a call by a wide margin. He poured himself a single malt and sat in his favourite chair thinking I will try one more time at ten thirty. However, at ten fifteen his telephone rang and a contrite Fran apologised for missing his earlier calls. 'Leo got some last minute tickets for a ballet performance and we expected it to end by nine thirty.' 'No need to apologise,' said Tom 'I do understand.' They chatted for a few minutes longer and then arranged for Fran to call him on Saturday. 'I will be on time,' she promised. Afterwards he sat musing, what kind of chap likes ballet, he wondered and how last minute were the tickets acquired. You have no right to question, he told himself, Fran has every right to lead a normal life. But he could not help feeling some pangs of insecurity.

Chapter Thirty Seven

On Thursday morning Tom telephoned his GP's surgery and was told by a rather impatient and uncooperative receptionist that 'There are no more appointments available this week but you could see one of the doctors on Monday afternoon.' 'Supposing I was seriously ill,' he asked her in a mild manner, 'would I still have to wait four days?' 'In that case, you would have to go to the accident and emergency department,' she said, her manner indicating that she was not the least bit interested in his problems, as did the abrupt way she terminated the conversation and put the phone down. Do all the patients get that sort of response, he wondered. Perhaps she does not like men or perhaps she is not happy at home. Many people must take their unhappy domestic lives into their workplace but it is even more unfortunate when their jobs entail them working with the public. Still, I am not seriously ill so next Monday will be perfectly satisfactory. He occupied himself for the rest of the day on housework and laundry.

He had no plans for Friday so he spent some time pottering in the garden. It was not a huge garden but he had very little idea about preparing it for the winter. He thought he might ask Jim if he could spend a few hours helping him, he may be glad of the money, he thought. Little did he know how true that thought was. On Saturday morning he went into town and then wished he had not bothered. He sat drinking coffee in the same café that he and Fran had used and all the memories of that weekend came flooding back. He had never considered himself to be a weak or sentimental man but then nothing had prepared him for falling in love at the ripe old age of seventy four. Most of my peers are contented grandfathers, considered by their relatives to be rather delicate on account of their age, here I am feeling all the angst of a lovelorn adolescent just because she has a new friend called Leo. He decided that when Fran called him in the evening he would be a bit more business like, even a little distant. He had to give her space to get on with her life. She simply cannot be tied to an old fool like me. He finished his coffee and any shopping and headed for home.

He thought about calling in at the pub for lunch but then decided it would be rather busy so he went home and made himself a toasted sandwich. The afternoon dragged, he had bought some paperbacks in town but he tried to start two and just could not settle so he watched the television, switching between the soccer results update and a programme on wildlife. His evening meal was a ready made one, purchased in a supermarket and at nine thirty his telephone rang. Right, he reminded himself, as he picked the phone up, brisk and businesslike. Unfortunately, the moment he heard Fran's voice and the way she seemed to be pleased to hear him, all his resolve crumpled. She told him about some of her research and he talked about the Christmas project, it was the longest telephone conversation they had ever had. I have been waiting to call you since five o'clock she told him. 'I am calling you from mummy's,' Leo has gone to London for the weekend and dropped me off on the way.' 'Mummy and Auntie have said they would love to meet you, so we must arrange for you to visit sometime in the future. Perhaps after I've stayed with you for the New Year.' Tom glanced at the clock and realised it was about ten o'clock, he didn't want the conversation to end but he said 'I had better let you go and make the cocoa.' They said their goodbyes and he thought that she sounded as warm and loving as ever. Afterwards he wondered what she had told her mother and aunt about him and whether they would get a shock when they met him.

On Sunday morning he woke just after six but it was still dark so he got up and made a cup of tea and took it back to bed with him. He half hoped that he might fall asleep again but he did not, so he got up about half past seven and prepared himself for what he expected to be another boring day. Wrong again Tom, he said to himself much later. After breakfast he walked round to Lennys for the morning papers, he asked about the health of Mrs. Patel and Lenny told him rather sorrowfully that she seemed to be getting a lot worse. 'She has had one visit from the community nurse,' he told Tom 'but the doctors seem very unwilling to visit her. 'I really don't know what to do, he said.' Tom said he would be going to see the doctor on Monday and if Lenny didn't mind he would mention the problem. 'I would be very grateful,' Lenny told him.

When Tom got back home he was just about to make some coffee when his doorbell rang. Harry Baines was standing on the doorstep and Tom said 'This is a nice surprise, please come in I am just making coffee.' It was a pleasant morning so Tom opened the French windows flooding the sitting room with sunshine. 'Mind it wipes its feet,' he murmured. Harry looked surprised and said 'Sorry, did I not?' 'Oh no,' Tom laughed 'I was thinking of a line from Under Milkwood, Mrs. Ogmore-Pritchard said to her husband "and before you let the sun in mind it wipes it's feet". Harry also laughed, 'Oh that's a relief, I thought you were telling me off.' They drank their coffee and munched some biscuits, Harry seemed reluctant to say why he had come. Eventually Tom said, it's nice to see you Harry, is this just a social call?' Harry seemed relieved that he had been given an opening, 'Well actually, I have a bit of a problem and I wondered if I could discuss it with you and perhaps get a little advice.' 'We can discuss it by all means but I cannot promise any sensible advice until I know what the problem is.'

'Right,' Harry said taking a deep breath, 'I was just locking up at the club on Friday evening, Jenny had left earlier as she was expecting her boyfriend down from the Lake District, I heard a noise along the side of the building so thinking it was kids messing about I took my bicycle lamp and went to see what the noise was about. Well, it was kids, but not as I expected. There's an old tool shed towards the back of the building, the gardener/odd job man keeps his mower and other tools there. The noise was coming from the shed so I opened the door and found two of the club members. They both had their trousers down and looked as if they were masturbating each other.' 'So what did you do?' asked Tom. 'Well I shouted at them and told them to get dressed and clear off home. I think I might have called them dirty little buggers, which leaves me with two problems. What do I do next and does it mean I could be called homophobic.

Tom thought for a couple of minutes, 'Let us try and answer your second question first. The point about you being homophobic is only relevant if the boys were indulging in homosexuality. How old were they?' 'One was fifteen and the other was fourteen,' replied Harry. 'Did either of them look as if they were being forced by the other boy?' 'No, I think it was mutual.' 'Well I would describe it more as a case of adolescent curiosity, many boys and possibly girls for all I know go through a stage in early adolescence when they are curious about their own bodies and the bodies of other people. I remember naval cadets who indulged in mutual masturbation but they didn't become adult homosexuals, indeed if Freud is to be believed we are all bisexual to some extent. What disturbs me more is when small groups of lads assault young girls, that can be really unpleasant. I believe that many schools go way over the top with their so called sex lessons, teaching children who are nowhere near puberty about sexual behaviour including homosexuality. But as for you Harry, nothing you did could be described as homophobic.'

'But what is my next move?' asked Harry still very anxious. 'Well, I believe you have to discuss the incident with Jenny, as she is officially the club leader, and then if she agrees, the two of you could sit down in confidence with the boys and talk the matter through. There does not seem any reason why you should involve the parents at this stage. Indeed the boys would be mortified and it may cause more harm than good. You will have to appear open minded and non judgmental in your discussion.' Harry looked relieved and said 'When I was a young copper, homosexuality was still a taboo and certainly illegal in public places. I had to arrest a few in my time but I wasn't happy about that. I do not understand their predilection for anal sex but then there are many other things I do not understand.' At this point Harry stood up and shook Tom warmly by the hand. 'Thank you very much,' he said 'it has been worrying me since Friday and talking it through has definitely helped.' 'Well, let me know how it works out,' said Tom 'I am sure you have a good leader in Jenny and between the two of you it will be sorted out without any unpleasantness.'

After Harry left, Tom cooked himself a simple lunch and decided he would spend the afternoon reading one of the books he had just bought, but it was not to be. About two thirty his doorbell rang for the second time that day and on his doorstep he found Alice and Vicky. 'Come in,' he said enthusiastically 'this is my second nice surprise of the day.' 'How do you mean,' said Vicky giving him a hug. 'Well, Harry came round this morning and now you two lovely ladies.' 'Did you have a nice holiday Alice?' Alice looked very subdued but she managed to smile at Tom and give him a little hug. 'The holiday was quite nice,' she replied 'but I was very disappointed when, after a few drinks, Jim decided to unburden himself about his predicament.' Oh Lord, thought Tom rather wickedly, don't tell me he couldn't rise to the occasion. I don't know if I can cope with two sexual problems on the same day. Behave yourself; he immediately remonstrated with himself. 'I'm sorry to hear that Jim has a problem and that it obviously spoiled your honeymoon.' 'He's just as bad as my old man,' growled Vicky. 'Oh no,' thought Tom 'not you too,' but he kept a straight face and said to Alice 'how can I help?' There's a leading question, he thought.

However, the problem was rather different from what his own rather fertile imagination was anticipating. Alice explained that Jim had told her his mother had left him a few thousand pounds and he had received five thousand more from her insurance policies. 'But how is that a problem?' Tom asked. 'Well, as you know due to the kindness of the Windmill Club members, our wedding was not very expensive so I thought Jim would at least offer to pay half the honeymoon costs.' 'And,' prompted Tom. 'And he says he's bloody well broke,' blurted out Vicky, and the indomitable Alice burst into tears. 'But how,' said Tom 'I don't understand?' 'Gambling,' said Vicky bitterly, putting her arm around Alice's shoulders. 'Just like my old man.' 'What kind of gambling, in the casinos?' 'No,' mumbled Alice 'horses and dogs in the betting shops. Before his mother died he used to bet a couple of pounds a day but when he got the money he started betting in twenties and fifties and then chasing his losses. He woke up one morning just before the wedding and realised he'd blown the lot, now I wonder if he married me so that he could have a comfortable home and an easy life. Perhaps he doesn't love me at all.'

'Oh I'm sure that's not true,' said Tom, 'I know from what he has told me that he is mad about you.' 'He's mad alright,' said Vicky 'men are always mad about gambling, alcohol or sex. Well perhaps not all men,' she said a bit sheepishly looking at Tom. 'Let me make some tea,' said Tom 'and then we can talk about it.' He went into the kitchen and made a pot of tea and then took a tray with the tea and biscuits back into the sitting room. Vicky had helped Alice to regain her composure and while they drank their tea she gave Tom some more details. It appeared that when Jim had apparently been going off to the cemetery to work he had been spending most of his time in two of the local betting shops instead. He had started by betting fairly small but as he saw his money beginning to dwindle he started chasing after it with ever larger bets. After a couple of early wins he thought he could double or treble his money and impress Alice but of course he simply kept losing. He then lost his job at the cemetery and now his only income was his old age pension. 'What do you think I should do Tom?' asked Alice in an appealing tone. 'Well first of all,' Tom replied 'don't give up on him; I'm sure he does love you and we will work something out. The difficulty is that he is quite a proud man and he will not want everybody knowing that he has a problem. Have you told anyone else?' 'Oh no, there's only you and Vicky, I have not spoken to anyone else.' 'Good,' said Tom, smiling at her, 'let us keep it just between the four of us. It seems as if there are two problems, one the gambling addiction and two the job situation. There is no way that any elderly person today can manage on the ordinary old age pension and be reasonably comfortable and I am quite sure Jim would not want to feel he was sponging off you. I will have a quiet and completely confidential word with the cemetery superintendent, I know him slightly and he is a very reasonable man. We could also ask around to see if Jim could do some gardening for different people. I can certainly offer him a few hours a week and he would only need three or four jobs like that a week to supplement his pension.'

Alice was very pleased with Tom's suggestions 'But what about the gambling?' she asked. 'Well, we could try to have a discussion with Jim and see if we could plan a system within his means. I will arrange something with him when we meet next Wednesday. I will be tactful because we don't want him thinking I am an interfering old busybody or that we are ganging up on him.' Alice and Vicky got to their feet, 'Thank you Tom,' said Alice 'I do feel much better now.' Vicky gave him a hug and a kiss 'Any excuse,' she said with a wink. 'Don't forget our date next Thursday.'

Chapter Thirty Eight

After his visitors had gone Tom sat slumped in his armchair, his headache had returned with a vengeance and he thought, 'It is not surprising with all the problems spinning around in my head.' He slept very badly that night but he was not sorry when it was time to get up. He remembered that he was going to see his doctor that afternoon and briefly wondered whether he should chicken out and cancel the appointment. He decided on balance that he had better not cancel or that damned receptionist would put him on the black list. When he got to the surgery after lunch, he was relieved to see that instead of the usual woman on reception there was a tall, bespectacled young man who said that he was a medical student on a placement at the surgery and that afternoon he was standing in for Mrs. Taylor, who was not very well. There were three doctors at this particular surgery and Tom was pleased to see that he had been allocated the one to whom he found it most easy to relate. He explained his present problem; Dr. Mason was familiar with the problems Tom had experienced with his wife and he knew that his patient was not a man to make a fuss about nothing.

He decided that Tom should see the neurologist at the local hospital, 'We won't jump to any conclusions until you have seen Dr. Jenson, who is an excellent consultant,' he told Tom. 'We will arrange an appointment for next week.' As they were shaking hands before Tom's departure he raised the question of Mrs. Patel. 'I hope you don't think I am interfering,' he said 'but Mr. Patel is very concerned. He has asked on three occasions if a doctor could visit his wife.' Dr. Mason scrolled through his computer and said 'I am sorry but there is absolutely no mention of Mrs. Patel, there must be some kind of communication breakdown, leave it with me and I will see she gets a visit tomorrow.' Tom left the surgery feeling a little more reassured, he was obviously in good hands.

On Wednesday the meeting seemed to reflect the gloomy weather outdoors it was cold, damp and misty, indoors some of the members seemed to be rather subdued. Tom knew that several of them were struggling with problems but even Bill and Mr. Wong were not their usual cheerful selves. The meeting was largely concerned with the Christmas project and here at least there was reason to be cheerful. Everybody they had contacted had been in favour and willing to help, Jenny Porter had said they could use one of the small rooms at the youth club to collect the boxes and gifts and some of the youth club members had offered to help decorate the boxes and pack them. During tea Tom had a word with Jim and they arranged a meeting for Sunday, including Alice, 'But not Vicky,' said Jim quietly 'she gets on my nerves.' Then Tom asked Lenny Patel if they had heard from the doctor. 'Ah yes,' Lenny replied 'Dr. Mason came round yesterday, he was very nice and prescribed a new drug which has apparently just come on the market. He told me they were having communication problems in the surgery.' 'They need to sack that awkward receptionist,' Tom growled.

Finally, he spoke to Harry who told him that he had spoken to Jenny and they were hoping the boys would turn up on Friday. Just before they broke up Bill asked if anyone had any ideas about their exercise on retirement homes. Alice said that she thought if they widened their remit to all the homes south of the city they could produce a directory. They should ask the homes for basic information such as the name of the head of the home, number of beds available and any special recreational facilities. 'It may be that some of the proprietors will take advantage of the opportunity and give us a lot more information. There may be, of course, some homes that just ignore us but if we made it a proper guide then most of them will not want to be left out. We could decide what grading system to use, perhaps stars such as used by hotels.' Bill said that he thought Alice's idea was very good and he asked the members if they had any objections. They were unanimous in their praise of their new councillor and Alice blushed. Tom proposed that they start work on the guide in January and this was agreed. The meeting broke up with Vicky reminding Harry and Tom of their date the following day. When he telephoned Fran that evening he had a lot to tell her about and they chatted until ten o'clock. When they said their goodbyes he put the phone down and had his usual sense of loss.

Chapter Thirty Nine

On Thursday evening Tom went round to Harry's and then they went to collect Vicky. 'You don't mind using your car?' Harry asked Tom. 'No, I don't intend to drink much; I am going to concentrate on my gambling. I thought I would try my hand at Blackjack as well as Roulette.' Vicky must have been waiting at the window because as soon as Tom pulled up the door opened and she came out and ran quickly to the car. Tom got out and opened the rear door for her, 'Evening boys,' she said gaily, as she settled onto the back seat. She was wearing a pleasant perfume and Tom thought how nice it was. When they got to the casino Tom dropped off the other pair and went round the corner to park his car. He got back to the casino just as Harry had ordered drinks. 'Vodka and tonic for you Tom,' he said. Tom thanked him and said 'I will make this last a long time.' He then looked at Vicky; she had taken off her warm coat and was wearing a white dress which contrasted vividly with the ebony of her arms and throat. She and Alice had been going to the gym to tone Alice up for the wedding but the greater change was in Vicky, she looked at least twenty years younger than her age and Tom said 'You look beautiful.' 'Hear, Hear,' said Harry and both men meant it. Vicky looked embarrassed but pleased, 'I had to dress up for you boys,' she said 'so I bought the dress specially.' 'It was money well spent' said Harry gallantly.

They went over to one of the roulette tables and Tom knew it was going to be his lucky night when he put his chip on red and let it ride for three spins, each of which came up red. He then went over to the blackjack tables and taking a seat he began to play better than he had ever played before. His pile of chips mounted and he became aware of Vicky's perfume just behind him. 'You look just like James Bond sitting there,' she whispered. The dealers were just changing so Tom turned round and said 'How are you doing?' 'Oh I've lost all my chips,' she said. He gave her five, five pound chips and said 'Put these on your lucky numbers and we'll share the winnings.' He turned back to the table, the new dealer had not changed his luck and he continued to win. Suddenly he heard a squeal and Vicky came running over to say she had chosen lucky seven and they were now one hundred and eighty pounds richer. Tom decided that it was a good point to call it a night. Harry had been drinking steadily and looked slightly the worse for wear. When Tom cashed his chips he discovered that he had won just over nine hundred pounds and when Vicky offered him the half share of her winnings he said 'No, please buy yourself something nice.' 'Oh no,' she said, 'we agreed to go halves and it was your money we used.' 'Please,' said Tom 'I have also won, so I would like you to keep it.' 'If that is what you want then thank you very much,' said Vicky graciously. They collected Harry from the sitting area; Harry and Vicky waited in the entrance while he got the car and then drove them home. Vicky was bubbly and excited but Harry seemed rather tired. After they had dropped Vicky off and received a smacking good night kiss each Tom took Harry home. He said, 'I haven't been very good company, but I'm a bit preoccupied with tomorrow night.' Tom said 'Try not to worry; I think you have a very good ally in Jenny. Let me know how it goes.' He drove home and for a change he had a good night's sleep.

Chapter Forty

Towards dawn he had a most disturbing dream; it started with him and Fran house hunting. Fran said they would need a bigger house if Leo was to join them and they were to live ménage a trois. Tom said well why does it need to be bigger, surely three bedrooms are enough. Oh no Fran replied, Leo and I want several children and my biological clock is ticking. At that point Evelyn appeared, she was laughing and saying I did warn you. He woke up sitting bolt upright, he was sweating and shivering at the same time. He suddenly felt very lonely and thought, you are alone when you're lost in a dream. But then dreams are often just a reflection of need or anxiety he told himself and I am sure that that particular dream will not come true.

The rest of the day was uneventful, Vicky phoned him in the afternoon to thank him for the evening before. She told him that she had just rung Harry but he seemed off hand and distracted. 'I would not worry about that,' said Tom 'Friday's are his club night and there are always things for him to think about.' 'Oh that's alright,' said Vicky 'I thought it was me.' 'Not likely,' replied Tom 'you were a lovely companion and we both enjoyed ourselves.' After he put the phone down he thought about Harry and hoped the problem with the boys could be resolved without any unpleasantness.

Saturday morning was bright and sunny if rather more cold than the last few days. He decided to go to the cemetery and take some flowers for Evelyn's grave. The trees were losing their leaves and the paths were strewn with them, they crackled under foot as he walked to where Evelyn lay. 'Good morning,' a cheerful voice broke his reverie, he looked up and saw

Mr. Pickles, the cemetery supervisor. 'Good morning to you,' Tom replied 'this is a bit of luck, I was hoping to see you.' 'Not another complaint about vandalism,' Mr. Pickles said wearily, 'I'm afraid you will have to get in the queue.' 'No, nothing like that,' Tom said 'although I know some of the local kids are being a damn nuisance. No, I wanted to talk to you in confidence about Jim Williams. I gather he has been recently dismissed.' 'Not so much dismissed,' said Mr. Pickles 'as constantly absenting himself. He was a very good worker until the last few months but he seemed to lose all interest.' 'Have you replaced him?' Tom asked. 'No, not yet, I thought I would leave it until after Christmas when we start preparing for the Spring.' 'Well I do hope you won't think I'm interfering but is there any chance you could reinstate him if he promises to work conscientiously again.' 'Tell you what,' said Mr. Pickles 'I was just going to lock up the office and go over to the pub for my lunch, meet me there in fifteen minutes and you can buy me a pint.' 'Splendid,' said Tom 'I'll see you shortly.'

He made his way to Evelyn's grave, 'Can't stop long dear,' he said as he placed the flowers, 'I have to meet Mr. Pickles.' He briefly outlined his dream to her and then said 'but of course you were there.' There was no response from Evelyn and as he said goodbye he wondered if he was going mad himself. Luckily the pub was an oasis of sanity, warm and noisy. George had two pints of foaming ale lined up on the bar, 'Mr. Pickles said he would order for you,' laughed George. Tom paid for the drinks and made his way to the fire where Mr. Pickles was already seated. 'Cheers,' he said as Tom passed him the drink. 'Now, about Jim, I believe in the saying better the devil you know, well of course I would, working in a cemetery and Jim was a good worker until he fell in love. I knew about the wedding of course.'

Tom thought he would leave the blame to love rather than go into the complicated question of gambling. So he said 'I am sure he has settled down now and will work well.' 'Fair enough,' said Mr. Pickles, 'we'll give it another go. Tell him he can start back a week on Monday and let us hope you are right.' They then chatted about football until George brought over Mr. P's lunch. 'I will leave you in peace,' said Tom, 'and thank you very much.'

He walked home, feeling much happier than he had on the day before. While he was preparing a simple lunch the telephone rang. It was Harry Baines sounding very relieved. He said that he and Jenny had talked to the boys the night before. They had pointed out that it was very unwise to behave that way in a public place or indeed anywhere that might embarrass anyone else. Harry said that it might have been Jenny that was locking up and would have seen them. The boys were very contrite and assured the club leaders that it would not happen again. They were very relieved when Jenny said that the matter need go no further and there was no need to involve their parents. Afterwards Jenny laughed and said to Harry that there were not many adolescents who have not experimented, 'I know I did,' she said with a little smile. Harry told Tom that he was sure he felt himself blushing when she said that. 'She's such a pretty girl,' he added. Tom laughed and said 'You mustn't let your imagination run away with you.'

After they rang off he finished his lunch preparation and found himself humming a happy tune. Things are working out well he told himself and then remembered his dream of Thursday night. I hope Fran is in tonight he thought. In the event she answered her phone on the second ring and said 'Tom darling, what a pleasant surprise.' 'Why, who were you expecting,' he asked.

'Only you,' she laughed 'I was just being facetious.' She asked how the Christmas project was developing. He told her that it was going well. At the last count they had forty seven parcels to deliver and of course forty seven deliveries of fish and chips. 'You are going to have a very busy Christmas Eve,' she said 'I wish I could be there to help but mummy and auntie are expecting me. Oh by the way, while I remember, Leo is going up to the Lake District for the New Year and will give me a lift up to you. We haven't fixed on an exact date yet, probably the day after Boxing Day, would it be alright if Leo stayed overnight with us before travelling on to the Lake District?' 'Of course it will my dear girl, you don't have to ask, this is your home also.' 'Oh Tom,' she answered, 'I do love you.' He could feel the warmth of her love even though they were many miles apart. Then he told her briefly of the problems with which he was assisting. 'Please don't use up all your energy,' she said 'leave some for me.' 'No problem,' he replied 'you will always come first.' They said their farewells and he went to bed a much happier man.

On Sunday afternoon Tom was just finishing a crossword in one of the Sunday newspapers when his doorbell rang; on his doorstep stood a rather unhappy looking Alice and Jim. He invited them in and as he stood aside Alice gave him a hug and said quietly 'He did not want to come.' Jim merely nodded and they sat him down in the sitting room while Alice helped Tom to make some tea. 'He's not in a very good mood,' said Alice 'and he's got a thing about Vicky.' They took in the tea and Tom said 'Here we are Jim, the cup that cheers.' He inadvertently hit the right note because Jim smiled and said 'My mum used to say that, she loved her cup of tea.' 'Most of us do,' replied Tom. 'I see that you have not brought Vicky.' Jim scowled 'We see too much of her as it is.' Alice sat upright 'That's not very fair Jim, she is my best friend and I have known her a lot longer than I have known you.' 'Yes, but does she have to live in our pockets,' Jim retorted. Tom leaned forward in his chair and said in a placatory manner 'We all know how ladies place great importance on best friends, much more so than men in my opinion.' 'Well, for a start they are more dependable than men,' said Alice glaring at Jim. 'I think Jim hasn't fully appreciated the fact that you and Vicky have been friends for a long time and of course, you and he are still adjusting to each other.'

'Not having a job to go to will not have helped the situation, Jim has been around the house more and therefore more aware of Vicky calling in. If you were out at work again Jim then Vicky and Alice could see more of each other and go shopping etcetera.' 'Aye, but I haven't got a job,' said Jim bitterly. 'Ah well, that maybe where I can help, I saw Bert Pickles yesterday and he said he has not replaced you and he would be happy if you started back again in the cemetery.' For a moment Tom thought Jim was going to explode and tell him to mind his own business instead he sat up and said 'Did he really, that's great I hate being out of work.' Alice beamed 'That's marvellous,' she said to Tom, 'when can he start back?' 'A week on Monday,' Tom replied and then he led the discussion on to gambling, and Jim agreed that it was a mugs game. He told them he had already decided just to have a bet on Saturdays and if he was working he would hand his pay packet over to Alice as a contribution to the housekeeping. 'Just like my dad used to do.'

He stood up and looked out of the French windows 'Your garden needs a bit of tidying up, I could do some this week to get my hand in again.' Tom glanced at Alice; she looked really happy and silently mouthed

'Thank you Tom.' He thanked Jim for the offer and then walked with them to their car, they were a much happier couple than the pair who arrived as they waved and drove off.

Just as he was dropping off to sleep that night he distinctly heard Evelyn say 'You're a regular little busy body nowadays, everybody's helper, it is a pity you did not help me more.' 'But I did,' he protested 'at least I tried to help you, but it was rather difficult.' 'And now you have replaced me with that red haired trollop.' 'She is not a trollop,' he shouted 'and nobody has replaced you. You just won't let me be happy.' 'Oh diddums' she replied 'children are happy, old fools should just be waiting quietly to die.' The wardrobe door slammed, he sat up and realised that he had left both the door and the window open. 'I must be going mad,' he told himself 'Evelyn is dead and gone.' But he was not convinced.

He spent most of Monday worrying about his appointment with the specialist on the following day. In the event everything went rather smoothly, he arrived at the hospital at nine thirty and instead of waiting around for a long time he was ushered into the consultant at nine thirty five. Mr. Jenson, the neurologist, was a pleasant man, younger than Tom had expected. On other occasions, particularly when he accompanied Evelyn, he had felt either intimidated or patronised by doctors. But there was none of that on this occasion. They had a long chat and Mr. Jenson conducted some simple tests and then asked Tom if he would be willing to have a scan. A male nurse accompanied him down a series of corridors and then he was asked to lie down on a kind of stretcher and move into a tunnel. He briefly wondered if it would feel like this lying in a coffin and then reminded himself that he would never know the answer to that.

After the scan the nurse took him back to the

consultant's office while Mr. Jenson examined the scan results Tom looked round the office, metaphorically keeping his fingers crossed. He listened to the various noises the consultant made and then after a few minutes Mr. Jenson looked directly at him and said 'I am afraid we have a problem. I will not beat around the bush, as I am sure you are a man who prefers straight talking.' Tom cleared his throat and said 'Yes, I would prefer to hear the unvarnished truth.' 'Yes well, in that case, you appear to have a tumour on the brain. The problem is that I cannot say without further examination whether we can do anything about it. I will ask your GP to provide some morphine based drug which will help with the pain and I would like you to come into hospital overnight in about two weeks time. Shall we say a fortnight yesterday? We can then explore further, can you do that?' Tom stood up 'Yes I can manage that Mr. Jenson, thank you for your concern.' They shook hands and Tom walked out of the hospital in a daze.

He sat in his car and said to himself well now, there is a problem to conjure with, what was it Spike Milligan wanted inscribed on his headstone? "I told you I was ill." The trouble is in my case, I did not believe it until now. Still, doctors do make mistakes and I should wait for the next test before I start to worry. He did worry though and he lay in his bed that night trying to guess what the future may hold. Here I am, in love and as happy as I've ever been and wallop, fate throws me a savage right hook. Eventually he fell asleep still worrying about the future.

The meeting at the Windmill Club was a much more cheerful occasion than the previous week. Alice and Jim seemed to be relating well and Harry was the life and soul of the gathering. He and Bill had collected fifty boxes, just in case there are any last minute additions,' he said. 'You know, lonely old folk like you

Tom,' he said with a smile. 'Oh Tom won't be lonely,' said Beryl quickly 'I thought you and he could spend Christmas Day here with me and Bill.' 'That's a lovely idea,' said Tom 'but can we leave the arrangements a bit nearer the time in case something crops up.' 'Something or someone,' said Harry 'perhaps a certain young lady is visiting Tom for Christmas.' 'No,' Tom answered 'Fran will be spending Christmas with her mother and auntie.' He changed the subject by asking Harry how the box decorating was going. 'Some of the youth club members are really getting stuck in,' was the reply. 'All the boxes should be ready for packing in another week or so.'

The meeting was getting rather ragged so Bill called it to order, 'We have just under four weeks to Christmas so I suggest we spend next week planning the delivery schedules and the preliminary visits, and the following week we can pack the boxes.' 'The preliminary visits are essential and must be done by adults. For one thing there may be some elderly people who will not want a Christmas parcel and secondly if we have not made them aware that a parcel is being delivered they may well be alarmed if a young person carrying a box turns up unannounced. If you have no objections, Tom and I will draw up lists based on the geography of who lives near whom, it should work out at four or five preliminary visits each but less for the deliveries if the youth club members help.' Everyone agreed to these suggestions and Beryl went off to fetch the tea trolley.

While they were enjoying the refreshments as usual, Tom took the opportunity to ask Lenny about Mrs. Patel. Lenny looked relieved and said 'The new drug that Dr. Mason has prescribed seems to be helping her a lot and Dr. Mason has been to see her twice now. She is feeling much more cheerful.' 'Oh that's good,' said

Tom 'I think he is a very good doctor.' Alice then reported that she had recently had a conversation with the director of social services. 'He was a bit surprised to hear that I was a member of this group but he had no objection when I said we were going to produce a directory of retirement homes. In fact he said that if it was well received he might propose one covering the whole city.' 'That would be great,' enthused Bill 'perhaps other cities would then follow suit. I know there is a national inspectorate which has inspectors visiting all the residential homes but after the fiasco in Bristol many people are questioning the efficiency of it.' 'Some of the people employed as inspectors are not really suitable' added Tom 'they have had no personal experience of residential care. Such a system needs skilled advisors not power mad inspectors. People who need to go into residential homes deserve the best possible care.' The meeting broke up with everybody in a cheerful mood, although Tom had to pretend a little. That night, just before Fran rang, he wondered if he should mention his visit to the hospital, but decided to wait until he had more information. They chatted about the Windmill Club and Fran said how much she was looking forward to the New Year. 'Me too,' said Tom and he almost meant what he said.

Chapter Forty One

The next few days seemed to fly by for Tom, on Friday evening he went to the youth club to liaise with Harry about the boxes. It was also an opportunity to catch up with Jenny Porter and she was delighted to see him. The club seemed as happy and active as ever, some of the members were rehearsing for a pantomime that they were going to put on for parents and friends on New Year's Day. As Tom stood talking to Harry, he suddenly found himself being hugged by an attractive young lady dressed as Dick Whittington and it took him a few seconds to realise that it was Susie, his former climbing companion. She was obviously very pleased to see him and said 'You will be coming to the pantomime Tom?' 'Oh yes, I couldn't possibly miss such a treat,' said Tom 'and with any luck Fran will be able to come as well.' Susie was one of the volunteers to deliver the Christmas parcels and she asked if it would be acceptable for the youth club members to wear their pantomime costumes for the deliveries. 'That seems to be a splendid idea,' said Tom, turning to Jenny, who had just joined them. She said 'Oh good, I did tell them that we would have to consult the Windmill Club, but I think it would just add that extra Christmas touch.' Tom had a few words with Harry and then set off for home.

On Saturday, his head was so painful that apart from a walk round to Lenny's for a newspaper he stayed at home and tried not to feel too sorry for himself. He rang Fran in the evening and brought her up to date with the happenings involving the Windmill Club. She was particularly pleased that he had been able to help Alice and Jim. It was so nice that they got together so late in life,' she said. She told him that she and Leo

213

were working really hard because they were hoping to complete most of their work by the end of next term. Afterwards he wondered if there was any significance in her comments about Jim and Alice and late in life but he told himself that she was a girl without guile and she would always say what she thought about him and herself directly.

On Sunday he went round to Bill's to look at the visiting schedule, Beryl had telephoned him just after breakfast inviting him to stay for lunch. They decided it would be better if they worked in pairs for the visits. Lenny had asked to be excused, as he was so busy with the shop and his wife being unwell, so they paired Tom up with Mr. Wong. Bill and Beryl were obvious partners as were Jim and Alice and so that meant that Vicky and Harry would work together. 'All the preliminary visits will be done by us,' said Bill 'but at least half the deliveries can be done by the youth club members, those within reasonable walking distance of their club, if we do a couple of visits each day over a week that should cover it.' They also drew up a leaflet explaining who they were and what they were doing; better include both our telephone numbers so they can ring us if they want to,' said Tom. After their discussion, Beryl produced a traditional Sunday lunch which Tom declared was superb and Beryl blushed with pleasure. He went home and nodded in front of his fire. I am getting old he thought, but how do you define old, he asked himself. Some people are old at sixty and others still active into their eighties. All bodies inevitably age but the brain and the spirit can resist ageing and continue to enjoy life, but then I was one of the latter group until there were rumours of a tumour. 'To hell with it,' he said 'I will continue to believe I am simply middle aged.'

On Wednesday the Windmill Club was back to it's

214

cheerful self. As soon as Tom went through the door he could tell by the chatter and the buzz of excitement that everybody was looking forward to the Christmas project. Bill read out the visiting schedule, which he and Tom had drawn up. 'Is everyone happy with this?' he asked. Mr. Wong looked at Tom and gave a little bow. 'I will be honoured to work with you,' he said. Tom was slightly surprised but he smiled at Mr. Wong and said 'The honour is mine.' Then Bill distributed the draft leaflet, 'I have not run it off until you have all seen it.' Vicky scrutinised her copy and then said 'It is very good for information but it could do with being a bit more festive. What about some sprigs of holly or a little robin in the corner?' 'That is a good idea,' said Bill 'but I am not very artistic.' 'Well I will do the drawings,' offered Vicky 'I can come back in the morning and do them with you.' Beryl said 'If you do it now everyone can take their copies home.' So Bill and Vicky went off to the room he used as an office while others arranged their schedules with their partners. By the time Beryl had brought in the tea trolley Bill and Vicky had reappeared with fifty photocopies nicely decorated.

Tom explained to Mr. Wong that they would have to do their visits over the next four days, as he had to be away next Monday and Tuesday. Beryl, overhearing this as she usually did, said 'Are you going anywhere nice?' Tom smiled and said 'Not really it's just a business visit.' That evening when Fran rang he was feeling rather low. 'Are you alright?' she asked picking up a note of depression. 'Oh yes, I am just tired, I have been chasing about quite a lot lately.' 'Well slow down, I want you in good spirits for our New Year.' 'Don't worry, I will be fine after a good night's sleep,' he assured her.

Over the next four days, he and Mr. Wong managed

to visit all the people on their list. Nine of them were very pleased, after the initial surprise, but one couple said they were going away to their son's for the weekend and in any case, they never accepted charity. On Sunday afternoon, they completed their list, shook hands and said they looked forward to meeting again on Wednesday. Tom went home and spent the evening worrying and wishing he could share his worries with someone else. He had a very restless night and on Monday morning he got a taxi to the hospital.

He did not go in his car, because he had no idea what he would feel like on Tuesday, but he had no need to worry. He spent the morning having a series of x rays and another scan. Doctor Jenson introduced him to a colleague who was apparently a neurosurgeon and was referred to as Mr. Tom thought it was one of the odder aspects of the medical profession that somebody studies for several years and is given the title of doctor then after a further period of study they revert to the title of Mr. He was not allowed to have any lunch and about three o'clock he was wheeled along to an operating theatre and given a general anaesthetic. He awoke in bed sometime later with a shocking headache and a bandage around his head. He was very drowsy so he had a cup of tea, which the nurse offered to him and then he went back to sleep. When he awakened on Tuesday morning he was quite hungry, so he ate a modest breakfast and waited for the doctor.

At ten o'clock he was visited by Dr. Jenson who told him that the bandage could be replaced with a plaster and the good news was that he could return home in the afternoon after some more rest. However, the doctor continued 'I am afraid we achieved very little.' 'What does that mean' Tom asked. 'We have established the fact that your tumour is malignant and that the location means we are unable to operate safely.

We could of course try chemotherapy or radiotherapy but we doubt it would make much difference at this stage. Unfortunately it means that you have a limited period of life left.' 'How limited; are we talking weeks, months or years?' Dr. Jenson stood up and patted Tom on the shoulder. 'Very unlikely to be years, my best guess would be six to nine months; although I have had patients with a similar condition who lived a little longer.' Tom lay back on the bed and took a deep breath, 'Thank you doctor, I had better start sorting out my affairs.' Dr. Jenson said that he would talk to Tom's GP about the best help that they could give with painkillers. 'Do go and see him tomorrow. Presumably you have someone at home to care for you.' 'Oh yes,' said Tom 'I will be fine.' He lay on the bed for awhile after the doctor had gone then he got dressed and told the nurse he was going home. He went down to the reception area and telephoned the same taxi firm that had brought him to the hospital.

Chapter Forty Two

When he got home the house felt very cold and very empty. He soon rectified the former problem by switching on the central heating but could do nothing about the emptiness. He felt lost and bewildered but he was determined not to feel sorry for himself. 'I have had a good life and it is not over yet. Who knows how long I have left? Best to make the most of it he told himself firmly.' That night he took his painkillers and a sleeping tablet and he was surprised when he woke to find it was seven thirty. That's surely a good sign he thought as he stood shaving in front of the mirror. Look at me, I don't look much different from the way I looked twenty years ago, I will probably live into my nineties. When he arrived at the Windmill Club Beryl immediately asked about the sticking plaster above his right ear. 'Oh I slipped on the stairs and bumped my head, nothing serious just a small cut.' 'You have to be careful at your age' she admonished him. Everyone reported that they had completed their visits and the vast majority had been very positive. Naturally some people were surprised and in two cases, both elderly ladies, they were rather bewildered as to why they had been chosen.

Apart from the couple Tom and Mr. Wong had seen there were three other refusals. In two cases the potential recipients were going away to relatives and in one of the people Vicky and Harry had visited the man was very pleasant but not only did he insist that he did not need any help but he thought it was a good scheme and gave them a cheque for fifty pounds to help with the expenses. They all agreed that this was a very nice gesture and that Bill should write to him on behalf of the Club thanking him for his help. There were now forty three parcels to pack. 'I just hope we haven't missed anyone said Alice. Harry said that all the boxes were now ready for packing and most of the supplies were either at Lenny's or in Beryl's dining room. 'Yes I won't be sorry to have my dining room back' Beryl interjected much to everyone's amusement. Bill said 'well if Tom doesn't mind we can use his car and mine to transport everything to the youth club tomorrow morning then those of us who are available can pack them tomorrow afternoon.' 'Good idea' said Tom 'then deliveries can start this weekend. We will need another note to remind people that the fish and chip suppers will be delivered on Christmas Eve. Mr. Wong produced a carrier bag decorated in a festive manner. 'I have purchased these especially for the deliveries' he said solemnly and everyone spontaneously clapped. Mr. Wong looked very pleased.

During tea Vicky patted Tom on the knee and whispered 'you do not look very well. Remember what I said about if you ever need a carer, I am still your woman.' Tom smiled, 'thank you Vicky I will remember if the time comes.' Everybody declared that they would be available on the following day with the exception of Jim. 'My boss has asked me to do some extra hours' he told them 'there always seems to be more deaths at this time of the year.' 'Ah well, us old folks are a lot more vulnerable in the winter chaffed Harry. Tom looked round at the bright cheerful faces of the members of the Windmill Club, 'there are exceptions' he thought. He continued musing, presumably the answer is to stay as active as possible both in body and brain, they do say that mind can triumph over matter, whoever they are. Beryl tapped him on the arm 'you must be miles away Tom, Bill has asked you twice what time do you want to meet in the morning?' 'Oh sorry Beryl, how about ten o'clock

Bill?' 'That's fine,' Bill replied 'see you here then.'

The group broke up shortly afterwards and Tom walked up the road with Lenny and Mr. Wong. 'I am grateful for you speaking to the doctor my wife is definitely better,' Lenny told him. 'Oh good,' Tom replied 'see you both tomorrow.' And he turned into his gateway. 'He is such a nice man,' Mr. Wong said to Lenny as they continued up the road. When he got in Tom wondered what he should cook for his dinner. He was still replete with Beryl's mince pies so he decided on the old standby of beans on toast. Afterwards he sat by the fire trying to read, he must have fallen asleep because the telephone ringing made him sit up with a start. Fran sounded rather anxious when she spoke to him. 'Are you sure you are alright, I am beginning to be a little concerned?' 'No, I am fine; I think I was just nodding off in front of the fire.' 'Well there are only a couple of weeks and I will be there to keep you awake. We are definitely coming on Boxing Day if that's alright.' 'Alright, it's marvellous,' he replied. They chatted for a little while, he told her of the progress with the Christmas project, and she told him that she was going to stay with her mother and aunt for four days including Christmas Day. 'I am sure they will be pleased about that,' he responded. After they had ended the call, he made himself a hot drink and took it upstairs drinking it in a hot bath. He lay listening to the cistern filling and he was sure he heard Evelyn chuckling and saying 'It serves you right', but he was too tired to respond. He got into bed and the combination of the hot drink and the painkillers meant that he slept like the proverbial log for the second night in a row.

Chapter Forty Three

Thursday was a cold, damp day and Bill and Tom worked briskly to load up their cars and take the supplies to the hall from Beryl's dining room. Tom stayed at the hall while Bill went to Lenny's and collected another load. Beryl had insisted that Tom should join them for lunch, 'Just soup and a roll,' she said; but inevitably followed by some of her delicious mince pies. Afterwards he felt more like sitting in front of the fire but he felt that he had to join the others in the hall to pack the boxes. 'Many hands make light work,' said Vicky cheerily and they had all the boxes bulging with goodies in less than two hours. In addition to the usual things like puddings and pies Tom had used some of his casino winnings to ensure every box had a bottle of good port, all that was now left was to distribute them. About a dozen were within easy walking distance of the club but the other thirty would have to be transported by car. Bill arranged for him and Beryl to take some on Saturday and Jim and Alice to take some on Sunday. Susie had asked Harry if she and her friend Jo could help Tom to deliver some; he was pleased about this because it meant he just had to drive the car and they could deliver the boxes. Harry had volunteered to be on duty at the youth club to make sure all the boxes went to the right addresses.

They locked all the boxes in the music room and Tom drove home feeling tired and depressed. His depression lifted when he found a card in his post box; it had a picture of Santa Claus on the front and Fran had written, "This picture reminds me of you and more importantly looking forward madly to Boxing Day. Lots of love Fran", with lots of kisses tacked on at the end. He spent the evening dividing his attention between the television and a book. On Friday morning, he went to see Dr.Mason who removed the plaster and said 'Well I don't really know what they did to you, but you will only have a small scar, you are obviously a good healer.' 'Unfortunately, the problem is still there,' said Tom. Dr. Mason was very sympathetic, 'I have had the report from Dr. Jenson and as you know the prognosis is not good. Still, we can never be certain.' He then asked Tom if the painkillers were effective. When Tom replied that they were, he said 'Well do not be afraid to ask if they prove less helpful due to familiarity.' Tom felt better for having had the opportunity to talk about his situation. 'You and Dr. Jenson have been a great help,' he said as he shook hands and left the surgery.

On Saturday morning he arrived at the youth club, Harry was there accompanied by two excited girls, Susie and Jo. They both looked very pretty in their pantomime costumes and Tom thought that they would undoubtedly cheer up the elderly people to whom they were delivering. They spent the morning on deliveries; some took at least twenty minutes because the recipients wanted to talk to the girls. Tom was happy to sit peacefully in his car. At lunch time both girls phoned their parents on their mobiles and said that Tom had invited them to lunch at the pub. George the landlord was delighted to see them and congratulated the girls on their costumes. They had a typical Christmas lunch and Tom was amazed at how much two slender young people could eat. After lunch, they did two more visits and then Tom took them to Susie's home, arranging to pick them up on Sunday morning to deliver the last of the boxes. Susie's mother remembered Tom from the outing to North Wales and thanked him for being so kind to Susie. 'It is a pleasure,' he assured her 'she is a charming girl.' On

Saturday evening he rang Fran and told her of the days activities, she sounded quite envious 'I have had a very dull day, all day in the library. Leo went off to London again, being very mysterious,' she added. They chatted for awhile and when Tom put the phone down, he felt the usual sense of loss. He wondered about Leo being mysterious, perhaps he has got a woman friend in London and does not want to tell Fran, or perhaps he has gone to buy an engagement ring.

On Sunday morning, he and the girls finished their deliveries. Beryl had invited them round to her house for coffee and mince pies. 'You could learn a lot from Beryl,' he told the girls with a smile, 'she is the perfect hostess for any occasion.' 'Don't listen to him girls, he's just a silver tongued flatterer,' said Beryl blushing. The girls laughed and Susie said 'Well I hope I can find someone like Tom to marry me, I think he's gorgeous.' Now it was Tom's turn to blush, 'You've got a lot of things to do before you think about marriage,' he said. Just then Bill came back with Harry 'All done and dusted,' he said 'all parcels delivered.' 'And you just had to come back via the pub,' said Beryl sniffing. 'That was Harry's fault,' said Bill with a grin. 'He was ever so thirsty, weren't you Harry?' 'Of course,' said Harry loyally; 'I twisted his arm Beryl.' 'Twisted his little finger more like,' she retorted. Tom said that he had better take the girls home and thanked Beryl for her kindness. She replied that he was welcome any time.

The next three days passed very quickly and Tom spent a lot of time buying Christmas presents for the ladies in the club and not forgetting Susie and Jo. The men would have to be satisfied with bottles of a good brandy, as his imagination would not run to individual presents for them. The rest of his casino winnings came in very useful. On Wednesday the Windmill Club met for the last meeting of the year, Beryl had surpassed herself and the tea was positively sumptuous. Before tea, Bill summed up the year, 'Considering we did not start until April, we have packed quite a lot in, the highlights were the Christmas project and the trip to North Wales. The low light was probably the depressing visits to the residential homes. Of course, the icing on the cake was helping Alice to become our very own councillor.' Everybody clapped and cheered and Alice held her fists above her head like a boxer, 'They aint seen nothing yet,' she said. Then the gifts were handed round, Tom had bought each of the ladies a hand painted silk scarf with a silver brooch to hold it together and the men each received their brandy.

He had a variety of gifts, from malt whisky from Lenny to a hand knitted sweater from Beryl. Jim, Alice and Vicky had clubbed together to give him gloves and slippers but the oddest present was a large box of cigars from Harry. 'I know you don't smoke,' he said with a grin 'but I love a good cigar and you can offer me one each time I visit.' He then repeated the Groucho Marx quote *"a woman is only a woman but a good cigar is a smoke"*. There were cries of 'Shame,' from the ladies. Mr. Wong got the biggest cheer of the day when he gave them all a specially printed voucher which promised a free fish and chip supper twice a month for a year. When Tom said 'That is very generous,' Mr. Wong replied 'No more generous than the friendship you have all given to me.' Their last meeting of the year was a great success and they promised to reconvene on the first Wednesday in January. 'Wouldn't miss it for the world,' said Harry 'I can't believe that nine months ago we were practically all strangers.' As Harry and Tom left, Beryl reminded them that she was expecting them both on Christmas Day. 'Somewhere between eleven and twelve,' she said and they both thanked her and promised to attend.

That evening when Fran telephoned him, he was in two minds about telling her of his hospital appointments. She sounded so happy he decided not to mention it and instead told her about the afternoon and the presents he had received. 'Lucky you,' she said 'I feel positively deprived.' 'Don't worry,' he told her 'I am sure Santa Claus will have left something for you.' After some more light hearted chat, Fran said 'I will be at Mummy's on Saturday, so I will ring you from there. 'Can't wait,' he replied and they said their usual tender farewells.

He woke early on Thursday morning; when he opened the curtains there was a fine dusting of snow, making everywhere look fresh and sparkling. It was now only five days to Boxing Day and Tom decided he had better make the house look a bit more festive. He had not bothered the previous two years, last year he was on his own and the previous year Evelyn had said 'We don't want to be bothered with that nonsense'. He decided to buy a new tree and use the lights he had in the cupboard but when he tested them half of them didn't light up so he went into the town centre and bought a six foot tree and some lights. He also bought some lights for the porch. He stood the tree in the hall and decorated it with the lights and some baubles from the previous years. The fairy, which Evelyn had always put on the top, looked a bit battered put he kept it for sentimental reasons. He stood back and admired the tree 'Very nice,' he murmured 'but why on earth have I bothered.' But he knew that he did not want Fran and her friend Leo walking into a cheerless house.

He had just sat down when the telephone rang, he heard Alice's cheerful voice saying 'I hope I am not disturbing you, but I did not get a chance to ask you yesterday.' 'Ask me what?' he replied rather puzzled. 'Well, we're having a little party on Christmas Eve after the supper deliveries and Jim and I wondered if you would come.' 'Well, that is very kind of you but I am not much of a party person.' 'Oh, it's just half a dozen of us getting together for a few drinks.' Tom thought that Christmas Eve alone might be a bit dreary so he decided to say yes. 'Thank you very much Alice, I will be pleased to come,' 'Oh good, about seven thirty then.' After he had put the phone down, Tom realised that he had not asked if he should eat first, but then he guessed that there would be refreshments, so that was another meal he did not need to worry about. That night he was very restless and about two o'clock he heard a noise downstairs in the hall. He thought that he had better go down to investigate, when he got downstairs the fairy and several of the baubles were lying on the floor. I am sure I fastened them on properly, he murmured as he picked them up. He didn't feel like replacing them just then so he left them on the kitchen table and went back to bed. He tossed and turned for the rest of the night and when he went downstairs about six thirty to make a cup of tea the Christmas decorations were on the kitchen floor and some of the glass baubles were broken. He decided that after breakfast he would go and buy a new set and put what was left of the others back in the cupboard. He was too superstitious to throw them out.

On Saturday evening Fran rang him as she had promised; she was staying with her mother and aunt 'And believe me the sherry is flowing like water,' she said with a laugh. Tom told her of his two invitations, 'Oh good, I was hoping that you would not be on your own. Mind you behave yourself though,' she said mock seriously. 'I will try very hard,' he replied in the same vein. 'Remember, it is only three days to Boxing Day,' she went on 'I hope you are taking your vitamin pills.' 'I cannot imagine what you mean?' he replied, glad that she could not see the big smile across his face. He was still smiling after he had put the phone down and made his supper drink. On Sunday, Bill rang and reminded him that they were due to meet at Mr. Wong's the following day, Christmas Eve. There were a number of the parcel recipients that had declined the offer of fish and chips and a number who had asked if they could have theirs at lunch time. The final figures were fifteen at lunch time and twenty one in the evening, so Bill, Harry and Tom would meet at twelve o'clock to make the lunchtime deliveries. The deliveries took about an hour and afterwards the three men decided to go to the pub for a warming drink. George was serving hot toddies especially for the Christmas period and after a couple of these delicious brews, Tom felt both warm and cheerful. Apparently, Bill and Beryl had been invited out for dinner in the evening, which is why they were not going to Alice's, so Tom arranged to pick up Harry to save him getting out his trusty bicycle. He left the pair of them in the pub and went home; he spent the afternoon reading and dozing in front of a log fire. When he got to Harry's there was no sign of him and no lights on in his flat. Tom rang the doorbell and after a lengthy wait, a rather dishevelled Harry appeared at his door. 'Oh sorry Tom, I was asleep. Bill and I stayed most of the afternoon at the pub, please give my apologies to Alice, I really do not feel well enough to come out.' Tom chuckled and said, 'Right, I will see you tomorrow at Beryl's, you had better be sober by then or she will have your guts for garters.

Chapter Forty Four

When Tom got to Alice's neat bungalow, he rang the doorbell and stood on the steps, shivering in the cold December air. All traces of the snow had disappeared and it looked very unlikely to be a white Christmas. The door was flung open and there stood Vicky clutching a large piece of mistletoe. 'A merry Christmas Tom,' she replied and holding the mistletoe over his head, she hugged and kissed him with an enthusiasm which left him momentarily disconcerted and slightly out of breath. 'A very merry Christmas to you, he said as he recovered from the assault. She was wearing the cream dress she had worn for their casino visit and once again, looked very attractive. Alice appeared in the hall and after one of her breath squeezing hugs she asked if Harry was not with him. 'No,' he chuckled 'I gather he and Bill spent most of the afternoon in the pub and he is feeling rather delicate. He asked me to tender his apologies. If Bill's in the same state, Beryl will not be at all pleased.'

They went into the sitting room and Jim thrust a glass of warm punch into Tom's hands saying 'Merry Christmas Tom.' There were three other people in the room and Tom recognised them as Alice's neighbours, Mary from the one side and Mr. and Mrs. Ward from the other. They remembered him from the wedding so he shook hands with them and wished them a very merry Christmas. It proved to be a very pleasant evening, Alice provided plenty of food which she described as nibbles and Jim offered a wide variety of drinks after the punch ran out. Tom was careful as he had to drive home but he entered into the spirit of Christmas and regaled an interested audience with some of his naval and climbing experiences. Alice and

Jim seemed much happier than they had been and Vicky was her usual bubbly, vivacious self. On a number of occasions, she put her arm around Tom's shoulders or patted him on the knee. On one occasion he saw Alice looking in their direction, she looked slightly bemused and then gave him a friendly wink.

About eleven o'clock he decided that it was reasonable for him to make his farewells. Vicky saw him to the door and this time without the mistletoe, she gave him another hearty kiss. When he got home the contrast between his empty house and the cheerful group he had just left was almost painful. He had drunk enough alcohol so he made himself a cup of tea and as he went upstairs, he said aloud 'A merry Christmas Tom and a very unpromising New Year.'

On Christmas morning he awoke about six thirty and decided to go downstairs, make a cup of coffee and bring it back to bed. As he lay in his bed, drinking the coffee, his mind drifted back to Christmases past. He had been born just before the Second World War and his early recollections were of austerity and anxiety; his father had been in the army and his mother constantly worried about her husband's welfare. Her own father had been killed in the First World War and she was convinced that she would be a widow before the war ended. Then of course, there were the air raids, Tom had an older sister, Iris, and some of his early recollections of the war were of his mother carrying him into the air raid shelter followed by his sister, clutching an armful of dolls and teddy bears. Like many families they had an Anderson shelter in their back garden, this was made out of sheets of corrugated iron covered with soil and sandbags. It was always cold and damp and his mother would go back into the house for more blankets and hot drinks. On Christmas Eve 1941, they had to spend the night in the shelter while bombs were raining down on a nearby industrial estate.

The best Christmas was in 1945 when his father was at home for the first Christmas in six years. There was still rationing and money was very short but they had a proper Christmas tree and the nicest of Christmas dinners. Tom had his best present ever when he received a model railway and his dad to play with him. He lay back smiling at this memory; then he remembered the saddest Christmas that they had ever had. He was sixteen years old and waiting to go for his naval training. His sister was due to be twenty one in January and was engaged to be married. Late on Christmas Eve, Tom and his parents were sitting in front of the fire when there was a loud knock on the door. When Tom's father opened the door, standing on the step was a large policeman who asked if he was Mr. Burton. When Tom's father said that he was, the constable said, without any further ceremony, "Well, I am afraid your daughter Iris has been killed in a road accident". Tom's mother, who was standing in the hallway heard this and screamed so desperately that Tom knew he would never forget the sound.

They later learned that Iris's fiancé had purchased a motor bike as a surprise and they were in the process of riding home to show her family when they collided with a lorry, killing them both instantly. After that, Christmas's seemed to come and go without any special meaning. Now, thoroughly depressed, he decided to get up and make himself a small breakfast, he knew that Beryl would expect him to eat an enormous lunch.

He spent a couple of hours tidying up his already tidy house and checking on the spare bedroom. Every time he thought of tomorrow he felt a frisson of excitement, 'Why is it that I have had to wait until now to experience these intense feelings?' he asked himself.

At quarter past eleven, he set off for Bill and Beryl's house, as he went out of the gate he almost slipped over because after a heavy frost the pavement was extremely slippery. 'Careful old chap, you do not want a broken leg on top of everything else,' he murmured. He was clutching a bottle of champagne, which he had bought especially for the occasion, 'And you don't want to drop the fizz either.' As soon as he rang the bell the door opened and Beryl, looking rather flushed after her efforts in the kitchen, gave him a hug and a kiss, 'Merry Christmas Tom,' she said. 'And to you too Beryl,' he replied.

'Those two reprobates are in the sitting room,' she said loudly. When Tom went in Bill and Harry were drinking coffee and looking rather sorry for themselves. Beryl followed him in and said 'They are just about sober now, but you should have seen them at four o'clock yesterday.' 'Do stop going on,' Bill said wearily 'it is Christmas after all.' She poured Tom some coffee and then bustled off to the kitchen muttering, 'And don't some of us know it. I will put this champagne in the fridge.' Tom heard the account of the previous afternoon, 'George and his damned hot toddies, we must have had at least half a dozen,' said Bill. 'More like eight,' added Harry. 'Sorry about last night Tom, but there was no way I could have come to Alice's.' 'What about me, Beryl insisted we went out for dinner, she made me shower and drink gallons of black coffee.' Tom smiled sympathetically, 'It sounds as if I left in time, there is no way I would want a hangover just now.' As he spoke he realised that he had not had a headache for several days, must be the magic of tomorrow he thought.

Beryl's Christmas lunch was as lavish as he had expected, the turkey was delicious and her Christmas pudding seemed to melt in the mouth. 'Wonderful,' the three men declared and they toasted the chef with Tom's champagne. Beryl was pleased by their compliments and the afternoon ended on a much happier note than the morning had begun. About four o'clock Tom said his goodbyes, having refused the offer of tea and mince pies on the grounds that he was absolutely full. He made his way home, stoked up the fire and fell asleep sitting in front of it.

The telephone ringing woke him, and when he glanced at the clock he was surprised to see that it was almost seven o'clock. He picked up the telephone and heard 'Merry Christmas Tom darling.' Immediately he was fully awake 'And a merry Christmas to you too, Frances my love.' Fran apologised for ringing earlier than usual but explained that her mother had invited friends in for the evening and it might be difficult to ring later. Tom replied that the time did not matter 'Just to hear you is enough, what time are you leaving tomorrow?' 'Leo is picking me up at ten o'clock and reckons we should be with you between two and three.' Tom suddenly had a feeling of deja vu, recalling the incident of his sister and a motor bike. 'Please ask Leo to drive carefully,' he said 'the roads may be very treacherous.' 'Don't worry, I will insist on the need for care,' she told him.

After their call he sat wondering about the sleeping arrangements for the following night. Perhaps he should offer to make up a bed on the settee for Leo. He had no idea how much Fran had told Leo about their relationship, then he started worrying about the roads and the motor bike. He heard Evelyn saying 'Yes, it will be most interesting tomorrow night, perhaps your little paramour will want to sleep with Leo. Maybe she has been having you on these last few months.' Tom angrily shook his head a first headache for several days was just starting to make its presence felt. He decided to have a hot, strong toddy and a sleeping tablet. He had a quick bath and five minutes after getting into bed he was soundly asleep.

Chapter Forty Five

On Boxing Day morning he awoke just after seven o'clock feeling refreshed and ready for whatever the day would bring, or so he thought. After breakfast he found himself clock watching. He was a bit like a cat on hot bricks, as his mother used to say. At ten o'clock he thought they would be leaving, at twelve o'clock he thought they must be north of Bristol on the M5, he had a very simple lunch and wandered round the house checking everywhere was tidy. At two o'clock he thought they must be very near and at two forty five he heard the sound of a powerful motor bike outside his house. He peeped through his front room window and saw two, leather clad and helmeted figures pushing a distinctive motorcycle into his drive. Fran took off her helmet and shook out her beautiful red hair. Then the second figure, who was slightly taller than Fran, took off their helmet and shook out their long blonde hair. 'Oh no,' he groaned, 'not one of these long haired fellows.'

He went to the front door just as his bell rang, Fran threw her arms around him and kissed him passionately then she rather self consciously unwrapped herself and said 'Tom this is my friend Leo.' Tom blinked because it was obvious that he was a she, Leo held out a slim hand and said 'Hi Tom, glad to meet you at last.' They turned back to retrieve their bags off the back of the bike and Tom went to put the kettle on. Over tea, Leo explained that she was christened Leonie but because she was such a tomboy her brothers called her Leo and the name had stuck. Tom felt like hugging her but then how would he explain that he was so happy because she was a female.

He took the tea tray back into the kitchen and Fran

followed him in. 'Is it alright if I show Leo up to my room so that she can tidy herself up?' Tom paused; this could be awkward he thought. 'If Leo is in your room,' he said 'where will you sleep?' 'Why in your room you silly man, I have thought of nothing else for days. That is if you want me to?' Tom's heart soared he pulled her into his arms and said 'My darling there is nothing in the world that I want more.' They stood clinging to each other until there was a discreet cough at the door. 'Is it OK if I go up?' 'Oh I am sorry, of course, I will take you up now, you're probably bursting.' And with that the two girls went off giggling together. When they reappeared Tom thought that both young women looked radiant. He and Fran settled Leo in front of the fire browsing through his books and they went into the kitchen to prepare dinner. Leo was a vegetarian like Fran so they cooked mushroom omelettes and chips. 'We have so many things in common,' Fran explained 'I feel I have known her for years.' 'We have one of Beryl's Christmas puddings to follow,' said Tom 'so I will put it to heat through while we are eating the omelettes.'

After dinner they drank some of the port which Tom had bought for the parcels and Fran got out the chess board. 'Leo and I have been playing chess quite a lot,' she said 'why don't you give her a game while I have a bath and then I will play the winner?' Tom was a little surprised; it seemed as if Fran had become more competitive in the last few months, or was there an ulterior motive? 'She is just trying to make a fool of you,' said Evelyn. Tom ignored her and said 'Well I will have a go but I have not played since you went to Exeter.' Fran went upstairs and Leo and Tom faced each other across the chess board. Tom half expected to be thrashed but he found that Leo did not offer the same challenge as Fran had in the summer. They agreed to play the best of three but Tom won the first two games so they sat chatting until Fran came downstairs. It was obvious that Leo thought a lot of Fran and she said that her friendship had been invaluable during the last term.

Eventually they heard footsteps on the stairs and Fran seemed to float into the room in her nightwear. Tom thought that she smelled delicious, 'Well, who am I to play?' she asked kissing Tom lightly on the head. He wanted to grab her and pull her down to him but he could not with Leo sitting there. Leo said, 'Tom won easily, so you will have to play him.' 'No problem,' Fran replied 'it will be interesting to see if I have improved.' Again they decided to play the best of three; Fran won the first game and Tom the second which made the third game very interesting. After a dozen moves Tom decided that he did not want to win, so he made a couple of elementary mistakes and found himself check mated. Leo said 'Well done Fran,' but Fran just smiled and said 'Just lucky.' They talked some more and Tom kept looking at the clock wishing it was bedtime. Fran offered to make everyone a bedtime drink but Leo yawned and asked if they minded if she went to bed. After she had gone upstairs Tom did what he had wanted to do all evening and pulled Fran down beside him. 'I have missed you so much,' he told her and she snuggled into him and murmured 'Me too, let's go to bed.'

While he was in the bath Fran, went in to say goodnight to Leo. As he lay in the bath he could hear the trickling of the cistern and an occasional burst of laughter from the spare room. Evelyn said 'They are laughing at you, you silly old fool, I bet they think you are a randy old goat,' Tom abruptly pulled the plug so that a swirl of water drowned her jeering comments. Later, when he was lying in bed, Fran came in and he watched as she removed her dressing gown and nightdress. He marvelled again at her beauty and his good fortune.

Fran pulled back the duvet and started to get into bed then she paused and said with mock indignation 'How dare you sir, trying to lure me into bed when you are practically fully dressed.' In fact he was only wearing pyjamas but he sat up and said 'Sorry madam,' and quickly took them off. Then he pulled her into bed and they clung tightly to each other. Tom could feel her warm and tender body pressed against him, he ran his fingers down her spine and felt there was nowhere in the world he would rather be. After a few minutes of holding each other he kissed her passionately and said 'Dear girl, I love you so much.' 'I know,' she murmured and they then made love with an intensity neither of them had ever previously experienced. It was so intense that neither of them had made a sound until they reached a mutual climax and Fran gave a very small cry.

It was almost midnight and Tom whispered 'I do not think we will have disturbed Leo.' 'I hope not,' Fran whispered back 'she feels rather protective towards me and does not fully understand our relationship. I have tried to explain but she just sees the age gap as too wide.' Tom thought for a few minutes, he knew that sooner or later someone would ask the question aloud, as a number of people must have thought about it. 'Leo is not the only one to be puzzled,' he whispered, 'I do not understand how a beautiful girl like you can possibly love someone like me.' 'That is one of the reasons I love you,' she replied 'you simply do not understand what an attractive man you are, you have no vanity.' 'And the other reasons?' he asked. 'Well, you are very kind, extremely interesting, thoughtful and tender, you make me laugh and most of all you make me feel cherished.' 'That last is because you are cherished, you are the most precious girl in the whole world.' She kissed him and said 'Show me again how much you love me.' So he did.

The following morning he woke about six thirty. Fran was still fast asleep. He lay for awhile watching her in the dim early morning light, she looked even more beautiful in repose and he wanted to kiss her awake. Instead he slid slowly out of bed and collecting his pyjamas and dressing gown he crept out of the room. He dressed in the bathroom and then went down to the kitchen to make himself a cup of coffee. To his surprise he found Leo already there. She said very quietly 'I hope you don't mind but I have been awake for ages so I came downstairs a few minutes ago.' Tom assured her that he did not mind, he made coffee for them both and they took it into the sitting room. They sat quietly in what Tom would have described as an awkward silence. Then Leo cleared her throat and said 'Actually, I was hoping to speak to you alone.' 'Well' he replied 'now is your opportunity, Fran is still fast asleep.' Again there was silence and she murmured so quietly that he could hardly hear her, 'I know you are in love with Fran and I don't blame you, in fact I am in love with her myself.'

Tom was slightly taken aback but then he said 'I can understand that, she is a very lovable person. Does she know about your feelings?' 'Well not completely, I'm sure she suspects about how I feel but I have not mentioned it because she is completely besotted about you.' 'And you don't think that is a good idea. Would she be any better off with you?' 'Well, for a start, I will almost certainly live a lot longer than you. Fran and I are only five years apart, I am thirty seven. I was in a long term relationship with another woman for about ten years but we broke up just before I went to Exeter.'

Tom felt a mixture of anxiety and anger. 'So, let me get this clear, you are looking for someone to replace your previous lesbian relationship and you think I am unsuitable for Fran so you would like to take her from me.' 'Well, I would not put it so crudely but yes I would like her to fall in love with me.' 'Surely we have to leave Fran to make her own decisions,' said Tom 'she is after all a grown woman.'

Just then the sitting room door opened and Fran said 'Good morning both,' and then she paused. 'Am I interrupting anything?' 'Not at all,' said Tom, rising to his feet 'come and sit down and I will make you some coffee. Would you like some more Leo?' 'No thanks, I had better go up and pack my bag.' When Tom came back with Fran's coffee she said 'It seemed a bit tense when I came in, was everything alright?' 'Of course, it was fine,' Tom reassured her, 'oh good because I would like you two to be friends.' Tom hugged her and said 'I will go and get dressed and then sort out breakfast.' As he went upstairs he felt sure he heard Evelyn whisper 'It sounds as if you're losing her.' 'Rubbish, mind your own business,' he said. And realised he was speaking aloud. 'What was that,' Fran called 'oh nothing, I just stubbed my toe.'

Whilst they were having breakfast Leo said 'I am not sure which day I will be coming back to pick you up.' 'Oh, don't worry about that,' Tom quickly replied, 'I will bring Fran down to Exeter and maybe stop off at Bournemouth to meet her mother and auntie at the same time.' 'Oh that's a good idea,' said Fran 'they have been asking about you such a lot.' Leo did not look too pleased but she said 'Oh well, in that case I will see you in Exeter.' After breakfast she put her bag on her motorbike, she gave Fran a big hug and a kiss and Tom a perfunctory peck on the cheek then she roared off up the road. They stood watching her go and then Fran said 'Thank you for your suggestion, to be honest I found the trip here very cold and rather nerve racking. The winter is no time for motorbikes.' They went into the house, Tom closed the front door and said 'I will make a cup of tea and then get my revenge on the chess board.' 'Or, we could go back to bed,' said Fran with a mischievous smile 'that is if you're up to it!' So they went back to bed.

Chapter Forty Six

Later, while they were enjoying a simple lunch Fran said 'It was Wednesday yesterday, did my coming stop you going to the club?' 'No, we agreed to shut down until the New Year,' Tom told her. They decided to drive down to the river and walk along the bank, the air was crisp and clean and the grass and leaves crackled under their feet. They walked along hand in hand and Fran suddenly said 'I can see us doing this twenty years from now, although I may have to help you a little.' 'It is not an unpleasant thought,' Tom replied 'but somehow I cannot see it happening.' There was a silence and he thought, is this the right moment to tell her about the tumour. But then he decided it was not. On the way home they stopped at the bakers and bought some crumpets then when they got home they toasted them sitting in front of the blazing logs.

'Should we have a little get together with your friends in return for the hospitality they gave you?' Fran asked him. 'That's a good idea,' said Tom 'what did you have in mind?' 'Well, I thought it would be nice if we were alone for New Year's Eve so how about we invite them round for drinks on Sunday evening, it is a bit short notice but if you ring them while I cook dinner you can at least see what they say.' Tom made the telephone calls; Beryl and Bill were very pleased to accept his invitation and Harry Baines said yes, providing there were no hot toddies. When he rang Alice, Vicky was there as Jim was not yet home from work, Alice said she was delighted to accept for the three of them. Lenny was very apologetic but explained that most of his family would be with him for the weekend. Mr. Wong was also very pleased because he said he had no intention of opening on Sunday evening.

When Tom relayed the information to Fran she responded by saying 'Jolly good, now all you have to do is worry about the food and drink.' 'Thank you,' said Tom 'what exactly will be your contribution?' Fran smiled and said 'I could provide the entertainment. You have never seen my song and dance act and I do a speciality act with balloons. Only you have to promise not to burst them.' Tom smiled 'On reflection I think I would rather you helped me with the refreshments. You can do your speciality act after the guests have gone home. More importantly, what's for dinner?' Fran laughed 'You just do not want to share me with your friends.' 'Well, no not if you're only wearing balloons. Dinner?' 'Well I found some prawns in your freezer so we're having prawns and pasta.' After dinner Tom got out his treasured chess set and suggested that they should play a couple of games. He started to set them out on the board and realised that the white queen was missing. 'Oh hell,' he muttered 'where could that be?'

When he told Fran what he was muttering about she said 'We must have dropped it somewhere, down one of the cushions perhaps.' They searched the sitting room but there was no sign of the missing chess piece. I have an old plastic set upstairs; we can borrow the queen from that. They played a couple of games but Tom's heart was not in it and he lost both. Where can it have gone he asked himself, it cannot be Evelyn, she just talks. They sat watching television for awhile and then decided to go to bed. About midnight a little voice whispered in his head 'It must have been Leo and it is a symbolic gesture, for white queen read Fran'. He fell asleep, still troubled.

When Tom opened the bedroom curtains on Thursday morning the rain was lashing against the windows and the sky looked almost black. 'Not a pretty morning,' he said to Fran who was still huddled under the duvet. 'Well a nice man would go and make some coffee and then come back to bed was the muffled response.' He had another of his bad headaches and this was not made any better when Fran said 'How would you feel about my going round Europe on Leo's bike? We would only be away for a couple of months.' 'When are you talking about?' he replied. 'Well we are both trying to finish our PhDs for Easter, so it would probably be June and July.' Tom swallowed some coffee and then said, 'It sounds exciting, you must tell me more.' Just then the telephone rang and when he went downstairs to answer it he heard Leo's voice. She said that she had been trying to get Fran on her mobile but she must have it switched off. 'Hold on, I will give her a shout.' Fran called back that she was just getting dressed, 'Tell her I will ring her back in half an hour.' Tom relayed this information and Leo said 'Thanks, bye,' and switched off her phone. Tom was a bit dismayed by this curt response but he went upstairs and told Fran he was going into the bathroom to shave.

As he did so he looked in the mirror and murmured to himself 'You are not dead yet, keep fighting for her.' Later, as he was going downstairs, he heard Fran talking on the telephone in the little used front room. He had no intention of eavesdropping but as he passed the door he heard Fran say 'I do not want us to fall out Leo, but I cannot accept you saying things like that.' Tom went into the kitchen and a few minutes later Fran came in and kissed him. 'What was that for?' 'Just to show you how much I love you,' she murmured. After lunch it had stopped raining so Fran said 'You have never shown me your wife's grave.' 'Well I did not honestly think you would want to see it.' 'Oh yes, I would like to,' Fran responded. Tom said 'It is only fifteen minutes away and as it's stopped raining we can walk there.' As they walked through the cemetery gates the first person they saw was Jim. 'Hello you two,' he said 'nice to see you again Fran. Are you stopping for long?' 'No, unfortunately not Jim, I have to be back in Exeter in early January.' Jim then addressed Tom ',Your wife's grave is nice and tidy Tom, I have been giving it special attention.' 'Thanks Jim, that is very kind of you, the vandalism is very depressing.' They said goodbye to him and soon arrived at Evelyn's grave. Fran read the inscription and said 'Do you miss her very much?' 'I have to be honest and say that the sadness grows less every week. You cannot live with someone for twenty years and not miss them but I believe that her death came as a relief to both of us.' Fran tucked her arm into his and said 'Perhaps we should not have come if it stirs up unhappy memories.' Tom half turned and kissed her 'No, I think it is necessary to remember our loved ones from time to time.' They then went to the pub for lunch and George welcomed them with a beaming smile and said 'The hot toddies are on me.' 'Oh lovely,' said Fran but Tom said 'You have to beware, just the one, they are lethal.' Then he said to George 'You realise that you helped to put Bill and Harry in the doghouse just before Christmas.' George laughed and said 'Yes, Harry did tell me, Bill has not been allowed out without Beryl since.' Fran and Tom settled on scampi and chips for lunch and then spent the rest of the day reading and watching television.

The remainder of the week passed far too quickly for Tom's liking and on Sunday morning he woke just before eight o'clock to see Fran standing beside the bed holding a breakfast tray. 'Coffee and croissants for my master,' she said with a smile. 'Super,' he replied and they sat in bed happily munching the croissants. 'We had better sort ourselves out for the evening,' Fran remarked, 'I am quite looking forward to seeing everyone.' By mid afternoon everything was ready and Fran said she would go and have a bath. 'Oh good,' said Tom 'I will come and wash your back.' So fifteen minutes later they were both splashing about in the bath followed by a trail of water across the landing and finally making love in the bedroom. Afterwards Tom lay in the bed marvelling once more at his good fortune, having found someone like Fran. Then came the gloom of the tumour and the realisation that, sooner or later, he would have to tell the woman he loved so dearly that he was only on borrowed time. Not today though he thought, and getting out of bed he said 'I will go and put the kettle on while you sort the two bedrooms out for Beryl's benefit.'

Just before seven o'clock the doorbell rang and the first guests arrived. These were Bill and Beryl accompanied by Harry. Mr. Wong closely followed, carrying a large bunch of flowers for Fran. There was a gap of about twenty minutes and Beryl said 'I wonder where Alice and the others have got to.' A minute or two later the doorbell rang and in came Alice and Vicky followed by a flushed and slightly dishevelled Jim. 'He had to change the wheel,' announced Alice 'only noticed as we were leaving that he had a flat tyre.' 'Yes, I am sorry Tom,' said Jim but Tom assured him that there was absolutely no problem and offered him a drink. They had put out the food and drink in the front room and everyone sat initially in the sitting room. At first the group seemed reserved and subdued and Tom thought it was a bit odd, because they chatted happily every Wednesday. Then he realised that the difference was probably due to Fran's presence as she had only been involved with the Windmill Club on their outings. He suggested that Bill should recite the little verse about the pig and the man in the gutter. He did so and everyone laughed, none more so that Vicky who said 'How did they know which one was the pig?' This seemed to break the ice and everyone chatted much more freely.

Then Fran said she would introduce the entertainment. For one awful moment Tom thought 'Not the balloons!' but he had not realised that Harry was a very useful guitar player and Fran had asked him to liaise with Vicky who had a very fine voice which she had demonstrated on their youth club evening. The result was a pleasant hour of music from the duo with occasional songs for everyone to join in. Afterwards they went into the front room and enjoyed the food, which Fran had prepared and which Beryl declared was really very nice. About ten thirty Tom started to feel very tired and his head was beginning to throb. He was not sorry when Alice decided that Jim should not drink any more alcohol as he had to drive her and Vicky home. Fran made some coffee and by eleven fifteen the party had dwindled down until only Bill and Beryl were left. Tom and Fran walked them to the gate and watched them walking down the road. As they got to their own gate Beryl waved and they went indoors.

As Tom shut the front door Fran yawned and stretched theatrically. 'Gosh, I am really shattered,' she said. Tom knew exactly how she felt, 'It has been a tiring day, let's go to bed. Can I get you a drink or anything?' Fran refused his offer although she said she was almost tempted by the anything. Within half an hour she was fast asleep and Tom lay listening to her gentle snoring. He was still worrying about when and if to tell her about his medical problem, which was how he thought of the brain tumour. Eventually he fell into a dreamless sleep and awoke to find Fran clutching mugs of hot coffee. 'Come on sleepy head, it is the last day of the year and we have much to celebrate.' 'We do?' he

246

murmured sleepily. 'Of course, this year was the year we found each other and I for one will always be grateful for it.' He sat up and took the coffee from her. 'Well, as you put it like that I just have to agree.' Fran had opened the curtains and it was a beautiful day, sunshine and blue skies. 'It could be Spring,' she said 'quite amazing.' They sat side by side drinking their coffee and planning the day ahead.

Chapter Forty Seven

They decided that straight after breakfast they would set off for the Peak District and find a pub there to have lunch. They were just about to put their coats on when the doorbell rang; Tom opened the door and was confronted by two beaming faces, Susie and her friend Jo. 'Morning Tom,' said Susie 'we just called round to see Fran, Harry said she would be here.' 'Indeed she is, you had better come in and see for yourself.' Fran was delighted to see two of her former club members, she ushered them into the sitting room and Tom went into the kitchen to make coffee. When he took it in they were engaged in an animated conversation. Fran was telling them that after Easter she was going for a trip around Europe. 'Then when you come back will you marry Tom?' Susie asked. Tom realised that the girls saw no problem in the age gap, probably because they saw everyone over thirty as elderly.' 'Oh, I do hope so,' Fran replied 'but we mustn't embarrass him because he hasn't asked me yet.' The girls stayed for more than an hour and after they left, with hugs and kisses all round, Tom said that his head was spinning with all that chatting. 'Oh, girl talk is always too much for mere males; in any case that has slightly dented our plans.'

'It will be dark by four thirty so shall we just drive into Cheshire and find a nice pub there,' Fran suggested. Tom thought this was a good idea and he headed for the walled City of Chester. They found the City rather busy so they drove south until they found a small village with a delightful black and white Inn. Tom had, what the proprietors called, a late Christmas lunch and because Fran gave one of her most winning smiles the chef cooked her a delicious omelette, which she pronounced to be the best she had ever eaten.

Afterwards they drove slowly back arriving home mid afternoon. Fran produced some maps and tried to show him the route she and Leo would take on their extended holiday. Tom realised that the plans were a little more advanced than he had previously thought and he tried to show some enthusiasm for Fran's sake. 'That was a bit of a surprise,' she said 'Susie asking if we were getting married when I get back.' 'Ah, well at her age everything seems more logical and people proceed from A to B.' 'I am not sure what that means, but I hope it does not mean that you think marriage is a bad idea.' 'My darling girl of course not, I cannot think of anything I would like more, but who knows what may happen while you are away. For example you may fall in love with a dashing Spaniard or dour but very rich German.'

'You are a funny man; I will never fall in love with any other man as long as you are available.' Aye, there's the rub, Tom thought but he simply said 'Oh that's alright then.' Neither of them was particularly hungry after their good lunches so they agreed to make a pot of tea and have mince pies and some of the Christmas cake which Beryl had given to Tom. 'Talking of Beryl,' said Fran 'is she still as protective about you as she was when I first moved in here?' 'No, I think she is more relaxed now, although I think the problem is the relationship between her and Bill and my role is simply accidental.' 'There you go,' laughed Fran 'selling yourself short as usual.' 'Right, well for that remark madam I will thrash you at chess.' 'Oh sir, do we really need the chess as an excuse?' 'You are a very naughty girl and later you may just regret what you asked for.' The evening passed pleasantly and at ten o'clock the telephone rang; it was Leo, and after a fairly brief conversation Fran told Tom that she had rung to wish them a happy New Year.

At eleven o'clock Fran said that she wanted to ring her mother. 'I cannot leave it any later,' she said 'or they may have gone to bed.' When she rang, her mother answered and after a few minutes Fran covered the mouthpiece and said 'Mummy would like to speak to you.' Tom took the phone with some trepidation, 'Hello Mrs. Summers, Tom Burton here, how do you do.' They chatted for a little while and then Fran's mother said, 'You sound very nice but I know you are a lot older than my daughter, you will look after her because she is very precious to me.' Tom found himself smiling and he said 'I can assure you that she is very precious to me, she is a wonderful young woman.' Fran took the telephone from him and said, 'You must not take what he says too literally mummy, he wears rose tinted glasses.' Tom could hear Fran's mother laughing at the other end. 'Well make sure you bring him to see us soon,' she said. Then Fran spoke to her aunt and by the time she put the telephone down it was eleven thirty. Tom got out his best brandy and they toasted each other and held each other lovingly.

Just before midnight Tom went out of the back door and walked along the side of the house to the front door. He had explained the custom of first footing to Fran and he carried food for the table, fuel for the fire and money for the purse. On the stroke of midnight he rang the doorbell and when Fran opened the door they wished each other a happy New Year and then stood on the step listening for the church bells. It was a crisp moonlit night with a fair array of stars and as they stood with Tom's arm around Fran she said 'I am so happy, these last few months have been the happiest of my life.' 'You mean while you have been able to get away from me in Exeter,' he said smiling at her. 'You know I mean no such thing, you wicked man. I mean, whenever we have been together, particularly in

250

Derbyshire and North Wales.' 'Me too,' said Tom 'and I am going to miss you when you tour Europe.' 'I do not have to go if you would rather I stayed at home.' 'No, you must go, it will be a wonderful experience for you.'

They went indoors and decided to have one last drink before retiring to bed. Later they lay side by side, neither of them wanting to sleep. Fran whispered 'I meant what I said; I do not have to go.' Tom had been trying to work out just when he might die, but of course it was impossible to calculate accurately. He believed that it could well be while Fran was away. He had always been a fan of western films and he particularly liked Butch Cassidy and the Sundance Kid. There was a line in it which somehow seemed very appropriate; Robert Redford was asking his girlfriend, played by Katherine Ross, to go to Bolivia with him and Butch. She replied, "I will go with you, but I won't watch you die". Tom realised that he did not want Fran to watch him die. Their brief time together had been full of life and love and he did not want to break her heart. 'Hey,' she suddenly said 'don't tell me you have fallen asleep, that's not very flattering.' 'No my darling, I am not asleep just thinking about the future.' She kissed him and whispered 'Just as long as your future includes me.' He assured her that it did and thought, am I now telling lies, would it be better to discuss the problem with her? But instead he whispered 'I love you sweetheart.'

'Do you realise,' Fran said 'we have done a lot of whispering together, usually around midnight. Then she whispered 'Shall we make love to welcome in our brand New Year?' They made love with such intensity and passion that afterwards Fran said 'Gosh, I thought my heart was going to burst.' And Tom replied, 'I think mine did.' They fell asleep in each other's arms and when Tom woke he could see daylight peeping through a crack in the curtains. He thought of a quote from Romeo and Juliet "But, soft! What light through yonder window breaks? It is the east and Juliet is the sun". Well Frances has certainly been my sun and if there ever were a pair of star crossed lovers there were none more so than Frances and me.

His reverie was broken by a mumbled question, 'Is that coffee I smell.' 'No, but I'm just going madam, back in five minutes.' It was actually more like fifteen minutes before he returned bearing coffee and toast. While they were having their simple breakfast Tom asked the question he had been dreading. 'When do you want to go back to Exeter?' 'Oh hell, must you go and remind me? As a matter of fact I have an important meeting next Monday; why don't we travel down next Sunday, meet mummy and auntie for lunch and then stay overnight somewhere between Bournemouth and Exeter. My meeting is at eleven o'clock, how does that suit you?' 'That suits me fine,' he replied, 'I can't wait to meet your mother and aunt.'

In the afternoon they went to the pantomime, which was staged by Fran's former club members. It proved to be excellent entertainment and Susie played her part brilliantly. Afterwards they went to compliment her and Tom told her that she was a born actress as well as a born climber. She blushed and kissed him and Fran.

The next few days passed far too quickly, on Friday they went round so that Fran could say goodbye to Lenny and Mr. Wong followed by tea with Alice, Jim and Vicky. On Saturday they had lunch at the pub with Bill, Beryl and Harry and George was most solicitous in his treatment of Beryl. Saturday night was painful for both of them, Fran cried for the first time in their relationship and although Tom hugged and consoled her he felt like crying himself. It was well into the early hours before they fell asleep. On Sunday morning they were up before seven o'clock and on their way just after eight. Fran had suggested that they took her mother and aunt out for lunch but her mother had insisted that she wanted to prepare lunch for them. They stopped three times on route, ostensibly for tea from flasks Fran had prepared, but actually to give themselves the opportunity to kiss and murmur sweet nothings.

When they arrived Tom pulled into the drive and admired the very pretty detached house which was a bit larger than his. It was set on a hillside and had a view of the sea. The car had barely stopped before the front door opened and mummy and auntie stood on the step. Fran introduced Tom, they first of all shook hands, and then he kissed their proffered cheeks. They gave no indication of surprise or dismay at Tom's appearance and it was obvious that Fran had prepared them for the age difference. They had a very pleasant lunch and discussed a wide variety of subjects. Fran's mother told Tom that it had been very nice for them to have Fran home for Christmas. 'She has never missed but this time she did seem to spend a lot of time looking at the clock,' she said with a smile. 'Please mummy, no more secrets,' said Fran looking at her watch, 'we must be off shortly.' As they made their farewells both ladies said to Tom, 'You must come and stay in the summer when Fran gets back from her travels.' 'I'll look forward to that,' he said, knowing that it would never happen.

As they drove off the ladies waved and Tom said 'They seem very happy.' 'Oh yes, they have always got on extremely well and once they were both widowed it seemed like a good idea for them to live together. I am glad you like them,' she added. 'I like them very much, but then I knew I would if they were your family.' Fran knew of a small hotel just before they reached Lyme Regis and when they enquired there, it was open,

although very quiet after the Christmas holidays. The proprietor, a Mrs. Thomas, managed to produce a good simple meal, steak for Tom and scampi for Fran followed by a delicious fruit trifle. They sat in the small lounge for awhile afterwards but decided to go to bed early, as they were both very tired. When they kissed goodnight only one of them thought that it may be for the last time.

Chapter Forty Eight

Tom woke just after seven o'clock and saw Fran making coffee with the kettle and coffee provided. When she realised that he was awake she opened the curtains and handed him a mug. 'Careful, it's very hot,' she said. He took the coffee and smiled his thanks, but his innards felt like lead and he knew the next few hours were going to be some of the hardest of his life. They showered and dressed in almost complete silence and as they were going downstairs Fran said 'You're very quiet.' 'Sorry, just a miserable headache, I will be better after breakfast.' Mrs. Thomas had prepared a full English breakfast for Tom and Fran settled for cereal and toast. 'Your breakfast looks very nice but you obviously do not feel hungry,' Fran commented. Tom pushed the food around his plate and he ate a little. They went to the kitchen and he apologised to Mrs. Thomas assuring her that there was nothing wrong with the food but he did not feel very well.

They packed their bags, paid their bill and were on their way before nine o'clock. They passed through Lyme Regis and a few minutes later Tom spotted a lay by with a view of the sea above the Jurassic coast. He pulled in and as he stopped the car they threw their arms around each other and clung together with an air of desperation. Fran started to cry and said 'Please tell me why you are so troubled, this is surely not goodbye.' The ever efficient Tom took out a clean handkerchief and dabbing her eyes he said 'Of course it's not goodbye, but it will be a long time before we meet again; six months or more.' 'Well I have said before, I don't need to go travelling.' 'And I have also said before,' he replied 'that of course you must. After all, we have waited all our lives to find each other, a few months is a mere bagatelle. If you start worrying, you will not enjoy the opportunities that the travelling will give you.' Fran smiled through her tears, 'I suppose you are right as usual,' she murmured. Tom set off again and they stopped for coffee at a café just outside Exeter. At five minutes to eleven they pulled up at the building where Fran's meeting was due to be held. They kissed each other tenderly and Fran said she would telephone him at nine o'clock just to make sure he had arrived home safely.

Fran got out of the car, collected her bag and walked quickly to the entrance to the building. She paused briefly on the step, turned and blew him a kiss then she was gone. Tom started the long drive home; he found the motorway and drove north. After a couple of hours he forced himself to stop at a service station and bought an almost drinkable cup of tea from one of the several counters, then he continued his journey home. He arrived home just as it was going dark. He put the kettle on and then he put a match to the already laid fire. Within a few minutes he was sitting in front of the fire with a cup of tea on one side and a large brandy on the other; his head seemed to be splitting in two. As he sat there he heard a voice say quietly 'Loves young dream over then?' He did not reply. The voice went on 'How could you ever expect such an affair to have a happy ending? You are an old man and love is for the young.' 'Not true,' he murmured 'everyone needs to love and be loved and I am no exception. Whatever happens now cannot take away the memories of the last few months which have been wonderful.' 'What happens now,' said the mocking voice 'is that you will die alone and miserable.' Tom swallowed his brandy in one large gulp 'Go away Evelyn; I will never listen to you again.' With that he threw his precious brandy balloon into the fireplace where it shattered in a myriad of fragments and sparks.

That was silly, he told himself, and then he got out of his chair, fetched the vacuum cleaner from the cupboard under the stairs and cleaned up the mess. The last thing he felt like was cooking a meal, so he made himself a sandwich and settled down with the newspapers that he had bought at the service station. He started, as always, at the back of the paper reading the sports pages. Like most men, he was tired of politics and politicians and depressed by many other aspects of the reports on the front pages. It was always easier to lose himself in the sporting reports. One bright spot, as far as he was concerned, was that United had been winning all their matches during the Christmas period and they were comfortably at the top of the league. He remembered from his working days how those workers who supported a specific club were always more cheerful on a Monday morning if their team had won over the weekend. He read both his newspapers and was surprised when the telephone rang.

'Good Lord,' he said 'it is nine o'clock already.' He picked up the telephone and said 'Good evening the lonely hearts hotel here.' 'Oh don't say that,' said a voice at the other end, 'I feel bad enough already.' Tom swallowed and immediately apologised. 'Oh I was just joking,' he said 'please ignore me.' He realised that he would have to be sensitive and empathetic in their future telephone conversations because the last thing he wanted to do was to spoil Fran's holiday plans. They chatted for awhile and he asked her how the meeting had been. Fran told him that she and Leo had reached agreements to finish their work by the end of April. 'It is unusual,' she said 'and it means we are going to have to work very hard if we want to get away in May.' Tom assured her that he had every faith in her ability to complete the work on time. Although in truth he was not entirely sure what this entailed. After a few minutes Fran yawned and said she was very tired and needed to go to bed. 'Me too,' Tom agreed, 'I will telephone you at the usual time on Wednesday evening.' He concluded by saying 'Goodnight darling, I love you very much.' Fran replied 'Yes so do I, goodnight Tom.'

While he was getting ready for bed he realised that, apart from the reference to their work, Fran had said nothing about Leo. I wonder how their relationship stands, he murmured to himself, perhaps she was there while Fran was making the telephone call, and certainly her final words were a little more distant than usual. But then he told himself to stop being silly and imagining things unnecessarily. Tomorrow I will pay some attention to the Windmill Club; I have been a bit neglectful of late. He took a sleeping pill and a painkiller and he was soon soundly asleep.

Chapter Forty Nine

When he opened the curtains the following morning he thought that it had snowed but in fact there had been a very hard frost. Everywhere was crisp and white and the sky was virtually cloudless. His head was throbbing and he would have given anything to hear a cheerful voice or activity in the bathroom or kitchen. But no such luck, the house was heavy with silence and he thought about getting back into bed and staying there. Come on Tom, shave and shower and you will feel like a new man. He followed his usual routine but as he went downstairs he said to himself 'More like a battered old man I'm afraid.' He made himself some toast and boiled and egg, after this simple breakfast he felt a little more human and he decided to ring Bill Harris. Beryl answered their telephone and when he wished her a Happy New Year she said she was delighted to hear him. Her next words were to enquire whether Frances had gone back to Exeter and when Tom confirmed that she had Beryl invited him round for lunch and said 'No leftovers, I promise.' Tom thanked her for the invitation and said he would be with them about twelve thirty. Then he set about tidying the house, he vacuumed the bedrooms and changed the beds. 'New Year's broom eh Tom,' he murmured as he worked. He worked his way downstairs and by twelve o'clock he had had just about enough of housework.

At twelve thirty he walked down to the Harris's, Beryl opened the door and embraced him warmly. Bill was just behind her and said 'Blimey Tom, I thought we had a VIP arriving the way Beryl rushed past me to open the door.' 'Don't exaggerate Bill,' said Beryl 'I did not know if you had heard the bell.' 'Anyway, come in Tom,' chuckled Bill shaking him warmly by the hand, 'a very Happy New Year to you.' Beryl was as good as her word; no leftovers. Lunch was mashed potatoes, peas and some very tasty lamb chops followed by a freshly baked apple pie. Afterwards, Tom leaned back in his chair, 'Thank you Beryl that was superb.' He helped her carry the dishes out but she would not let him help her wash up. 'That's what dishwashers are for Tom, now go and talk to Bill and I will bring the coffee in.' They had a long discussion and agreed that, so far the Windmill Club had proved it's worth. They made plans for the meeting on Wednesday while Beryl bustled in and out with coffee and then home made biscuits. As Tom walked home he felt positively bloated but much happier than when he woke up that morning.

The first meeting of the Windmill Club in the New Year was a pleasant afternoon. Everyone was present and everyone seemed in good spirits, Bill opened the meeting by greeting them all and said that the first business was the possibility of a new member. He reminded them of the man who had given the contribution to the Christmas parcels. His name was Charles Wright. When Bill had written to him thanking him for his contribution he had replied and asked whether there were any vacancies in the Windmill Club. A discussion followed; Beryl reminded them that she had suggested a maximum of ten and there were only nine of them. Alice pointed out that the men already outnumbered the ladies by two to one and she had been going to propose her neighbour, Mary. Tom sat listening to the discussion; he was the only person who was aware that there would be a vacancy in the next few months. He said that he thought Beryl and Bill had been extremely generous in allowing the meetings to be held in their house and he thought they should have the final word about enlarging the group. 'We could have some of the meetings in my house but we would have to knock down the wall between the sitting room and the front room,' he said with a smile.

Beryl stood up drawing herself up to her full height of five feet two inches, 'Well I like the sound of Mr. Wright and it would be nice to have another lady so I suggest we invite both.' 'Then we will have a full hockey eleven,' laughed Vicky 'I used to love playing mixed hockey.' They agreed that Beryl had made two good points and authorised Bill to issue the invitations. They then discussed the register of the residential homes and it was agreed that Bill, Tom and Vicky would be responsible for producing it. Finally, they discussed the need for a follow up programme for the recipients of the Christmas parcels. Harry was very keen that the question of loneliness and isolation should not just be a once a year job. It was agreed that he, Alice and Beryl would be responsible for this with perhaps help from the new members. Jim, Lenny and Mr. Wong were all working full time so could be excused, 'And' said Tom 'we must not forget that our councillor will have plenty of work coming her way from the council.' 'Good job we are getting some new blood,' said Bill. People were standing up to go and Tom suddenly had one of his blinding headaches. 'Oh my goodness,' said Vicky 'you don't look very well Tom, you are as white as a sheet.' 'Just a headache,' he said 'nothing to worry about.' Lenny said that he and Mr. Wong would escort Tom home, so they did and Tom thanked them and went indoors. There were a number of club members who worried about Tom that evening.

The first thing he did when he got in was to take a couple of painkillers; the second thing was to pour a large brandy. He acknowledged that the first was necessary and that the second was possibly unwise, then he revived the fire and sat in front of it until he fell asleep. He woke about eight o'clock and decided he had not got the desire or the energy to cook properly so he settled for the old standby of beans on toast. As it was then almost nine o'clock he decided to ring Fran. When she answered the phone she sounded almost as tired as him. 'Are you alright?' he enquired. 'Yes, I have just had a very busy day.' Tom told her about the developments at the Windmill Club and she said 'It sounds as if you are also going to have a busy time.' 'Keep me out of mischief,' he said with a chuckle. 'I do hope so,' she replied 'but mind you do not overdo things.' After a few more minutes she was just going to say goodbye when she remembered to tell him that her mother and aunt had told her how much they had enjoyed meeting him and how much they liked him. 'A very strong vote of approval from both of them,' she added. They reluctantly bade each other good night and after he had put the phone down he brushed his teeth and got straight into bed. 'Goodnight sweetheart,' he murmured and fell into a restless and dream strewn sleep.

Although his headaches were getting worse he managed to hold everything together until the last Wednesday in February. Then, at one of the meetings, matters went rather awry; Bill had just reported that the group compiling the register of residential homes were just about ready for publishing. They had managed to include nineteen homes ranging from very good down to one which Bill described, as abysmal. Some of the homes had been extremely helpful and had even supplied photographs, a small number had been quite difficult and in three cases the information consisted of the name, address and number of residents. Alice made an impassioned speech, probably prompted by the treatment her aunt had received, although she had now moved to a better home. 'Old people who have lived their lives contributing to society deserve a decent standard of life in their final years. There is still too many care staff that see the residents as a damned nuisance and a small minority who actually bully the more vulnerable residents. Old people should be neither pitied nor patronised, but treated with respect and care.' 'Hear, hear,' said Tom, 'well said Alice.'

Harry then got to his feet 'I agree with everything Alice said but we must also be equally conscious of the elderly people who do not go into care but live at home. They are all too often neglected by society; many of them feel isolated and rejected. This is where our programme comes in, food parcels at Christmas are fine but they are not what most elderly people want.' Jim then added 'There's a lot of talk nowadays about food banks and a lot of well meaning people who are collecting and distributing food because they say people are in poverty. Well I am sure that some of them are, but I know of a few who are just scrounging and using their grocery money for other purposes. Two chaps who come in the pub every night for example, haven't worked for years and think that the benefit system is great. Now they get free food, what could be nicer than that?'

'We must not get sidetracked,' said Bill 'I also agree with everything that has been said but there will always be people willing to help and other people who will take advantage. Now what has your little group decided Harry?' 'Well, as you may know, that group that some of you were in at the beginning has dwindled enormously. They still meet in our hall but when I have looked in on the last couple of weeks there were less than twenty people there.' 'The winter and the cold weather don't help of course,' commented Beryl. 'But it's more than that,' Harry continued 'many elderly people do not want to sit on hard chairs in a draughty hall and be "entertained" what we are suggesting is that each one of us becomes friends to the people who are isolated and lonely but prefer to stay at home. We have identified about thirty two people and if we each took three or four, visited them once a week, telephoned them occasionally and just gave them a regular contact this would be very useful.' Everyone agreed that this would be a good idea and Bill suggested that the following weeks meeting should be devoted to allocating the members as suitable friends. 'These allocations will not be written in stone and we can change them around as appropriate, some ladies will prefer female visitors and vice versa.' The group then broke up for tea and everybody sat chatting and enjoying Beryl's cakes.

Tom had been listening to all the discussions but his head was throbbing, he decided to go to the bathroom but as he stood up the room whirled about him and he fell back in his chair. The next thing he knew there was a group of his friends standing around him and looking very concerned. 'Shall we call an ambulance,' said one; 'No please don't,' he mumbled, 'I just fainted; I will be alright in a minute.' He felt embarrassed and ashamed, 'How could I be so stupid?' he thought to himself. Beryl was ushering everyone out but Vicky and Alice refused to go, 'We have to stay and see that he is alright,' they said. Tom spoke, 'Another cup of tea would be nice,' he said. Beryl bustled off to the kitchen while Bill and Harry cleared away the tea things and Alice and Vicky sat either side of Tom holding his hands. He wondered just how far he should go to explain things to his friends. Beryl brought in a tray of tea for all six of them and Bill said 'Now come on Tom, level with us. Have you got a problem we don't know about?' Tom had by now recovered, 'Apart from old age you mean,' he chuckled. 'Well I do suffer from these rather unpleasant migraines and they have been getting worse lately.' 'Have you seen a doctor?' asked Beryl. 'Oh yes, he's given me some tablets and he's keeping an eye on me.'

You must tell us if you need a hand or anything,' said Alice 'after all that's what friends are for and you are always willing to help others.' 'Thank you Alice, thank you everyone, I promise to let you know if I cannot cope. Now I had better get home.' Alice and Vicky said that they would walk him home; Jim was outside sitting in his car waiting for them so he turned his car around and cruised up to Tom's gate. Vicky and Alice insisted on going into the house with him and Vicky got his fire going. He had laid it that morning as he did every day. 'Now ring us if you need anything at all,' said Alice, 'we will be round in a flash.'

After they left he sat in his chair and closed his eyes. 'It's been a funny month,' he thought. On February 14th he had received three Valentine cards, more than he had ever received. One, he knew from the postmark, was obviously Fran and he had sent her one, telling himself what a sentimental old fool he was. He guessed one was from Susie, judging from the handwriting, the quantity of kisses and the fact that she addressed it to Monty. The third one was a mystery; he had also remembered that it was Fran's birthday on the twenty second, good old Interflora came to the rescue there, he thought. Now the month was almost over and he would almost certainly not see another February. He fell asleep and awoke with a start when the telephone rang. Not Fran, he thought, but he looked at the clock and it was only seven o'clock. It was Beryl, enquiring if he felt any better. He reassured her that he did and she invited him for lunch the following day. He thanked her and said he would be delighted. After he put the phone down he decided not to go to sleep again before Fran telephoned. He made himself a sandwich and when he spoke to her at nine o'clock he thought that he sounded alert and normal. She must not know before she goes away, he reminded himself. 'Tell you what,' he said 'I might fly over to Switzerland and meet you in Zermatt as we discussed that time in Derbyshire.' 'That would be wonderful,' she said 'we must try and sort it out before Leo and I leave.' They said their goodbyes and Tom decided to have a nice warm bath and read in bed. He took a book upstairs, had his bath, and got into bed and the next thing he knew was when his alarm clock went off at seven o'clock.

Chapter Fifty

March was a very cold month; keen winds, flurries of snow and hard morning frosts. Easter was at the end of the month and Tom and Fran discussed whether they would get together during the Easter break. Tom desperately wanted to see her but on the other hand he knew that just by looking at him Fran would know there was a problem. Another factor was that he was not at all sure he should be driving any distance. For her part, Fran believed that if she worked through the Easter break, she and Leo would get away that bit earlier. 'The earlier we get away the sooner we will be back; I have persuaded Leo that six weeks will be enough. Also there is still a possibility we can meet up in Zermatt.' 'Yes, we can plan that before you go in May,' he replied. And so the dream was left floating in the air.

Meanwhile, the Windmill Club continued to flourish, the directory of residential homes was considered to be a great success and Nigel Lomax, Mrs. Brooks' successor, contacted Bill and asked if he could meet the Windmill Club to thank them for it. He would also like to learn about their befriending project. When Bill tactfully enquired about Mrs. Brooks, Mr. Lomax said she had retired. There was a full attendance at the meeting in the middle of March; one of the topics was whether the club could arrange a holiday weekend for some of their elderly friends. Money would be a problem and Mr. Lomax said he did not think the social services department could help. They decided to aim for September, just out of season when it would be cheaper. Tom thought wistfully that he would not be around in September, but he knew that there was something he could do so he said to Bill 'I have an old

Navy contact that could get us a grant of five thousand pounds.' 'That would be wonderful,' Bill replied and everybody applauded. As Mr. Lomax was leaving he told Bill that he was very impressed by the level of debate and he thought it would be splendid if there could be more Windmill Clubs. 'I am going to a conference next week,' he went on 'and with your permission, I will speak about your club.' 'Delighted,' said Bill. When he passed the information on to the group there was more applause. Tom saw Beryl, Vicky and Alice looking at him and talking quietly together. 'There is something in the wind,' he thought. 'Beware the ides of March.'

However, the meeting broke up as usual at about five o'clock and apart from Alice, asking him how he felt, nothing else occurred.

On Friday morning he got up at the usual time, but he felt very lethargic and got dressed without changing his shirt or bothering to shave. As he went downstairs he was conscious of the fact that the house seemed dustier and less tidy than it normally did. Right, he thought, after breakfast a good spring clean. Breakfast was only cereal or toast nowadays; he could not be bothered with cooking just for himself. His head was throbbing and he felt terrible. 'I could go back to bed,' he said aloud. That was another change, now that Evelyn was not appearing as much, he had started talking more to himself. He was still sitting at the table when the doorbell rang; he stood up rather stiffly and went to open the door. On the step arranged in a half circle were Beryl, Alice and Vicky. Oh Lord, he thought, now what! But he smiled a welcome and asked them to come in, and then he led the way into the sitting room. 'Sit down ladies and I will make some coffee.' 'No, no,' Vicky said 'you sit down and I will make the coffee.' Tom had not got the energy to resist so he sat with Beryl and Alice until Vicky reappeared with the tray. 'I can't find any biscuits,' she said. 'No I think I'm out of biscuits.'

They sat drinking the coffee and then Alice leaned forward and said, 'Tom dear, we are worried about you.' 'There is no need, I'm fine,' he replied. Beryl then sat up straight and said, 'No Tom, you are not fine. You look terrible and it looks as if you are letting your standards slip. Please tell us what is wrong.' He knew that he could not hide it from them any longer. 'If I tell you three, it must stay only with you three for the time being.' 'That's fair enough,' said Alice 'but we cannot promise any length of time until we know what the problem is.' The words came tumbling out, 'Yes, well, I have a brain tumour and apparently I have only two or three months left to live.' There was a stunned silence and then Beryl said very quietly 'How long have you known?' 'Since a couple of weeks before Christmas.' 'That plaster on your head,' said Vicky 'I knew it had some significance.' 'Does Frances know?' Beryl asked. 'No, you three are the only people I have told.' Alice, the so called tough member of the group sat with her hands over her face, she was almost certainly crying and Tom realised that she was the only lady present who had suffered a really close bereavement. Vicky then said 'And that's what these headaches and fainting have been about, why haven't you told us?' Tom was not sure how to answer, part of him wanted to say 'Because it's my business,' but he knew they were concerned for him and such a response would have been unkind. 'I'm very sorry, but I did not want to burden anyone else with my problem.' 'Oh, you proud, foolish man,' Vicky expostulated. 'That is exactly what friends are for, to share burdens. Look at how you have helped some of us.' Alice wiped her eyes and said 'Please Tom, let us help now, we would never forgive ourselves if we let you slip quietly away.' Tom swallowed hard; he was very touched by their genuine concern. 'I must confess that I could probably do with a little help and support.' 'More than a little I would say,' said Beryl. While Tom went to the kitchen to make more coffee the three ladies had an urgent discussion. When he came back they told him that they would tell their husbands only that Tom wasn't well and they were giving him some assistance. Alice said that she could organise some help through the social services but Tom firmly rejected that idea. 'I do not want people who are strangers to me and who are being employed to help me coming into my house.'

Vicky smiled and said 'Good, then we can use plan B.' 'And what I pray is plan B?' 'Me,' she replied, 'I'll look after you. I can keep the house tidy, cook your meals and generally keep an eye on you.' Tom thought rapidly, 'Now how do I deal with this?' A little voice seemed to say, just bow to the inevitable, these ladies will clearly not be denied. 'We could give it a try, I suppose.' 'Good man, you won't regret it,' said a beaming Vicky and both the others smiled their approval. As they went out Vicky said 'I will give you a few hours to think about it. See you tomorrow.' After he shut the front door he wondered what he had agreed to. It could be a disaster, but then I have felt very lonely since Fran went back to Exeter. Ever since he had been told about the tumour he had denied the likelihood of an early death and in the process denied that he needed anyone, apart from Fran. He slept fitfully that night, his dreams full of a collection of home helps and social workers all telling him what to do with the rest of his life.

He got up about seven o'clock determined to shave and dress carefully. 'I won't be caught out twice,' he told himself. He had just finished his meagre breakfast when the doorbell rang. He opened the door and found Alice and Vicky, he was not surprised but he was not prepared for the fact that Vicky was carrying a suitcase and a travelling bag. 'Good morning,' they both said cheerily, 'We hope you don't mind,' said Alice 'but we thought that Vicky could look after you more effectively if she lived in for awhile.'

Chapter Fifty One

To say Tom was taken aback was to put it mildly. 'Er, um, well I am not sure, what will people think.' 'Apart from we three and Beryl, nobody will need to know for the time being,' said Alice. 'What about Jim?' 'Oh, I will just tell him that Vicky is visiting a friend, which is not untrue.' 'After all,' said Vicky 'when Fran moved in as your lodger, nobody raised an eyebrow. Well, that is apart from Beryl. She has given me the seal of approval on account of my seniority.' Tom had to smile, 'Right, you have convinced me, let's celebrate with a cup of coffee, I will give you a month's trial.' 'And then throw me out I suppose if I don't come up to scratch.' 'Something like that,' he smiled. After Alice had made her farewells Tom showed Vicky up to the spare room, he did not think of it as Fran's room any longer, because Leo had been the last person to sleep in there. 'This is very nice,' announced Vicky 'I'm sure I will be very comfortable in here and I promise not to intrude upon your privacy.' 'Just one thing,' said Tom 'please let me answer the telephone. I do not want Fran to know that I need looking after, she won't go on her trip.' 'Agreed,' Vicky replied 'we will make this work.'

And work it did; the first few weeks went very smoothly. Vicky was very careful to ensure that the bathroom was always available for Tom. She was a good cook and accepted the fact that Tom was not keen on curries or very spicy food. For Tom's part, a cup of tea in bed every morning was very nice and Vicky had soon got the house looking clean and tidy once more. She didn't drive and providing Tom did not have a headache, he was still able to drive his car locally so they went shopping together. Easter came and went and they were soon in the middle of April. They agreed that it was time that the other members of the Windmill Club knew that Vicky was now Tom's housekeeper. He did not want them to know the nature, or seriousness, of his illness. After they had told the group, Harry patted Tom on the back and said with a smile 'That's the second woman you've pinched from me, you old dog.' Beryl knew it was Tom's birthday on the twentieth of April so she had arranged a birthday party. The twentieth was a Saturday so they all gathered together to celebrate 'Our senior member and founder's birthday,' as Beryl put it. Tom thought back to his birthday the previous year and how miserable he had been then and how much had happened to him since. He and Vicky left the birthday party together and not a single eyebrow was raised.

One evening when they were sitting quietly in front of the fire Tom was reading and Vicky was doing a word puzzle. Tom paused, because he suddenly had a thought. 'I keep meaning to ask you Vicky, are you still paying rent on your flat?' 'Well, yes,' she replied, 'I will have to have somewhere to live after....,' she paused, 'after you have left me.' Her face crumpled and she burst into tears. 'Please don't cry Vicky, you have been so brave I do not know how I would have managed without you.' 'That is why I am crying, I do not know how I will manage without you. I have loved you since our casino evening.' Tom realised who the third Valentine had been from, 'I love you too Vicky and I intend to see that you are not left homeless. I intend to leave this house in trust to the Windmill Club with the proviso that you will live here as caretaker for as long as you wish. I am sure you and the club will find ways to use it, a simple drop in centre for lonely elderly people, for example.' 'Oh Tom, are you sure? You are so thoughtful.' They agreed that Vicky would relinquish her flat, but they would not tell anyone apart from Alice, of Tom's intention.

That night Vicky told Tom that she would bring him a warm drink after he was ready for bed. She did this and sat on the edge of the bed holding his hand, she asked him if he was afraid of dying. He answered honestly that he did not think so, 'Curious more that afraid perhaps.' They did not discuss the question of death after that night and continued to live happily together. Vicky became more overtly affectionate, she would hold his arm sometimes when they were out and kiss him on the cheek at bedtime. She knew that he was in love with Fran and accepted this, at least outwardly.

The Windmill Club continued to flourish, the directory of homes was very well received and the social services department promised to produce a similar book for the other side of the city. There were a number of enquiries from different parts of the country and they learned of three other Windmill Clubs which were being set up elsewhere. Nearer home, although Tom had to withdraw from the visiting scheme, more than thirty older people living on their own were receiving visits from club members. At the beginning of May during one of their telephone calls Fran told him that she and Leo were planning to leave the country on the twentieth. 'Are you sure you don't mind me going?' she asked anxiously. 'Of course not my dear girl, please go and enjoy yourself, I will be waiting for you to get back.'

'What about us meeting in Zermatt?' she asked. 'Well, if I can get away we could meet there, but if not you and Leo must go into the Hotel Matterhorn and drink a toast to our love. You will find it has the most superb views of the Matterhorn and surrounding mountains.' Fran must have detected something in his voice. 'How do you mean if you can get away?' Tom lied for the first time in their relationship. 'Well there are a number of Windmill Clubs being started throughout the country and Bill and I will have to go to various meetings.' 'Well for goodness sake don't overdo things and do try to get to Zermatt if at all possible.' 'I will my darling, let us aim for the second weekend in June.' 'Agreed,' she said 'and Tom, I do love you so very much.' He remembered their whispered conversation in Hathersage and it seemed a lifetime ago. 'Just come home safely my dear girl.' That evening he put the telephone down with a very heavy heart, 'What a fool I am, perhaps Don Quixote really is my patron saint.'

The days seemed to fly by after that conversation, he was experiencing much more pain and Vicky was as much a nurse as a housekeeper. On the evening of the nineteenth Fran telephoned Tom and said that she and Leo were ready to move off the following day. They were planning to start off in France move to Spain and Portugal and then to Italy; after that it would be Austria and Germany followed by Switzerland. They were planning to be back in England at the end of June. 'Leo is not entirely pleased,' Fran told him. 'She would like to stay away until the end of July, but I am insisting on the end of June and if she insists on staying I will fly home anyway. Then we will be together for good.' Tom took the opportunity to tell her that he had transferred ten thousand pounds into her bank account. 'Please don't be offended, if you don't spend it you can use it for something else.' 'Like a wedding for example,' she laughed. 'Yes, something like that, but it is always useful to have an emergency fund when you are abroad.' 'Alright darling, I will not be offended but it is very kind of you.' They ended the call with the usual protestations of love. The following morning he did not want to get out of bed, his heart was heavy and his legs felt like lead.

Vicky came into his room carrying a cup of tea and wearing her usual smiling face. 'How are you this morning Tom,' she asked. 'Well, to be honest, I do not feel very good. Would you mind if I skipped breakfast and came down at coffee time?' 'No, of course not, would you like me to bring some breakfast up to you?' 'No, I don't think so; I will just rest for a bit longer.' As Vicky went downstairs she thought, is this the thin end of the wedge, the beginning of the last few weeks. Rather unsurprisingly, Tom was thinking along similar lines, he resolved to telephone Doctor Mason later and seek a second opinion. He pulled the duvet around him and for the first time he really felt a sense of despair. He realised that he had been denying the question of death but Fran going away had somehow aroused it. 'It might have been better if I had never met Fran, after Evelyn died there did not seem a lot to lose but now I am about to lose the most wonderful thing that has ever happened to me.' That thought seemed to summon Evelyn, 'Oh, feeling sorry for yourself now are you? Well perhaps you will understand how I felt sometimes, but now you have got that black woman to console you. It seems that you always come up smelling of roses, but soon it will be all over'. Tom shook his head and dismissed these thoughts; he remembered that he had to get the five thousand for the club holiday. If he got the bankers draft then no one would know it was his money. He got out of bed and made his way to the bathroom, Vicky heard him moving and smiled to herself. 'He must be feeling better.'

After coffee and biscuits he telephoned his bank and his doctor and made appointments with both for the following day. 'Then I must talk to my solicitor,' he reminded himself. Having things to do took his mind off his illness and he felt much better. He hugged Vicky and gave her a kiss. 'What was that for?' she asked.

'Just to show how much I appreciate all you are doing for me.' 'I would do much more if I could,' she said with a smile. She had cooked a very nice lunch of chicken casserole and they spent the rest of the day reading, watching television or just sitting and chatting to each other. It was the kind of day he needed and he went to bed that night in a much more relaxed mood.

Chapter Fifty Two

Tuesday morning was warm and sunny and Tom recalled that it was the kind of day his mother used to call a "glad to be alive day". When she did not feel too good she would call it a "nearer my God to thee" day. These memories made Tom wonder why he had not thought of praying and why he didn't worry about the possibilities of Heaven or Hell.

'In any case,' he thought, 'Vicky probably does enough praying for both of us.' She had asked him on a couple of occasions whether he would like to go to church with her, but he had very politely refused. He knew that some people turned to God and the church as they moved towards the end of their lives but he thought in his case it would be rather hypocritical. 'Too late now old son,' he told himself.

After breakfast, he and Vicky set off to keep his appointments. He felt surprisingly well so they took his car. The visit to the bank did not take very long and he collected the banker's draft for five thousand pounds. The visit to Doctor Mason took a little longer and although both he and the doctor knew there was nothing to be done he felt strangely comforted by their discussion and the doctor's concern. He did think about going to see his solicitor but he felt exhausted after only a couple of hours so he drove home carefully and let Vicky fuss over him.

On Wednesday morning Vicky asked him if he felt strong enough to go to the Windmill Club that afternoon. In truth he did not, but he said 'Of course, I am looking forward to it.' Something told him that it would probably be the last time he went. There was a full attendance of eleven and everyone seemed to be in good spirits. Most of the members asked him how he was and it was clear that there was genuine concern for him. He pondered, as he had done on a number of times before, about how valuable groups like this could be to older people. Everybody felt accepted and even more importantly, valued as individuals. Alice reported on the council debates about bus passes and free parking badges, which had been going on for months. 'I expect they will find ways to stop them eventually,' she said.

Harry had been looking at the possibilities for holiday weekends for their Christmas friends. He said that he had quotes from Colwyn Bay and Morecambe although his preference was for the latter. Tom produced the draft for five thousand pounds and received a round of applause. 'Now we can go ahead and book,' said Harry 'which is it to be.' After some discussion it was agreed they could take a coach load of thirty people to Morecambe in late September. 'It is much cheaper if we go Monday to Thursday,' Harry reported, so that was the agreed plan.

After tea the group broke up and Alice had to rush off to a meeting. This left Beryl and Bill with Harry and Vicky and Tom agreed that Vicky could tell the two men the reason for his illness. Both Harry and Bill were visibly upset and Beryl burst into tears when she realised that Tom's life was drawing to a close. 'Please don't be too upset, this last year has been one of the happiest of my life and I regard you all as wonderful friends. I may not get to our meetings again but I hope you will visit me.' They assured him that they would and watched him and Vicky walk very slowly down the road. Harry remarked that it was only a few months ago Tom had said he would trot down the road because it was raining. Beryl threw her arms around Bill and said 'Oh dear, we are all so vulnerable and he is such a nice man.'

When the telephone rang at nine o'clock Tom was

not surprised, 'It will be Fran,' he said to Vicky. He answered the phone and indeed it was. 'Where are you?' he asked. 'Floating down the Seine,' was her reply 'we have just had dinner on one of the cruise boats.' 'Lucky you!' he replied. 'I am just getting ready for bed.' He did not feel pangs of jealousy any more; he knew that Leo would never be able to lure Fran away from him. 'This is a lovely surprise,' he said and she promised to call him whenever it was possible. 'Bye darling, see you in Zermatt.' 'Goodbye sweetheart, do take care.' He put the phone down and Vicky could see that he was almost in tears. 'It is OK to cry Tom,' she whispered. 'I hardly ever cry Vicky, and I am not going to start blubbering now.' That night he had a number of troubled dreams, he awoke shouting at five a.m. because he had just dreamed about his sister and her fiancé being killed on their motorcycle. Vicky came into his room, obviously very alarmed. She sat on his bed holding his hand and making soothing noises. 'Shall I make a cup of tea?' she asked and he mumbled 'Yes please.' That morning his head was throbbing and he stayed in bed until lunchtime. This became the pattern for the next few days. Most afternoons one or more members of the club visited him and Doctor Mason also paid him a visit. Bill very kindly took Vicky to do their shopping and Tom reconciled himself to the fact that he was now housebound.

At the beginning of June he asked his solicitor, Sid Levy, to come and see him. They had known each other for a number of years and were on friendly terms. Sid was obviously shocked to see him and said, 'Tom I had no idea you were so ill.' 'Nothing a couple of aspirins won't cure,' Tom joked. He explained what he wanted to arrange about the house and Sid said he would draw up a trust deed. 'It had better include twenty thousand pounds to cover council tax and running costs,' Tom said. They worked out that there would be a balance of eighty thousand pounds and Tom said that this was to be given to Fran. He explained exactly who Fran was and said how much pleasure their relationship had given him. Sid was not much younger than Tom and he had seen many situations during his time in the legal profession. He congratulated Tom and assured him that his wishes would be properly carried out. When Vicky showed him out he shook her warmly by the hand and thanked her for looking after his old friend.

The morning after Sid had been, the telephone rang. Because Tom was still in bed Vicky answered it and then ran upstairs with the telephone. 'It's Fran,' she said, slightly out of breath. 'Who was that?' was the first thing Fran asked. 'Oh it was Vicky,' she and Alice are here because we are working on a holiday programme and I was just upstairs.' The answer obviously satisfied Fran and she went on to say 'I cannot remember whether it was this coming weekend or the following weekend we were hoping to meet.' 'Oh I am so sorry,' Tom replied, 'I will not be able to come to Zermatt, we are much too busy.' Fran was obviously disappointed but she said 'Never mind, it is not too long until the end of the month. We are just moving into Vienna,' she told him and promised to ring him from Zermatt. 'I must go and see your Matterhorn,' she said. Tom put the phone down with a strong feeling of foreboding. 'Are you alright,' said Vicky. 'Yes, just another bad headache I'm afraid.'

Tom was now drifting off to sleep much more and he had stopped getting up at lunchtime, but he would sometimes go downstairs in his dressing gown. One afternoon, when Beryl and Alice were visiting, he collapsed in the kitchen. Alice was still very strong so she and Vicky helped him upstairs and put him back to bed. As they were doing this the telephone rang and

Beryl answered it. She called upstairs and said 'Alice it is for you.' When Alice got downstairs Beryl said 'It is not really for you but it is the police for Tom.' Alice gingerly took the phone she explained to the policeman on the other end that she was a councillor and a friend of Tom's but he was too ill to come to the telephone. The policeman was satisfied by this and said that they had just heard from Switzerland that there had been a motorcycle accident. The driver had been killed outright and the passenger was in hospital in Zurich.

Alice's heart sank, 'Can Tom cope with this?' she asked Beryl. 'He has to know,' Beryl replied. Alice went upstairs; Tom had been propped up against the pillows by Vicky. He took one look at Alice's face and said 'I know.' She explained about the accident and said 'But Fran is in hospital.' What she didn't say was that Fran was critically ill in intensive care. Tom leaned back against the pillows, the last six months had been a trial but nothing had prepared him for this.

Vicky said 'Do you want us to stay?' he replied that he would like to be alone for awhile. The three ladies crept downstairs, Tom closed his eyes, he could see a sunbathed Zermatt and on one of the balconies of the hotel he could see Fran looking down and waving at him. He smiled and waved back and in far away Zurich someone said 'We may as well turn off the life support machine.' Vicky called up the stairs, 'Are you alright Tom?' There was no reply, so she and Alice decided they should go back upstairs. When they went into his room Tom was lying back on his pillows, his eyes were wide open and he was smiling.